At First Sight

Bran felt her before he saw her.

A woman with long black hair stepped forward, and he struggled to pretend indifference. The white shimmering band of her aura weaved its way over to him. Through the window it came, his magic calling it forth, beckoning it. She was strong, but there was a vulnerability there as well that engaged him, made him want to explore it. And she was passionate. He felt the desire, the longing for pleasure. The ache for sex. She wanted it but she would fight him, make him work to convince her to accept him. There was something so raw and primal about her; if he could make her submit to him, he felt he could survive off that energy for years.

It was so rare, a pure white aura. White meant perfect balance. He should probably fear it, but he was drawn to it—to her. He suddenly wanted nothing more than to take all her pleasure inside his body and convert it into magic.

Yes, this mortal female would give him great power. Tonight.

HEAT

Published by New American Library, a division of
Penguin Group (USA) Inc., 375 Hudson Street,
New York, New York 10014, USA
Penguin Group (Canada), 90 Eglinton Avenue East, Suite 700, Toronto,
Ontario M4P 2Y3, Canada (a division of Pearson Penguin Canada Inc.)
Penguin Books Ltd., 80 Strand, London WC2R 0RL, England
Penguin Ireland, 25 St. Stephen's Green, Dublin 2,
Ireland (a division of Penguin Books Ltd.)
Penguin Group (Australia), 250 Camberwell Road, Camberwell, Victoria 3124,
Australia (a division of Pearson Australia Group Pty. Ltd.)
Penguin Books India Pvt. Ltd., 11 Community Centre, Panchsheel Park,
New Delhi - 110 017, India
Penguin Group (NZ), 67 Apollo Drive, Rosedale, North Shore 0632,
New Zealand (a division of Pearson New Zealand Ltd.)
Penguin Books (South Africa) (Pty.) Ltd., 24 Sturdee Avenue,
Rosebank, Johannesburg 2196, South Africa

Penguin Books Ltd., Registered Offices:
80 Strand, London WC2R 0RL, England

First published by Heat, an imprint of New American Library,
a division of Penguin Group (USA) Inc.

First Printing, March 2010
10 9 8 7 6 5 4 3 2 1

Copyright © Sophie Renwick, 2010
All rights reserved

HEAT is a trademark of Penguin Group (USA) Inc.

LIBRARY OF CONGRESS CATALOGING-IN-PUBLICATION DATA:

Renwick, Sophie.
Velvet Haven / Sophie Renwick.
p. cm. —(The Annwyn chronicles series; bk. 1)
ISBN 978-0-451-22918-2
I. Title.
PS3618.E64V46 2010
813'.6—dc22 2009039627

Set in Adobe Caslon
Designed by Alissa Amell

Printed in the United States of America

VELVET HAVEN

Sophie Renwick

HEAT

To Fedora, for winning my contest.
Thanks so much for coming up with Immortals of Annwyn!
And to all those hussies who hang out at my blog, I hope Bran satisifies!

ACKNOWLEDGMENTS

Velvet Haven would not be here if not for the wisdom, patience, and hand-holding of my excellent editor, Tracy Bernstein. Thank you for helping me see the forest for the trees! It was sometimes a difficult task, but thanks for sticking with me and not giving up on either Bran or me!

VELVET HAVEN

PROLOGUE

In the beginning there was peace. Prosperity. The fertile lands of Annwyn flourished. The trees were bountiful, bearing the most luscious fruit. The forest teemed with life, and the streams ran cool and clear. The people of Annwyn lived harmoniously alongside the human world; the gossamer veil that separated the two spheres allowed Annwyn's inhabitants to see the mortal realm, yet protected us from man's poisonous ways. Greed. Lust. Avarice. Such mortal vices did not penetrate the veil, for Annwyn was above all temptations.

But now all has been transformed. Annwyn is no longer pure.

The Dark Times have come.

War will be waged between man and the inhabitants of Annwyn. Each side seeks a flame and an amulet that have been hidden away for centuries. Into whose hands these fall will dictate what will come—peace or annihilation.

And these Dark Times will bring betrayals, deaths, and utter blackness before the dawn of light might once again creep between the trees of the forest.

From this darkness will rise the sacred nine, bringing the beginning and ending of all things. But there will be one among them, a Dark Soul, whose ascent shall either be that of savior . . . or destroyer.

The Scribe of the Annwyn Chronicles.

CHAPTER ONE

Death. Even now it was bearing down upon him, its arrival thick, menacing. *Unstoppable.*

Kneeling on the ground, eyes closed, heart beating heavily in his chest, Bran waited for the inevitable. Just as he did every night when the moon rose and the winds stilled, he awaited his vision.

It was a gift, this ability to divine death. It had saved many of his people over the centuries. But now his gift was more a curse. To envision his own murder, but not when or by whom, left him wondering why the universe had allowed him this warning. Why bother, when none of the information necessary to protect himself from his untimely end was given to him?

When would his murderer arrive and who would it be? Those two questions had plagued him for months. Tonight, he *would* get answers.

Listening intently, he heard the shimmering birch leaves coalesce with the whisper of wind that swept through the dark woods. Combined, the two reminded him of a woman's sultry laugh. The sound made his body tighten with anger he found difficult to restrain. *Morgan.* She was the reason behind this. Even from the Wastelands her spell bound him to her.

Bitch.

He should have just married the witch and been done with it. Then his brother would not have been damned and lost to him. And he himself would not be carrying the Legacy Curse.

But now was not the time to dwell on the past. It was the future that brought him here tonight. A future he *must* find a way to alter.

As the minutes ticked by, the moon ascended higher in the sky, the beams creeping through oak branches, penetrating the grove slowly, a graceful arch across the black velvet that draped the altar before which he knelt. Once the silver rays illuminated the pewter chalice, filling the body of the cup, it would be midnight and time for him to die.

The silver beam, Bran noticed, had just crept to the rim of the chalice.

It was nearly time.

He stilled his mind. Quieting his breathing, he gazed deep into the glow of the candles that surrounded the altar. Almost immediately, he found himself at one with the grove, the trees, the animals in the forest. The life force of the elements wove around him, wrapping around his knees, then his body, until he felt the energy on his face. He harnessed the strength, the protectiveness, of the magick circle he had created, and watched the first glimmer of moonlight sneak into the chalice.

Seconds later, Death arrived.

As it always did, it claimed him in its cold, unrelenting grip. The familiar imagery floated before him and he swayed, trying to search deep within for the strength to hold on and divine as much as he could from Death's visit.

Bran experienced the precise moment of his death, when his lungs burned and his heart slowed. He buried the panic of waiting for the last thump of his heart, and the beat of silence where another thump should have been.

It didn't come. Only quiet. Followed by darkness.

He felt his soul lift, saw his physical form lying facedown upon a white cloth. His arms were spread out, his thick wrists shackled with iron manacles, his own athame plunged between his naked shoulders.

It was always the same. Night after night. His death coming to him in a vision that never revealed any more, or less. His death by an unknown hand and in an unfamiliar place.

The seconds of lifelessness hovered, started to fade. Air and warmth soon began to flow back into his lungs and veins. But he fought it. He was not yet ready to return to the land of the living.

Luring the bastard back, Bran refused to fall into any other state than the deep divination trance that would bind him and Death together.

Death had screwed him for the last time.

Pressing his knees to the cool, mossy earth, Bran grounded himself, sending the excess elemental energy into the ground to be dispersed. Eyes now opened, he focused on the black candles and inhaled the scent of incense as Death struggled in his grip. But Bran was stronger, able to hold Death in his grasp until darkness once again descended and he was dead once more.

Finally. This part of the journey was all new to him. He was hit by an onslaught of sensory stimulation. *Scent.* The smell of female arousal mixed with nightshade and male musk. *Sound.* The husky pant of a woman, his own heavy breaths. *Touch.* The sensation was everywhere, surrounding him from all sides. His sigils, which adorned his chest and arm, neck and temple, tingled with the incredible power he felt cocooning his body. Yet there was a weakness there, too. It was draining him. Making him vulnerable. Still he craved it, that haunting touch that hurt as much as it aroused.

Sight. He tried to see, to look deep within the flickering glow of the candles. Tried to reach out to Death, to use his strength to piece together the rest of the vision.

And then it happened. His sight swirled for the briefest second, then stilled. The pupil of his right eye dilated, allowing him to see his world. Annwyn was still. *Quiet.* His left pupil opened to the mortal realm. The same disquieting calm was seen there. But before he could close the portal, he was assaulted by the cries of a screaming woman. Splashes of red swam before both eyes. The acrid stench of burning flesh stung his nostrils, while a low chant of invocation swam in his ears.

A shadowy image followed, of a hand, delicate and pale, wrapped around the hilt of his athame. *A female hand.* He reached out to the vision but his fingers sliced through gray fog. The image was gone, having evaporated in tendrils of smoke. The sight, scent, and sounds of the vision were sucked out of him as though a separate entity, leaving him spent, panting, and wondering what he'd just witnessed.

He had never seen that vision before. There was a dark malevolence to it. In his previous visions, he had merely died. In this one, there had been suffering and pain—and a woman.

Death, it seemed, was fucking with him.

Head bent, Bran sought to slow his breathing while his body continued to hum with the life force that surrounded him. He still smelled the heavy perfume of a female nearing orgasm. His nostrils flared, taking it in, that heady, arousing aroma. Shuddering, he felt his skin flicker in awareness at an imaginary caress.

He was aroused, he noticed. His cock thick. Erect and straining. Pulsing with unspent desire. So this is how death would find him, the scent of a female clinging to his damp skin and her touch rippling along his flesh. He had been at someone's mercy. But whose? A female—that was all he could be certain of.

Morgan had cursed him to be brought down by a mortal. He had always believed the mortal would be male, but the hand on his athame was definitely a woman's.

Inhaling again, he drew the scent deep into his lungs and shuddered. He had never responded to a human female in such a way before. And yet what Sidhe female would kill her king? Morgan, of course, but he would never respond physically to her. The vision made no sense.

A twig snapped and he glanced up, snarling at the sound of someone approaching. No one dared interrupt him. Especially not here, in Nemed, his sacred circle of magick. No one would think to intrude on him, the king of the Sidhe.

"Your magick cannot keep me out, Raven."

Except her.

"What do you want, Cailleach?" he growled between great breaths of air. *The sex.* He could still smell it on his skin, taste its dew on his lips. It had been centuries since he had felt this kind of lust. And like a slave he was weakening to it. Its heady scent, like a drug, went to his head, making him crave more of it, making him lick his lips so he could taste the fine, teasing drops that lingered on his mouth.

Swallowing hard, he looked down between his thighs. His cock was near to bursting. He wanted to stroke it, to relieve himself of the ache that was growing in his shaft. He wanted to close his eyes and envision a female submitting beneath him while he got off with his hand.

He wanted it hard, to empty in forceful thrusts right here in the open grove where everything was primal and male. *Where everything was his.*

He needed this release, but he would not have it now that *she* had arrived.

"Clothe yourself, Raven, so that I may approach you."

"Does the sight of me not please you?" he taunted, knowing his consort, the supreme goddess of Annwyn, was a damn prude.

"I am not alone. Cover yourself."

Bran stood to his full height, his erection slowly dying. But his skin was still alive and vibrant with the remnants of sexual energy. His sigils glowed gold and pewter, especially the ones where the goddess was afraid to look.

"There is no need to flaunt yourself, Raven," she snapped in a crisp voice that was more hag than the beautiful woman she was. "I have no interest."

"Nor do I." He'd never been attracted to Cailleach. Not before he became king and coruler of Annwyn, and especially not after. "To what do I owe your visit?" he asked as he shrugged into his black cloak.

The tall, svelte woman dressed in a formfitting white gown

stepped between the trunks of two ancient oaks. At her side was a figure shrouded in black, a hood concealing his face. Only his hands were visible, and when he emerged from the shadows into the moonlight, their markings were suddenly illuminated, turning into whirls of curling lines. In his arms, he carried a woman, clearly dead.

"There is a Judas amongst us."

Cailleach's proclamation sent a ripple through the life force. Bran perceived the vibration along his skin, and the evil that seemed to gather in the grove that surrounded them. Even the candles on the altar flared.

As Cailleach and the stranger approached the magic circle he had crafted, Bran studied the body of the woman. Her white-blond hair caressed the dark sleeve of the man's cloak, her arms dangling at her sides. Her pale flesh, mottled in death, was marred by slashing cuts that crudely marked her arms and neck with the symbols of their world. The *Lemniscate*, or infinity knot as the mortals called it, was carved in the valley of her small breasts; the triscale, which was the symbol of Annwyn, was drawn above her navel. Streaks of dried blood the color of rust ran from flesh that no longer lived.

The lifeless form the stranger cradled so protectively in his arms was that of a woman of Bran's kind. A Sidhe. A youngling, only a few years into womanhood.

The goddess motioned to the altar and her companion placed the youngling atop the black altar cloth. Brushing her hand over the face and chest, Cailleach blessed the lifeless body before raising her brilliant green gaze to him.

"Like the others before her, she has been anointed by the Dark Arts."

Necromancy. It had returned to Annwyn after nearly two hundred years of banishment. The fact could no longer be denied that someone was practicing ancient death and sex magick. But why, when the punishment for practicing the banned art was so severe?

"May I?"

Nodding, Cailleach seemed to float gracefully away from the altar, allowing him to come forward. The stranger stood his ground, however, guarding the body, refusing to allow Bran to see her. "You are her *Anam Cara*?" Bran asked. The man inclined his head.

That explained his presence here and the protection energy Bran sensed radiating from the cloaked figure. The stranger was the youngling's Soul Friend. It was the *Anam Cara*'s responsibility to guide the soul through the passage of birth, life, and death.

"Were you with her when this happened?"

"No. It is not my purpose to change one's path."

"So you did not see who did this to her?"

The stranger shook his head. "I arrived just in time to keep her soul before it could be taken. It is here," he said, showing Bran his hands. The illuminations glittered, nearly blinding him.

"You do realize she is the ninth?" Cailleach asked, drawing Bran's gaze away from the youngling's body and the *Anam Cara*'s glowing hands.

"But the first woman. The other eight were males."

Cailleach met his gaze. "Is it of significance, do you think?"

"I don't know."

Bran walked the perimeter of the altar, taking in the woman from all angles. "May I?"

Reluctantly the *Anam Cara* nodded, stepping just far enough away to allow Bran near the altar.

The scent of burning flesh assailed him. On her mons, which had been shaved, a pentacle, point down, had been scratched onto her skin with the tip of something sharp. A knife? A sword? The jagged edges of flesh told him it might be from an athame, but the sacred knife of their rituals was never meant to shed blood. There was no greater insult than to use the sacred knife to cut flesh. And the significance of the pentacle? Inverted, it was pointing to the Shadowlands, otherwise known as hell to the mortals.

Her thighs were bruised as well, the tops bloodied and smeared with sexual secretions. Both wrists and ankles bore red excoriations. She had been tied down. *Spread.*

Bending closer, Bran inhaled the heavy perfume of incense. It was a cloying, oppressive aroma that coated her body. Pressing close to the woman's mouth, he smelled the sweetness of death, but there was something else there as well. The pungent, nutty scent of thorn-apple. Parting her lips, he found the pod of thorn-apple that had been placed inside her mouth. Bran closed his eyes, imagining this youngling tied up. The dark magick rituals performed as she writhed in pleasure, unaware that her death would follow orgasm.

"Where was she found?"

"The Cave of Cruachan."

The passageway to Annwyn.

At the eastern end of the stone corridor lay the glimmering gold veil that led to Annwyn. At the western end was an ancient wooden door that led into a nightclub where both mortals and immortals mingled. The corridor was long, shadowed, with alcoves perfect for hiding, or for carrying out clandestine meetings. Built deep beneath the club, only inhabitants of Annwyn knew of the cave. Unless, of course, the mortals had somehow discovered it, which posed a whole host of threats. But Bran doubted they had, for the human owner of Velvet Haven would never allow any mortal near the door that led to Annwyn. Besides, Bran himself had cast a protection spell on the door, keeping mortals away. Which meant, of course, they were dealing with something magical.

"What has you frowning, Raven?"

"Had she been inside Velvet Haven, then, if she was found in the cave?"

"Yes."

Then this dark mage was preying on immortals who came to the club. And this female, she was not the first immortal to return to Annwyn dead.

The previous eight bodies that had been returned had been that of males, old enough to know what they were doing. There had been signs of sex and bondage, but not gruesome markings. No symbols or incense.

Bran had thought the first two deaths might be nothing more than sexual experimentation by lovers not well versed in bondage. But after the third body had turned up, Bran had known something more sinister was lurking in the shadows.

"This is someone of our world," Cailleach announced as she came to stand beside him. "Only one who makes their home in Annwyn could know of these symbols."

Bran glanced once more at the woman's body. "That is clear,

but it's where they are placed on her body that puzzles me. And there is this symbol here," he said, pointing to her neck, above the red excoriations on her throat. "This is not of our world."

"Ancient Druid," Cailleach suggested. "Or perhaps an archaic symbol used in Black Magick?"

"No. It's Angelic."

He thought he heard Cailleach's breath catch. *Interesting.*

As he walked around the body once more, Bran studied not only the youngling, but the goddess as well. She was discomposed, though she tried admirably to hide it. Nothing unnerved Cailleach, but something about this particular situation did. Which, of course, made him even more determined to discover what the black magician wanted of them. For that was the purpose of the markings on the youngling's body. The mage had something to say.

"The third eye has been etched onto her forehead." Bran ran his fingers carefully over the mottled flesh. "That is a warning we are being watched."

"But by whom?" Cailleach murmured. There was true fear in her voice. He'd never known the goddess to fear anything— or anyone.

There were a few seconds of silence before the goddess addressed the *Anam Cara.* "You may leave us. Carry her soul with you, for I fear that the ones who have done this to her seek her soul for use in black magick."

Lifting the lifeless body from the altar, the *Anam Cara* moved silently into the depths of the forest, the blackness of night enveloping him. When he was gone and the grove had fallen silent, Cailleach turned to Bran. "We must speak in private."

Folding his arms over his chest, Bran studied Cailleach. "This is *my* sacred grove. None but you intrude here."

She did not blush despite the coldness in his voice. "I am aware of your opinion of me. But you must now see how this battle between us has brought the Dark Times. We have allowed evil to seep into our lives while we have warred between us."

Bran hated to admit the truth, but Cailleach was correct. They were supposed to rule Annwyn together, yet they had never once done so. For a hundred and seventy years, they had been at odds. But whose fault was that? It was she who had given him the Legacy Curse, damning him to a life without love. She who had made him king of the Sidhe, knowing he disdained the throne.

"Your hatred for me has clouded your vision, Raven."

"Your need to rule me has clouded yours," he snarled.

She smiled and stepped closer. "And this is the way it is between us. Always circling each other. Always fearing. Never trusting."

"I am Night Sidhe. Why would you trust me?"

"True, your blood is black and dangerous, but I sense in you such power. And above all, honor. Alas, your loyalty does not lie with me or with Annwyn, but with your brother."

"A brother I cannot find. A brother you allowed Morgan to curse."

Cailleach held his gaze. "And you have never forgiven me."

No, he hadn't. Nor would he ever. "I begged you most humbly to sever the marriage contract my father made with Morgan. Yet you did nothing."

"There are some things that even I cannot interfere with."

He snorted, feeling his hate and anger swell. "You had the power. But you sat back and refused to intervene. You allowed her to ruin my life and that of my brother."

"Have you no feelings for anyone other than Carden?"

He stilled, wondering at the soft tone of Cailleach's voice. Did she want his love? She knew he had no heart to give, nor love to share.

"Cailleach—"

"I speak of love not for me, Raven, but for your people. For *all* people of Annwyn. Have you no love for them and for what they hold dear?"

His head suddenly hung in shame. "I did. Once. Now I live only for two things, to feed the Legacy Curse that hungers within me, and to find Carden."

When she faced him once again, her eyes were saddened. "Will you allow the Dark Times to destroy our world? Or will you become the warrior you once were? Will you not fight this darkness with me? I cannot do it alone."

"Will you lift the Legacy Curse?"

"You know I cannot. It was your *Adbertos*, not a punishment."

Yes. He had offered her a sacrifice, his happiness for that of another's. He had sacrificed himself for his uncle, Daegan, then Cailleach's consort; had offered the goddess an *Adbertos* so that Daegan could spend his life with the mortal woman he loved. Cailleach had taken that sacrifice and given him his Legacy Curse. She had robbed him of a soul mate, stolen the sacred rites of his kind from him, for he could never have a Sidhe bride. No Sidhe female would share him with another. And there *would* be others. She had made him need the one thing he hated most. Humans. *Female humans.*

To keep his magic alive and strong, Bran needed to mate with human females. Their sexual energy was what made his magic so powerful. And he hated it. Despised having to pleasure them, touch them, to gain power, a power that had rightfully been his by birth.

"How many more of your people will you allow to be carved up? How many more need die before we act to vanquish this darkness that plagues us?"

He thought of what had been done to his brother, cursed to live as stone. He thought of the youngling whose body had been mutilated. She could have been his child. Could even have been his mate. "None," he said. "I promise, no more."

"So you will do it?"

"I will."

"You know where you will have to begin?"

"In the mortal realm," he spat. "'Tis where all evil begins."

"Be careful, Raven. For I cannot help you in that world. I am bound to Annwyn. I cannot leave."

And that grated his nerves. While Cailleach could do whatever she damned well pleased, he was bound by his curse to visit the mortal realm regularly. The prospect of staying there for any length of time made him feel violent. Away from Annwyn his magic was weak; he would need to mate with many human females to survive. He would find all he needed at Velvet Haven, but he despised the place, and the things he would have to do inside its walls.

"I will go to Velvet Haven and begin the search."

"I think I know what you must do first."

Bran looked at her expectantly, but she averted her gaze. "Amongst my kind, there is a scribe. A chronicler whose grimoire has gone missing. We *must* find this book, Raven."

"And how is this book connected to the killings?"

"You know that once, long ago, there was a goddess who betrayed her order to lie with an angel," Cailleach said, garnering his attention. "Their forbidden passion cost them both their powers. When you mentioned the angelic mark the youngling's body bore, it made me recall the prophecy the grimoire contains."

"What prophecy?" He knew the story of the fallen angel and the goddess, but he had never heard of a prophecy. When Cailleach spoke, her gaze remained on the ground.

"The tale of the amulet and the flame, and how to find them. The prophecy says that whoever possesses these will have the power to rule both Annwyn and the mortal realm. The angel swore retribution against Annwyn; perhaps he has found the book and is using it against us."

Bran eyed her skeptically. "An angel performing death magick?"

"Why not? The grimoire contains the necessary spells. It is most vital that you find this book, Raven, and bring it to me. Only then will we have the means to destroy this threat."

Extinguishing the candles, Bran stood in darkness while Cailleach seemed to glow and sparkle in the moonbeams. She looked like an angel, but he knew her for a succubus beneath her goddess guise.

"There is much you are not telling me," Bran accused. "I can sense your deception."

"I do not know all, Raven."

"So much for your pretty speech about fighting this darkness together."

"Some things you are not meant to know."

"Why? Because you enjoy having the upper hand?"

"Because it is not the right time to reveal them," she snapped. She pressed her eyes shut and struggled outwardly for control. When she opened them, she was steadied. Slowly she walked forward till she was standing before him. Once again she was the Supreme Goddess. "There is much I cannot tell you. Already, I have said more than I ought." Her gaze flickered before holding his. "But know this, Raven. Your time as a warrior has come. You will lead the quest for the flame and the amulet. This I have foreseen. You will command nine immortals whose powers will assist you in destroying this dark magician. It is a destiny that you will not evade, for it will find you. Already it is close."

He glared at her. "What if I don't want it?"

"It's too late. Besides, you cannot choose fate. It chooses you."

He growled, not liking her answer. He wanted to find his brother and destroy Morgan. He had no desire to be Cailleach's soldier, but he had no choice. He was king. It was his duty.

"And the significance of nine?"

"The beginning and ending of things. Be careful, Raven. There will be one amongst the nine who has immense power. Even more than you. That one will either save or destroy everything we love."

"You know a lot more than what you're telling me. Damn you, Cailleach—"

"Trust, Raven. You must learn it. In time I will reveal what you need to know. For now, you are ready to begin."

She smiled, then reached for him, bringing him close to her before placing a silver chain with a large fire opal pendant around his neck. "This is the only way I can help. Inside this pendant is all you need to protect you. Birch bark for purification and fortification, holly berries for protection and potency in your magick. Leaves of the ivy, for the vine that never fears to go into the dark will guide you through the blackness. Be well," she whispered, before fading into the mist.

The beginning and ending of all things. Casting one last look at the empty altar, Bran was left wondering what was ending and what the hell was just beginning.

CHAPTER TWO

Mairi MacAuley stroked the gilt edges, then traced the flowing words on the wrinkled vellum. The contact gave her an immediate rush. She'd never seen anything so beautiful, so rare. The detail in the artwork was amazing for such a little book. She'd never felt this amount of excitement over an illuminated manuscript.

But this one was different. Special in a way Mairi couldn't describe. She should probably feel guilty for taking it, but she hadn't been able to resist.

"So this place is, like, totally dead."

Mairi looked up from the illuminated manuscript to see the new student nurse she was training flop down beside her. "Probably not the best thing to say in a hospital," she replied. "Besides, the patients waiting behind the curtains don't want to hear the word 'death.'"

"You know what I mean. I thought the emergency department would be more exciting and have *waaaay* more hot doctors. All the docs here are dinosaurs."

"*Competent* dinosaurs," Mairi replied. "And you shouldn't date colleagues. Gets messy."

"Speaking from experience?"

It was a comment full of snark and Mairi refused to rise to the bait. Obviously people had been talking behind her back. Everyone thought it was a laugh that Mairi preferred musty old books to men. But she had her reasons. Reasons no one needed to know.

"I'm not stupid enough to get involved with on-the-job drama, and you shouldn't either," Mairi mumbled as she returned to the book that lay open in front of her.

"You didn't actually think I went into nursing to become a nurse, did you?"

Mairi looked over her student. From her highlighted hair, enhanced boobs, and acrylic nail tips, Mairi knew that Blondie, as she'd dubbed her, wasn't in it to help the sick and injured.

Her student crossed her long, shapely legs, not bothering to shove down the creeping hem of her already too short dress. She'd already given Blondie the dress-code rundown, but her student obviously didn't care. Which made Mairi not give a shit, either. Why should she put effort into someone whose only concern was landing a rich doctor?

"I bet you're one of those *real* nurse types, aren't you?"

"I care about people who are hurting, if that's what you mean."

Blondie snorted. "No way am I doing this gig all my life. I hate going home smelling of hospital and . . . people." Blondie actually shivered in disgust. "I can tell you've been doing this forever, though. The shift work shows around your eyes."

Mairi actually felt herself snarl, and was about to tell

Blondie where she could stuff her inflated boobs and empty brain when the chief of the ER came up to the desk, looking for a head to bite off.

"Where's the chart for the MVA in five?" Dr. Bartlett growled.

"I don't know," Mairi replied, refusing to be cowed. "I'm not assigned to trauma tonight. I'm working domestic violence."

Bartlett actually growled as he flipped through a pile of charts that lay on the desk. "Is it too damn much to ask you nurses to keep the chart outside the cubicle?"

"It's against hospital policy. The privacy act," she reminded him.

Bartlett growled, "I need a pen and the chart. *Please*," he said with mock sincerity.

Beside her, Blondie perked up. "Oh, let me get that for you, Doctor."

Rolling her eyes, Mairi went back to work on her book, separating the fragile vellum pages that had stuck to each other. Bartlett, while a good doctor, was an ass to nurses. It'd be a frosty day in hell before Mairi jumped to do his bidding.

"Here you go." Mairi saw the student nurse flip her long blond hair over her shoulder and stick out her silicone breasts. Old Bartlett's eyes almost bugged out of his skull, smacking against his eyeglass lenses.

"I could use a hand in trauma five," he murmured, not bothering to look at Mairi.

"I'd love to help," Blondie gushed.

Mairi watched her student leave and laughed to herself. If she was looking to marry a rich doctor, Blondie was barking up the wrong tree. Bartlett was a womanizing snake who was drained by alimony payments to his long-suffering ex-wife, not to mention those hush-hush child support payments he was making to one of the nurses Mairi worked with. There was very little left for the lifestyle Blondie was dreaming of.

"She know that Bartlett won't give her anything but a case of VD?"

Mairi grinned at the department's secretary. "Nah, I'll let her figure that one out for herself. All part of the learning curve."

"So, got yourself another one of those books, eh?"

Mairi flushed. "Yeah."

"Pretty girl like you should be getting herself a man."

Mairi groaned. She really didn't want to have this conversation again. Thankfully the phone rang and the secretary reached for it, allowing Mairi to go back to her manuscript. She'd collected the beautiful books for years, and this little gem was a prize. She'd found it hiding behind some books at the bottom of the antique rosewood bookcase in the library of Our Lady of Perpetual Sorrow. Opening it, she realized it wasn't just an ordinary manuscript, but some kind of diary. It was ancient, written in a language similar to Old English. Mairi knew as she held the worn leather book in her hand that she had to have it. Just to borrow, she had told herself.

The book had *spoken* to her. Like Gollum in *Lord of the Rings*, she would have stroked it and called it "my precious" if one of the nuns hadn't walked by, forcing Mairi to bury it in her work bag.

And since that day she'd been all but consumed by it, by the need to translate the story and understand it. And since that day in the library, not only had the book come into her life, but a strange dream had as well.

"I'm gonna go for break," Mairi called to Louise, the charge nurse for the shift. "I'll be in the sleep room if you need me."

Stuffing the book into her bag, Mairi picked up her coffee mug and headed to the back room that housed a twin bed and a bunch of extra equipment. The shift was relatively slow and she planned to take advantage of it.

The sleep room door creaked open and Mairi dropped her bag on the bed before flopping down onto the lumpy mattress. Digging out the book, she opened it to the page that contained the image of a Celtic triscale. Below it, in fancy gilt lettering, were the words "And so shall come the divine trinity, their numbers the sacred, elemental root of nine warriors."

With her finger, Mairi traced the exquisite work and the brilliant colors of the triscale as she mulled over the words. This was the fun of collecting manuscripts—deciphering them. Normally they were chivalric or biblical stories, but this book, this was far more interesting. From what Mairi could gather, it was written by a woman who was some sort of ancient seer. She had received a vision of the coming Dark Times of her world.

And there will be black magick and the resurrection of the Dark Arts. There will be sorrow and despair until one of the nine will emerge, either Destroyer or Savior.

Definitely the best reading she'd ever found. Most people thought she was a nerd to be getting a rush from old, dusty books, but Mairi didn't care what people thought of her, or her hobby. It was probably why she had few close friends.

Oh, she was friendly enough with the people she worked with and even went out the odd time with them for dinner and a few drinks, but she wasn't close to them. She had a hard time getting close to people. Trust wasn't something that came easily to her.

Checking her watch, Mairi realized she had only a half hour left on her break. She closed the book and placed it carefully back in her bag. Removing her stethoscope from around her neck, she hung it from an IV pole and kicked off her shoes. Man, she was exhausted. Too many late nights working on the book, and too many nights of interrupted sleep from those weird dreams she kept having.

With a yawn she fell backward and was asleep before her head hit the pillow.

❧

"Hey, MacAuley, Dr. Stud says he's got a stiff one for you in trauma three."

"Tell him if that's what he's dangling for bait, I'm not biting," Mairi grumbled from beneath the flannel blanket she had stolen from the warming cupboard in the hospital supply room.

"C'mon, you're not telling me that Pretty Boy Sanchez doesn't do it for you?"

"Look, Louise, I'm on break." Man, she had *just* fallen asleep.

"Get yer ass up, MacAuley. I need you."

Mairi groaned. Speak of the devil. "I'm on break!" she snapped, covering her head with a pillow as the room burst into a blast of halogen light. "You ignoramus! Turn the light off."

The husky male chuckle from the door made her teeth

grate. She so didn't get the whole Sanchez mystique. The guy was an asshole, and a mediocre ER doc at best.

"Vicky is covering me for break. Tell *her* to go."

"Yeah, the thing is, the cops aren't asking for Vicky."

Mairi sat up and shoved her hair back from her face. The light was bright and she squinted. "What'd you say?"

"The cops. They want to see you."

Great. What the hell could they possibly want with her? Maybe it was the overdose she'd helped with at the beginning of the shift. Or the suspected wife beater who'd taken his bruised wife home three hours ago. Bet that was it: The wife was dead. Whatever it was, it was damn rude interrupting her on break. A night at St. Michael's in which you even got a break was rare, and one to be savored. Obviously, she wouldn't be savoring this one.

Her gaze shifted to her bag, and suddenly she felt ill. Maybe the nuns had somehow discovered that she'd taken the book? Maybe it was a priceless artifact and now Mairi was going to be arrested for art theft.

Ah, hell!

"I'll be there in a minute," she grumbled, wiping her face with her hands. What the hell was she going to do? What was she going to say if they knew she had the book?

"Need a sponge bath?" Sanchez asked with a leer. "It'll wake you up."

"Like a physician's ever given a sponge bath."

He shrugged, watching her with his dark brown eyes as she tossed the flannel aside and reached for her shoes. "Hey, I can play nurse if you wanna play patient."

"Not in this lifetime," she mumbled as she swept past him.

Maybe all the other nurses fell for Dr. Sex, but she wasn't one of them. There was something about the guy that irritated the hell out of her. He was cocky, self-absorbed, and emotionally void. Perfect attitude for a trauma doctor. Horrible for relationships.

Not that she'd done any better. The guys she attracted were all the wrong sort. Besides, she wasn't into relationships. Based on what she saw rolling into the ER, it was better to stay single and wear out sex toys than get tangled up with the wrong man.

Out in the hall, two uniformed cops were waiting for her and she suddenly forgot all about sex and the irritating Dr. Sanchez. By the look on their faces, they meant business. *Serious* business. And Mairi had the sinking feeling that somehow she'd been found out. Hell, maybe the nuns had put a security camera in the library.

"You Mairi MacAuley?" the older officer asked.

"Yes."

"Detective Morris wants to see you."

Mairi followed them through the busy ER to the back, where their largest trauma room sat across from the ambulance ramp. A trail of blood streaked across the floor from the sliding doors to a cubicle where the curtains were drawn.

"What's this about, Officer?" she asked. "I'm not in trauma tonight. I'm assigned to DVSA."

"DVSA?"

"Domestic Violence and Sexual Assault," she clarified.

The curtain suddenly pulled back and a middle-aged man in a rumpled suit stood before her. "I'm pretty sure you'll agree that this qualifies." The detective glanced down at the laminated name badge that hung from her lanyard. "Mairi MacAuley?"

"Yeah."

"In here."

One of the cops moved her forward and Mairi froze, unable to step inside the cubicle. "What in the hell—"

"Hell was, indeed, the last thing she saw," the detective murmured. Mairi swallowed hard when she felt bile rise up her throat. "So, Miss MacAuley, you know this woman?"

She shook her head, unable to take her eyes off the naked body. Her torso had been used for a canvas, her skin marked with knife wounds. Symbols were carved in her skin, and her wrists, neck, and ankles displayed bloodstained rope burns.

In a pile on a chair next to the stretcher were a hot pink leather dress and a pair of shiny black thigh-high stiletto boots. The detective followed her gaze to the chair. "The clothes were lying beside her. Her purse was there too. Inside was this."

He handed her a crisp white business card. *Mairi MacAuley, RN, Crisis Worker, St. Michael's Hospital.*

Shit.

"You remember her now?" the detective asked. Shaking her head, Mairi approached the gurney, taking in the macabre artwork on her skin, noting the black wax that had been dripped onto the girl's breasts and mons. The stench of burning skin and hair made her want to gag, and she looked away, to the face that Mairi knew she would see in her nightmares.

Her eyes were open. She hated when they died like that. And the endotracheal tube that was sticking out of her mouth told her that she hadn't been dead when she arrived. She'd been alive, and . . . suffering.

"Well?"

The eyes were familiar, but she couldn't recall counseling

a young woman with fluorescent pink hair. She reached for the bangs and pulled the nylon wig off. A cascade of blond hair toppled out of a bun, and the wig fell from her hands.

"Lauren Brady," she rasped, recalling her meeting with the girl last week, right after Mairi had found the manuscript and stolen it.

"Remember anything about her?"

"Seventeen. No parents. Ward of Our Lady of Perpetual Sorrow."

"The home for troubled girls?" the detective asked as he flipped open his notebook and began writing.

"Yes," Mairi whispered, closing Lauren's eyelids so she wouldn't have to see the vacant stare. The action made the elastic cuff of her lab coat ride up, revealing the pale, jagged scars on her inner wrist. Nonchalantly, Mairi pulled it back down, securing it by curling her fingers around the elastic.

"When did you see her last?"

"Thursday afternoon. I volunteer at Our Lady once a week. She was my last appointment of the day."

The detective grunted as he wrote down everything she told him. "So St. Mike's has an outreach program or something with Our Lady?"

"No."

"No? You do this pro bono? You a saint?"

Mairi felt her face flush with anger. "There's still some charity in the world, Detective."

"Yeah? I ain't seen it in years." He looked her up and down, his eyes narrowing. "Our Lady had problems with narcotics last year. Know anything about that?"

"You don't have to work in a hospital to get your hands on

narcotics. Besides, the days of a drug cabinet and a set of keys are long gone. The dispensing is all computerized. No chance I'm signing out two Percocets and taking a handful, if you know what I mean."

He nodded, and Mairi knew he was just fishing, trying to bait her. Jackass. "So you go to Our Lady once a week. Why there? Why not some other place, in a better part of town?"

She shrugged. "The sisters were good to me and my mother. So I return the favor."

His shrewd gaze landed on her left arm, where her fingers still clutched the cuff of the lab coat. *He'd seen them—the scars.* "Were you one of those troubled girls, Miss MacAuley?"

Damn it. She didn't want to go into this.

"I don't see how that's pertinent."

His gaze shifted to the gurney. "Maybe *she'd* think it important."

Mairi tried desperately to look anywhere but at the mottling body beside her, but it was like trying to look away from a train wreck. God, why would someone do something so sick?

"Miss MacAuley?"

Mairi shook herself, trying to focus on Detective Morris and not the satanic symbols that had been drawn on Lauren's body, or the scars that marred her own wrist. "My mother was a cook there, and when my father took it into his head to beat the crap out of her, the nuns let us stay with them till he came around, begging for forgiveness."

The detective stared at her with knowing eyes. "Did he do that a lot?"

"Sometimes. Sometimes it'd be months and we'd be thinking he'd reformed. Then the hammer would drop."

His gaze once more dropped to her left hand. "And your world would collapse?"

She really hated cops. Detectives most of all. Far too perceptive. "Look, the nuns fed us, clothed us, and they helped pay for my education. I think I can give them back a day a week, Detective."

He nodded and dropped his notebook onto the bedside table. "Did you examine her last week?"

"Yes. And she didn't have the artwork. I would definitely have remembered that." Her gaze traveled over the pale skin that was marked so cruelly. "Who the hell would do something like this?" She'd seen a lot of shit in her career as an ER nurse, but this topped the list.

"Someone with a lot of time, and a place where he knew he wouldn't get caught."

"Where'd you find her?"

"On Sanctuary, in the middle of the road. The guy who nearly drove over her with his minivan stopped and called 911."

"Was she dressed?"

"Nope. She was lying on the ground, spread-eagle on an inverted pentagram that had been drawn on the road in chalk. Her belongings were dumped on the sidewalk."

Mairi pressed her eyes shut. "And she was still alive."

"Barely."

Exhaling, she looked at the young girl's body. "I write a report and file it every time I counsel the girls. You'll find my report at Our Lady."

He nodded, reached in his pocket, and unwrapped a piece of gum. "Do you remember offhand what you talked about?"

A shiver caught her unaware and she couldn't hide it before the detective saw. He was studying her as he popped the gum in his mouth.

"We talked about a man she had met," Mairi said. "She said his name was Aaron. She seemed . . . happy. She said he was nice. Treated her right. Took her out to dinner and bought her stuff."

"He was older?"

"Yeah. But it's common for these girls to look for older men. They want security. To know they can be taken care of."

He's so hot. He's a total gentleman, and, wow, is he good in bed. Way better than any guys my age are. He knows how to make me feel good, you know? His name's Aaron . . .

Mairi shivered again. The similarities were there: the same name, the same age. But Mairi had nothing more to go on, no proof that Lauren's Aaron had been the same Aaron who had stalked and terrified the hell out of her friend Rowan two months ago. It *could* be coincidence that both Rowan and Lauren had met a man named Aaron. Still, Mairi found herself wondering if Lauren had met her Aaron while he was visiting his niece at Our Lady, just like Rowan had.

The detective coughed, catching her attention. "Ah, she didn't happen to mention anything about being into the kinky stuff, did she?"

Mairi shook her head. "But I know she was into the rave scene. She and another friend used to sneak out of the house and down to the dockyards to the warehouse district. It's only a block away from the home. I'm sure that's where she met up with this guy."

"You ever seen this?" He was holding up what appeared to

be a bud of some sort. Mairi took it, knowing right away what it was.

"Thorn-apple. It's a deadly narcotic, part of the nightshade family. It's hallucinogenic and it apparently heightens sexual arousal."

"And how do you know that, Miss MacAuley?" the detective asked with a smile.

"You wouldn't believe the shit that crosses this threshold, Detective. I've seen just about everything, and drugs that get people off are the least of the weird. Trust me."

He laughed, then reached for his pad. "Do ravers use this?"

"Along with neo-pagans, occultists, rich people looking for a rush, and kids trying to be cool by experimenting." Mairi paused. "Any chance that goth club over in the East End might have something to do with this? It's close to Our Lady, and it's the right sort of scene for drugs like this."

"Velvet Haven?" he asked, obviously surprised. "I doubt it. The owner, Rhys MacDonald, is careful to stay within the law. He gets raided regularly and we never find anything. Besides, she's obviously underage. She'd never get past security there."

"She would if she was with a VIP member."

"Not at Velvet Haven she wouldn't. I know MacDonald. He doesn't want trouble. Customers who are VIPs are given that privilege because they don't cause shit. VIP status isn't bought like at other clubs. It's given, by him. That's how he keeps things in line."

"You hear stories," she murmured, trailing off. "I just thought—"

"Yeah, well. It's just a bunch of freaks getting their rocks off playing dress up. There certainly isn't any of this crazy shit going on," he grumbled, waving his hand toward the body. "I can tell you that much."

Shoving his notebook into his pocket, he said, "I'm heading over to Our Lady in the morning to check her file. If I have any more questions I'll be in touch. If you think of anything that might help us, anything she might have said, give me a call." He handed her his business card, his brow arching when she took it with her right hand, leaving her scarred wrist safely out of grabbing distance. Thankfully, he didn't comment or question her further; he just turned on his heel and left her alone with the dead body of Lauren Brady.

God, what a waste. Mairi reached into the stainless-steel cupboard for a white plastic body bag. Pulling on a pair of gloves, she touched the cold, lifeless body, positioning Lauren so the bag could slide beneath her. Her exam glove rolled down slightly, and Mairi's warm wrist touched Lauren's cool chest.

She hissed and jumped back. The body had . . . burned her. How was that possible? She looked at the symbol that had been carved between Lauren's breasts and then at her wrist as she felt the burning give way to a painful tingling, like a bee sting. Her wrist was red, the scars as prominent as they had been when they were fresh.

Louise poked her head around the curtain. "Want some help?" Mairi gasped and whirled around. "Sorry. Didn't mean to freak you out."

"It's all right," she rasped, sliding the cuff of her jacket down over her wrist. "You just surprised me, that's all."

Louise arched her brow, but let the comment slide. "I'll have someone come in to prep the body for the coroner."

"I'll do it."

With her hands on her hips, Louise arched her brows. "Five minutes ago you were bellyaching that you were on break."

"I know. Get Vicky to cover for me, and I'll do this."

"You want some help? It's creepy as hell doing death care by yourself."

"I'm good," Mairi whispered. "I . . . kind of knew her."

Louise glanced at the body. "Poor child. What the hell is this world coming to? You know, the cops that came in here told me she's the ninth one this month, but she's the only one that was carved up like a turkey."

"Yeah," Mairi murmured as she rubbed the elastic cuff against her wrist to relieve the stinging. "The whole world is fucked up, isn't it? Maybe it's a sign, Lou."

"A sign of what?"

"The beginning of the end."

The shop bells tinkled as Mairi pushed open the door, and Rowan looked up from the magazine she was thumbing through. "Hey, I was just thinking of you, and here you are!"

"Disturbing. I hate it when you do that."

Rowan laughed and closed the magazine, then tossed it onto the end of the counter by the cash register. "So, you just missed two of the hottest guys on the planet."

"Yeah?" Mairi drawled, looking around her friend's New Age store. "Was one of them your weekly Tarot Guy?"

Rowan flushed. Mairi swore that even the tips of Rowan's short blond hair glowed pink. "Uh-huh. He brought a friend this morning. Double the visual pleasure."

"Thought you swore off men for a while after the disaster that was Aaron."

"Yeah." Rowan sighed. "Still, it can't hurt to look and . . . dream. It's good for your mental health."

Mairi knew all about dreaming. Her subconscious had been conjuring up a hunk for the past couple of weeks. Man, the things the guy could do with his hands and tongue.

"So, what'd Tarot Guy buy this week?" she asked, making a beeline for the bookcase. Rowan watched her with interest as she scanned the Occult section of the case.

"His usual. A tarot deck. I swear, the guy must have hundreds. He says he gets different vibes from different decks so he has to have a lot to choose from to get the right reading. Today he picked out this really creepy black magick deck. The pictures were gruesome."

Mairi whirled around. "What do you mean, gruesome?"

"Well, really dark. Morbid, with a sexual edge. Normally, I don't carry that kind of stuff. Brings bad karma and energy, but it came by mistake. I had it on the counter, ready to pack up and send back to the supplier, but he saw it and went through the deck. I guess he liked what he saw because he bought it."

"I wonder what he wanted it for."

"Tarot readings."

"Well, duh, I know that," she snapped, turning back to the bookcase. "Ro, you got anything on satanic symbols?"

"Why, did you have that dream again?"

This was when Mairi really hated the fact she had confided in Rowan about her strange dreams. Rowan was just way too in tune with people and the shit they tried to hide. Maybe her friend really was psychic.

"Okay, I'll take the silence as a yes. And, no, I don't do satanic stuff. Enchantment is a New Age store with *positive* energy."

"Okay, then, help me out, Glinda the Good Witch. Tell me what these mean."

Pulling a piece of paper from her purse, Mairi set it in front of Rowan. It was a poorly drawn sketch of Lauren, complete with the symbols and their locations on her body. Rowan looked up, the sparkle in her jade-colored eyes gone.

"Is this what you dreamed about?"

Mairi swallowed hard. "If I tell you, you have to swear you won't breathe a word. It's confidential."

"Well, it's wearing on you, Mairi. You look exhausted. You can't keep it in. And of course, I won't tell a soul. We're best friends."

Mairi nodded. "Last night, one of the girls from Our Lady of Perpetual Sorrow arrived in the ER. She was found lying half dead on a chalk drawing of an inverted pentagram. Those marks"—Mairi pointed to the drawing—"were *carved* on her body."

"Oh, God!"

"And worse, I counseled her last week. She had my card. And I . . . I remember her." And worst of all, Mairi had dreamed of those symbols weeks ago, the night she started having the strange dreams of *him*. The guy with the magic hands and mouth.

"You're creeped out," Rowan murmured. "Look at you, you're shaking." Reaching for her hand, Rowan pulled Mairi around the counter and offered her a stool.

"A bit unnerved, yeah," she replied with a shaky laugh.

"I have a pot of herbal tea all ready to go. Let me get you a cup."

"You don't need to wait on me."

Her friend just glared. "I'm not an invalid—yet. Don't worry, you'll have plenty of opportunity to wait on me hand and foot next week after they operate on my brain. God only knows what will be left of me then. And you can be damn sure I'll milk it for all it's worth."

"That's not funny," Mairi snapped. "That tumor is going to be benign and you're going to be perfect."

"Well, I'll have a bad haircut, that's for sure." With a laugh, her friend disappeared behind the purple satin curtains.

She shouldn't be burdening Rowan with her problems, not when her friend was so sick. But Mairi had nowhere to turn. No one who would understand like Rowan understood. There was something almost ethereal about her friend. She virtually radiated goodness and light.

As Mairi sat quietly waiting for Rowan to return, she pulled up the sleeve of her denim jacket. Her wrist was still tingling, the kind that happened after a sunburn, when the skin started to heal. She scratched, watching the old, faded white streaks turn pink. Ever since last night, when she'd touched Lauren, that patch of scarred skin had felt strange. Kind of . . . Mairi swallowed as she looked down at the marks, which were now a brighter pink, despite the fact that she'd stopped scratching them. That patch of skin almost felt . . . *alive.*

"Sweet, just how you like it."

Mairi shoved her sleeve back down and straightened in her stool. No way was she going to come clean about her wrist.

Rowan passed her a delicate pink china teacup and saucer.

Under her arm, she carried a black leather book, its pages edged in gilt. "Okay, let's see what we can find here," Rowan muttered. "Symbols . . ." Licking her fingers, she flipped through the pages. "The placement on the body has to be as important as the symbols themselves," she mumbled as she thumbed through the book. "That's part of any ritual, getting the placement right."

"And how do you know this?"

"Just sip your tea." Rowan winked at her. "Okay, here," she said, drawing her finger down the page as she glanced at the drawing. "So, these symbols. They aren't necessarily satanic. They're occult."

"And the difference would be?"

"Well, it's not a devil worshipper, so you can get that thought out of your head, but there is magick involved. Both dark and light, I sense."

Swallowing her tea, Mairi prayed the symbols she dreamed about were of the light variety.

"The pentagram on her . . ."

"Pubis," Mairi supplied.

"Well, the pentagram can be innocuous. It really just represents the five elements—water, air, fire, you know, that sort of thing. Sometimes the circle surrounding it can represent the sixth element, which pagans call the element of self."

"What about when it's inverted, like it is on her?"

"Hmm, that's probably dark magick. It's pointing to the Underworld. But you know, in the pagan religion there is no hell or devil. It's just another world below ours."

"Uh-huh." Mairi wasn't buying it.

"And the infinity knot—"

"Which one is that?" Mairi asked, rubbing her inner wrist along her thigh. Thankfully Rowan was way too interested in deciphering symbols to notice she was scratching her scarred wrist.

"The one that looks like the number eight turned on its side. It's the most powerful Druid symbol. It represents the flow of all things—life, death, and rebirth."

That had been the symbol her wrist touched. Even as Rowan tapped the page with her fingertip, Mairi felt the coinciding thump against her skin. "Why is it between her breasts?" she asked, completely unnerved.

"Hey, I never said I had the answers to everything. But I do know that the infinity knot is really powerful, and positive."

Mairi found herself swallowing hard and asking in a hoarse voice, "Could it be used for evil?"

Rowan's expression clouded. "I suppose so. Perhaps in necromancy. You know, death and sex magick."

Mairi shivered, pressing her wrist into her thigh to relieve the burn she felt. "And what does a snake swallowing its tail mean?"

Rowan glanced at the paper, then back at Mairi, who looked away. That symbol had not been marked on Lauren's body, but it continually showed up in Mairi's dreams. It *always* preceded the image of the man. That, and the circle divided into three sections. Those were the hunk's calling card.

"The snake is called the Ouroboros. Like the infinity knot, it represents the circular nature of life, but it has more to do with the Underworld, the ancient knowledge and power to be found in darkness."

Tea sloshed out of her cup onto her jeans. Oh, goody, she was doing the devil in her dreams.

Rowan steadied her and took the trembling teacup from her hand. "You dream of this symbol, don't you?"

"Let it go, Rowan."

"Dreams are powerful, Mairi. They can be an omen. A warning."

"They're just stupid dreams. And I think I've had enough of this conversation," she muttered. God, she had goose bumps. To think that anything she dreamed might have a connection to Lauren's gruesome murder was just too much.

"Mairi," Rowan whispered, reaching for her hand. "I just want to help you better understand your dreams."

"It's stress, that's all. I've been working too much and I'm worried . . ." She glanced up at Rowan. "I'm afraid for you and what will happen after your surgery next week. It's all just manifested into these crazy dreams."

Rowan backed off, but Mairi saw the doubt in her intuitive eyes. "If you dream of this guy again, or any of these symbols, you let me know, okay?"

Mairi nodded. Even though she had started it, she wanted nothing more than to end this conversation.

"I've got something that'll put a smile on your face," Rowan said as she pulled away from the big hug she was giving her. "You're gonna love it."

"Yeah? What's that?"

"VIP tickets to the hottest club in town. Velvet Haven, baby!" she cried, waving the tickets before her. "And it's tonight. So get your sexy clothes on; we're going partying."

A shiver swept through Mairi's entire body as a vision of a man shimmered before her. Tall. Heavily muscled. Oozing sex and stamina, calling to the primitive female need inside her. Her body responded to the visual, wakening, craving his touch. *Sex*. Suddenly it was all she could think about, all she could see in her mind.

She heard a woman's voice whisper in her ear, "*You will find the warrior tonight and you will take him inside you.*"

The image of this man on top of her, driving into her as he pinned her to the bed with his heavy body, swam before her. She saw herself arching, her head thrown back in ecstasy as he thrust unrelentingly deep inside her. She could feel his strong fingers biting against her wrists, his harsh breath against her cheek, the sound of his dark, velvety voice whispering sex words in her ears.

Suddenly, there was nothing more she wanted—*needed*— than to have him between her thighs, giving her his body, his strength.

"*You will take him inside you.*"

"Mairi, you okay? You look like you're zoning out."

"I think I just need a nap," Mairi whispered, finding her way to the door. "See you tonight, Rowan. I'll pick you up at your place."

Outside, she leaned against the brick wall, trying to catch her breath, trying and failing to stop the images of a man on top of her. Her body was trembling in eager anticipation. It had been a while since she'd last been with a guy, but it shouldn't feel like this. Her urge for sex was as strong and primordial as her need for air.

Against her denim-clad thigh, her wrist tingled, and she unconsciously rubbed it against her leg, searching for relief.

Things were getting crazy. First her wrist, and now she was hearing voices and seeing her dream hunk when she was awake. Wishing he was real, despite the danger she felt.

She didn't do danger, she reminded herself. But she couldn't lie; she wanted to do *him*.

CHAPTER THREE

Bran had no use for humans, but this one, she was exactly the sort of mortal he was looking for—single, lonesome, and begging for it.

"This female will give you what you need."

Bran looked down at the man standing beside him. Though the music was loud and pounding, he could hear every word, as if they were the only ones in the room. Above the throbbing bass, he even heard the thump of his companion's heart. Steady, rhythmic; nothing to signal any impending betrayal or tricks.

His companion's serpentlike eyes shifted. The slit where the pupil should have been was long, elliptical. More than mortals had been caught up in those mesmerizing eyes, but Bran knew better than to look into them for more than a second.

Sayer was half-Selkie and used enchantment magic to interrogate and ferret out information, from immortals and mortals alike. Tonight Bran had need of that skill.

Rolling his shoulders, Bran shrugged off the tension that

had been steadily growing inside him since last night, when he'd seen the body of the butchered youngling.

Tension coiled as he rolled his shoulders once more, his long black hair sliding down his back as his knuckles rapped against the stone balustrade that overlooked the dance floor. Beneath the neon lights, the sigils on his left hand glowed, the pewter and gold reflections entwining like vines, casting shimmering images on the copper-tiled ceiling. Not wanting to draw any attention, Bran dropped his hand from the balustrade, hiding it beneath the sleeve of his coat.

Ignoring Sayer's inquisitive glance, Bran turned to look again through the stained-glass window, down to the street below, where hundreds of humans were lined up, vying for the coveted tickets into Velvet Haven.

If they only knew what lurked in the shadows of this place.

What did they know, these mortals, other than that Velvet Haven had been created inside an old mansion built in the ornate Victorian Gothic style? What lured them, besides the mystery and seduction to be found behind the arched iron doors?

Did they know the truth? Did any of them suspect that a diaphanous veil separated the mortal world from the Celtic Otherworld? Did the humans know that beneath the floor they danced and writhed upon was the *Cave of Cruachan*—the magical entrance to Annwyn?

Would they believe that here in Velvet Haven, mortals and immortal shape-shifters mingled? Danced. *Fucked.* Would it scare them to know the type of magick being practiced right beneath their noses?

Was it possible one of these mortals was practicing the dark arts? He frowned at the thought.

"Does she displease you?" Sayer asked as he caught Bran's black expression.

"No."

Sayer grinned and gazed once more at the dance floor. "You're a real buzz kill tonight."

"There is no 'buzz' in this for me, Sayer."

"There could be, if you allowed yourself the pleasure."

Bran grunted as he crossed his arms over his chest. "There's no pleasure in this curse. You know how I feel about mortal females. They're nothing but a necessary evil."

Sayer glanced out the window and stared down at the blond woman he had picked to service his king. "Mortals have their uses."

"You're sure she's clean?" Bran asked, getting back to the night's mission and his purpose for being in Velvet Haven.

"You needn't worry. She'll do you right."

Sayer suddenly stopped, his gaze sharpened like a predator's when it spied prey. His skin flickered; a brief sparkling of iridescent orange and pink ran up his neck; then it was gone, but the Selkie's watchfulness was still present, alerting Bran to a danger his friend had suddenly sensed.

At the same moment, Bran felt the pupil of his right eye dilate, swallowing up the gold iris. There was something going on in Annwyn. *Movement. Gathering. Darkness.*

"What do you see?" Sayer asked as he watched Bran's eyes glow in the dark.

"Annwyn. An unseen threat lurking in the forest. Magick. *Dark* magick." The portal that allowed him to see his home closed, leaving Bran with his mismatched eyes.

"Necromancy." Sayer spat the word as he scanned the hu-

mans and immortals below them. His skin absorbed every hum, every vibration. "I sense it here, in the club."

Bran searched the darkened corners, peering through the shadows for this necromancer he sought. Scattered among the humans were the rebels of the Otherworld. Shifters with no allegiances; magicians with great powers.

They were here, lurking in darkness, cloaked by shadows and magic. The Phoenix, the Griffin, the Shadow Wraith. Even the Fallen Angel had come out of his hiding place amongst the mortals to partake of the night. The only one missing was the gargoyle.

The gargoyle—*Carden*—his half brother needed to be found. And soon. But to continue the search he needed energy. He needed the sexual pleasure of a human female to recharge his power, and with it, the ability to perform the strongest of magic in Annwyn—destruction magic. With this magic he could destroy the dark magician who was preying on his people. He could destroy Morgan. And find Carden. *Someday*. But first he needed to find the book Cailleach spoke of, as well as the other immortal warriors he was supposedly going to lead.

"The female," Bran growled irritably. "I need her—*now*."

"You needn't sound so unhappy about it. Your own uncle fell in love with a mortal."

"No mortal will ever ensnare me. You can count on that."

Sayer only smiled and shifted to the left, allowing Bran full access to the window and a glimpse of the woman who was to be his evening's entertainment. "You're just pissed because your uncle's abdication made you king. You'd rather be playing war than ruling Annwyn."

Bran didn't bother to answer. "She is rather mousy, isn't she?" he muttered.

Sayer shrugged. "You gave me three requirements. First, she must be free of drugs; second, she must not be ovulating; and third, she must be hungry for sex. *Hours of it.*"

"And so I did." But a part he didn't want to acknowledge had secretly wanted to enjoy it. Although he didn't know why he still, on occasion, longed for the impossible. It was a futile wish to desire the humans. It was only the need for power that aroused him.

"I don't know about mousy," Sayer murmured with obvious appreciation. "Her body is rather delicious. All those curves."

She moved to the left, out of the way of some shoving mortal males. She nearly disappeared among the crowd. From his vantage point, Bran tracked her. A cloud passed and moonlight suddenly illuminated her aura.

"Her name is Rowan. Keir introduced us this morning. He goes into her shop all the time. I thought she—"

"She won't do," Bran said, leaning closer to the window to get a better view.

"And why not?"

"She's marked."

"Marked?" Sayer squinted, his eyes narrowing, the pupil-like slit elongating, allowing him keener sight. "I don't see anything."

"Her aura." Bran motioned to the halo of color that arched around her body. "I've never seen a mortal with two colors before."

"Well, I'm no Sidhe, so I can't see auras. In fact, I can't see a damn thing, other than a pair of fine tits in a corset."

Bran furrowed his brow in annoyance. Sayer *would* notice those. "The colors meld, black and indigo. Black means illness, possibly imminent death. Indigo represents a highly intuitive and spiritual nature. A seeker."

"And you can't sleep with her because?"

"Because it is a bad omen to take a woman who is marked for death. And even if she is not, then the intuitive side of her is dangerous. What if she senses I am not like the men she is used to?"

Sayer looked him up and down, noting his height, his long hair, the glittering markings at his temple, and the ones on his neck that disappeared down the front of his black T-shirt. "I think it's safe to say that any female will find you different, seeker or not."

"I'm not taking risks. This one won't do."

Sayer sighed with displeasure. "Well, then, what about her friend? Here, I'll show you."

Closing his eyes, Sayer lifted his chin. His skin changed from its golden hue to a luminous mix of gold and orange. Pink flickered over the cords of his neck as the strobe light waved over them, the luminescence of the Selkie shifting and writhing over Sayer's human form.

"You've enchanted her already?" Bran asked with disgust.

"I'm not opposed to your leftovers," he said with a sly grin. "Now look down. I think I have persuaded her to show her friend."

Bran felt her before he saw her.

Hiding the way her aura hit him in the gut, he gathered his control. He trusted Sayer, but not completely. Alliances only went so far in the world of Annwyn. There was no need for anyone to know just how weak he became without his mortals.

"What do you think of her?"

A woman with long black hair stepped forward, and he struggled to pretend indifference. The white shimmering band of her aura weaved its way over to him. Through the window it came, his magic calling it forth, beckoning it. She was strong, but there was a vulnerability there as well that engaged him, made him want to explore it. And she was passionate. He felt the desire, the longing for pleasure. The ache for sex. She wanted it but she would fight him, make him work to convince her to accept him. There was something so raw and primal about her; if he could make her submit to him, he felt he could survive off that energy for years.

Scanning her frame, he saw that she was of small stature, even with the heels. Her body was curvy, with heavy breasts and rounded hips. Her shape was so very different from the females of his kind, who were tall and lithe, with small breasts and narrow hips. He'd always preferred the Sidhe ideal of beauty, but suddenly he was considering the merits of feeling those soft curves beneath his body.

From where he stood he could not tell if she was pretty or plain. But that did not matter. What mattered was her aura. White meant perfect balance. It was so rare, a pure white aura. He should probably fear it, but he was drawn to it—*to her*. He suddenly wanted nothing more than to take all her pleasure inside his body and convert it into magic.

Yes, this mortal female would give him great power. *Tonight.*

"And where are you going?" Sayer called as Bran left him standing at the balustrade.

"Outside. To have a closer look at my evening meal."

"And you think *this* place is a den of inequity? Wait till you get beyond the doors and into *their* world."

"I assure you, I would *never* allow a mortal to be the death of me."

The Master stepped silently into the shadowed alcove. In one fluid movement his knees were bent, palms pressed together in a mockery of a prayer, black cloak concealing any identifying features. Like a huge black crow, he sat perched on the stone balustrade, hidden in shadows, watching the humans and immortals gyrating against one another, committing every cardinal sin. Normally the vision was arousing, but it wasn't the sinning mortals and wayward immortals that turned him on tonight. It was the motley gathering of shape-shifters.

From the darkness, he watched them struggling with their inner demons. His gaze skipped to each one of them, studying them: the raven, the Shadow Wraith, Selkie, Griffin, and the morose phoenix. Everyone was there, even the gargoyle, hidden well out of anyone's sight. But he was there nonetheless. And the Fallen Angel. He inhaled deeply. Ah, yes, Suriel was there, too.

Out of all of them there was one who screamed for the Master's attention. Closing his eyes, he used his other senses to find his new apprentice. Behind closed lids, the image flared to life.

Yes, that's what he wanted. That beautiful Dark Soul he lusted for. The Dark Soul who hadn't a clue what possibilities lurked inside him. The Master would show him what blackness was there, bubbling just below the surface.

All that hate. All that pain. *The rage.* Oh, yes, the Dark Soul was going to be beautiful once he was turned. And it would not take much. The seed was already there, taking root—growing, until the day he, the Master, the *Soul Stealer*, could come and pluck it, control it.

The aroma of his new apprentice was intoxicating: a mixture of helplessness, fury, and perhaps a hint of desperation. Inhaling deeply, the Master felt a deep stirring. It was an exhilarating elixir, much more potent than alcohol or sex. An aphrodisiac made for the devil. And it was sweating off the immortal's body in rivulets.

So much pain. So beautiful in his emotional prison, waiting until the day the lock was sprung open, freeing him. The hatred he would unleash against his kind—against the world—would be utterly breathtaking.

He had waited so long to hold such power, to unleash it to do his bidding. But soon the Master would have what he needed to destroy both worlds: Annwyn and the mortal realm.

He was aroused just thinking about the mayhem and pain they would cause. Every master needed an apprentice, and this one was utterly perfect. Together they would have immense power, and the rituals . . . the black magick rituals would be even more exciting when he had someone to share them with.

"Hi there."

He closed his eyes, inhaling the scent of aroused female, which made his cock throb behind his leather pants. "Hello."

Jumping down from his perch, he reached for the woman, wrapping his hand around her slim waist.

"Love the jacket," she said, rubbing her hands along his chest, then down the pocket of his trench coat. "What's this?" she asked in a coy, sexy voice. She pulled the silver satin cord from his pocket, her eyes rising slowly. From beneath her long eyelashes, he saw her pupils dilate with excitement.

"What's your name?" he asked as he cupped her breast in his palm.

"Trinity," she answered in a husky breath that immediately had him leaking from the tip of his cock. He hid his smile as he pulled her to him, fitting her lithe body against his. "How appropriate," he murmured into her ear. "I happen to be looking for a divine threesome." *The Sacred Trine.* That was what he was searching for. And he would find it, all three women, right here in Velvet Haven. Perhaps this woman could lead him to them.

Trinity giggled and wrapped her leg around his calf as she shoved her breast farther into his hand. "Mmm," she moaned, "sounds like my kind of time."

He smiled, trailing the back of his hand down her cheek, angling her head so he could watch the bounding pulse of her carotid. *Stupid human.* She had no idea what he meant.

"Did you bring a friend?" she asked, rubbing up against him.

His gaze flickered to his apprentice. "Not tonight."

"Oh." She pouted, then brightened. "I have some friends."

"Have you?" He circled her nipple, which was protruding through her thin top. "I'm searching for a particular threesome."

She looked up at him, batting her lashes. "A Trinity?"

Indeed he was, but not this kind of Trinity. No, the one he wanted was much more important. One he couldn't allow to slip into the wrong hands.

"What I'm looking for," he whispered as he flicked his tongue along her neck, "are three women. A healer, an Oracle, and a Nephillim." She pulled back, her eyes glazed. "Have you ever heard of such women? Do they come here?"

She shook her head. Her eyes were as vacant as her thoughts, consumed with the need for sex. She might be a regular at Velvet Haven, but she was not connected in the way he needed. Unfortunate for her. He might have kept her alive if she had more than her pussy to offer.

As he swept the club with his gaze, he searched once more through the crowd. He needed that Trine. And he needed it soon if he was going to find the key that unlocked the flame and the amulet.

Dangling the silver rope between them, she licked her lips. "Ready to play?"

Mentally he undressed her, imagining his markings imprinted on her body. She was going to be exceedingly amusing.

This one would be different, he would make certain of that. After he fucked her, branded her—*terrorized* her—he would make her into a billboard that no one would fail to understand. Not Suriel, and not Cailleach. Both worlds would suffer his wrath for what they'd done to him. Both would know that they were now his enemy. No one was safe from him and his wrath.

"What's your name, sugar?" she asked as she raked her nails

down the heavy shaft of his cock. He smiled as he bound the rope around her wrists. Her breath rushed out. Apprehension and sexual need perfumed the air, arousing him to the point where he could have come just by thinking of what he was going to do to her.

He smiled. "Just call me Aaron."

CHAPTER FOUR

The gargoyle, with its bulging eyes and grotesque mouth, leered down from the eaves, making a mockery of the neon welcome sign that flashed below it. The creature was the most hideous thing Mairi had ever seen, yet somehow it managed to seem right at home, carved into the gray stone portcullis of the mansion's elaborate Gothic entrance.

On the other side of the gargoyle was the carving of an angel, its wings spread wide, its head bent in prayer. The whole angel-and-demon thing was totally appropriate, given the mansion's history and the mystery surrounding the couple who had lived there for an unnaturally long time.

The house, it was said, had been built by an eccentric Scotsman, Daegan MacDonald, for his wife, whom he had adored. The mansion had seen many lavish parties over the decades since its construction in the 1870s. There was something dark and otherworldly about the architecture and the stained-glass windows that were covered with Druid mythological symbols Mairi had seen in one of the manuscripts she collected.

There was no denying that Velvet Haven, as the mansion was now called, held some magical, enthralling quality that sucked you in and held you captive. It lured, even though the feeling of danger was persuasive, seducing even as it frightened. The distant roll of thunder rumbling across the heavens only added to the menacing atmosphere.

Glancing once more at the statue, Mairi shivered despite the warm spring air, which was growing heavier with the threat of rain. She could have sworn that the eyes of the statue were tracking her as she shifted in line, trying to get beneath the blossomed canopy of an apple tree before the rain came.

The very idea of a stone statue capable of watching her was completely irrational, not to mention stupid.

Something strange was happening to her. She wasn't her logical self. *Fatigue.* It was exhaustion, that's all. Swinging back and forth from the night shift to the day shift, not to mention sleepless nights worrying about Rowan's health. And the dreams, she thought darkly. The dreams kept her up all night.

Well, at least her wrist had stopped bothering her. She'd gone home and taken an antihistamine and lo and behold it had worked. It must have been an allergic reaction to contact with Lauren, maybe from the thorn-apple.

As another tremor snaked down her spine, she looked up once more into the taunting face of the gargoyle, unable to deny that despite her rationalizing pep talk, she was still spooked. The past twenty-four hours had been nothing but weirdness. And nothing was stranger than the dream she'd had that afternoon after visiting Rowan.

She'd fallen right to sleep after taking a Benadryl. Immediately she'd been visited by the man of her dreams. As usual, he had pleasured her, made her cry out in ecstasy. But the dream had taken on a different tone than the ones before it. After her orgasm, a darkness had swept over her. Images of blood and the sting of betrayal assailed her until Mairi had forced herself awake, terror filling her as her sweat-drenched T-shirt clung to her breasts, the nipples still hard from her dream.

She was still kind of freaked out, and it didn't help her current state of mind to know that she was standing on the sidewalk in the city's notorious downtown east side. No one but drug addicts and vagrants came to this part of town. No one except the hundreds of eager people around her who were lining up, trying to get inside the old Gothic mansion.

"This is going to be so cool," Rowan squealed beside her. "I can't believe we're actually going to get in."

"How did you manage to score VIP tickets to the hottest club in town, anyway?" she asked, watching a big black bird land on the shoulder of the gargoyle statue. The thing was huge. But then, if the east side was his home, there was lots of garbage to dine on.

She watched its head cock to the left, its sharp, predator eyes honing in on something. Was it just her, or was the bird scanning the crowd as if it were looking for a midnight snack?

"I told you, my Tarot Guy brought a friend along with him this morning. He gave them to me."

The flap of the raven's wings drew Mairi's attention away from Rowan. She watched the bird lift from the statue's shoulder and fly to a branch of the apple tree above her. The branch wavered as the bird landed, and the sweet scent of apple blossoms wafted over her.

She was never one for bird watching, but this one had a

strange silver streak on its back that captured her attention. It was extremely focused, astute, as it watched the crowd. Its head would cock sharply to the left and then to the right, as if it were listening. But always its sharp eyes came back to—her—if she allowed herself to admit it. But she couldn't.

The bird is not watching me, she muttered over and over, but still, she felt that rapacious gaze on her, even when she kept her eyes firmly lowered.

"Are you sure you should be accepting tickets from a guy you don't even know?" Mairi asked.

"I swear," Rowan gushed, "he was totally normal."

"Yeah, well, we thought Aaron was, too. Till he turned into a stalker and we had to hide you for weeks."

"That was months ago, and he's in jail, remember? Besides, you know I've always wanted to get inside this place. How could I turn down free tickets?"

Was Aaron still in jail? Mairi wasn't so sure. Not after what Lauren had told her. "So, tell me about this man," Mairi said as she watched a pair of guys with Mohawks and silver chains dangling from their nostrils to their lips saunter past them.

"His name is Sayer," Rowan answered, watching the guys go by, "and, my God, is he hot. He came into Enchantment this morning with the Tarot Guy. Who, by the way, is überhot, too. He simmers with mystery and totally oozes sex. I bet he's wild in the sack, once he lets go of his reserve."

"I know. You talk about him every week."

"Do I?" Rowan sighed. "He doesn't notice me. At least not that way."

"So a guy you've never met comes into your store and offers you tickets to Velvet Haven, and you accept them—and don't feel a bit worried about that, especially after what I showed you happened in the city last night?"

Rowan paused. "Did it happen here?"

Mairi glanced at the bird, then at the facade of the club. "No."

"Then what's to worry about?"

"I don't know." And truly, she didn't. But she felt like they should worry. This wasn't their usual scene. And her dreams . . . they were dark and disturbing and somehow in her mind she had linked them with this place. Even though she'd never been inside the club.

Something brushed by her, skating down her arm. It was a black feather from the raven, which had just flown off the branch. Goose bumps sprang up and she shivered. Her body tingled where it had touched her. She felt warm—aroused.

"Hey, look, the line's moving," Rowan announced.

Within five minutes they were standing before a brute of a bouncer who scowled and looked them up and down as he took their tickets. "You're VIP," the bouncer muttered as he unhooked the velvet rope and waved them through. "Sign in, name and phone number. Then take the stairs and turn right. Mr. Macdonald will show you where to go from there."

"Cool!" Rowan squealed as they entered the club and scribbled their name on a clipboard. "It's even better than I thought."

The doors suddenly shut behind them, creaking on the old rusted hinges. Inside, neon blue and pink beams of light flickered over the dance floor, illuminating the gyrating dancers. The music was loud . . . pulsing . . . the techno beat hard and heavy. In the shadowed corners were shimmery fabrics in fuchsia and black. The furniture had a Victorian Gothic vibe that reminded

Mairi of an old burlesque club. Only it wasn't occupied by men in tuxes and ladies wearing feather boas. The clientele at Velvet Haven were in leather and PVC. Mohawks and piercings and long *Matrix*-like coats replaced the tuxes. There were cyber Goths wearing their silver wigs and metallic costumes, as well as those creepy Babydolls who dressed like little girls and walked around sucking their thumbs. Some Metal Heads were holed up in a corner, their leather jackets covered in spikes, their necks adorned with dog collars. A group of women dressed in long black gowns that looked like something out of the Victorian age floated past them. One of them had two little puncture holes on her throat with two drops of blood dripping from the openings.

Talk about taking things seriously.

Against a wall filled with gilt mirrors, the DJ was spinning records, his shoulder-length black hair streaked with electric blue dye, his arms bulging with muscles and tats. He was at least six feet five and the expression on his face was beyond intense.

"Oh my God," Rowan gasped, looking at the DJ. "That's *him*! The Tarot Guy."

Mairi swung her gaze to the wall to check out the man who came into Rowan's New Age boutique on a weekly basis. She got an eyeful, all right. In the reflection of one of the mirrors behind the DJ was a couple making out, the guy's hand steadily moving down the woman's belly, only to escape beneath the waist of his date's black leather skirt. Beside them, another couple watched eagerly as they fondled themselves.

Holy shit! Just what the hell had they walked into? What was this place, some sort of fetish club?

"Are you seeing what I'm seeing?" Mairi yelled over the loud music. Rowan nodded, swallowing hard as she watched the couple in the mirror. The man was now sinking to his knees.

"Rowan, who exactly is this guy who gave you the tickets?" Mairi's eyes widened to three times their normal size as she watched the guy shoulder his way between the woman's thighs, his palms sliding up her fishnet stockings, lifting her skirt. Nervously, Mairi glanced around and noticed that no one else was watching the show in the mirror. Everyone else was so blasé.

"I know I have a terrible history of picking up the wrong sort of man," Rowan said uneasily. "But I swear, Sayer is . . ." She trailed off as another guy came into the reflection of the mirror to join the busy couple. "That is . . ."

"C'mon, we're leaving. This Sayer is obviously a twisted pervert, just like that other asshole you've finally gotten away from."

"I'm not twisted. Nor am I pervert."

Jumping, the two of them whirled around, only to find themselves looking up at a giant. A beautiful, golden giant with eyes that shimmered in the strobe lights. His beauty was beyond anything Mairi had ever seen. And his body . . . Her gaze slid over the tight black T-shirt that showcased his pecs and arms.

Obviously hard-core in the workout department.

There was something inhuman about him, he was that drop-dead gorgeous.

He smiled, a slow sensual grin that was almost hypnotic. "Welcome to Velvet Haven. We've been expecting you."

"We?" Mairi glanced back at the DJ, who was still playing music.

The man grinned and moved to the left, revealing the most

dangerous, sexiest man Mairi had ever laid eyes on. When he looked at her from across the room, her entire body jolted and images flooded her brain. He was dark, brooding, intense, reminding Mairi of a black thundercloud. Menacing yet strangely fascinating.

There was a fierce storm brewing inside him. Mairi could feel it, a strange energy radiating off of him. Her body lit up like a nuclear power plant and her breasts suddenly grew heavy. She was aroused, and her arm tingled where the feather had landed on her.

Their gazes locked as he began to walk—no, *stalk*—slowly toward her through the crowd. An instant connection was made, one Mairi felt deep into her core. The way he looked at her, the way he made her insides tighten with longing was the same as her dream lover.

But this man wasn't a fantasy; this man was flesh and blood and warmth. This was for real, and so was the desire she felt suddenly taking over.

The scent of the woman clung to his fingers. Bran hadn't been able to resist flying past her, allowing the tip of his wing to graze her soft skin. The zap of sensation had taken him by surprise. He hadn't expected to feel so much with only the barest of contact. In fact, his fingertips still tingled from the brief brush of her arm.

He could still smell her, despite the scent of cigarettes, booze, and sweating bodies. As overpowering as those scents were to him, the woman's was still more powerful. As sweet as the apple blossoms, but spiced with something more exotic. She smelled of woman, and sex, and the unmistakable pungent odor of unease.

She was perceptive, this female, her instincts keen and clear. Yet she buried them, hiding them beneath a suffocating layer of disbelief and rationalization. *Mortal thinking*, he thought with disgust. It had been many centuries since humans believed in the Otherworld. As much as he despised their narrowed vision, Bran counted himself fortunate that the humans didn't see past their own kind. If they did, he'd have more to worry about than keeping Annwyn safe from within. He'd have humans to keep out.

He did not need mortals creeping about his world, causing havoc and mayhem. They would not understand magick, or Annwyn. And when humans didn't understand, when they feared something they could not explain, their natural inclination was to destroy.

As king of the Sidhe it was his duty to protect Annwyn and its secrets. And to do that he needed to lie with a human female to sustain his magic. A bitch of an irony, but there was nothing to be done about the Legacy Curse now. He needed this woman.

"The two of you better be keeping your noses clean tonight."

The gruff voice of Rhys MacDonald stopped Bran and he turned and faced his cousin. That this human was part-Sidhe burned him every time he thought it. His uncle had been a fool to give up his throne and his powers for a mere human. To know his uncle's essence swam in the veins of this mortal made Bran feel savage.

"What are you up to, Raven? And it's not your usual sex fest."

"Nothing you need concern yourself over."

"Don't bother to hide it. I already know about the bodies that have shown up in Annwyn."

"The Shadow Wraith, no doubt. He needs to learn to keep his mouth shut."

Rhys shrugged. "He doesn't need to tell me things. We're connected. I already knew of the killings before he told me."

"You're an abomination," Bran spat with disgust. "Your bond with your wraith is unnatural."

"Screw you, Raven." Rhys took a step closer to him. "If you've come here looking for revenge, you can sheath your talons. The murders didn't happen in my club."

"No, just beneath it."

Rhys' gaze narrowed. "That's your domain, King. I haven't gone near that door since you put the spell on it. You can look to your own kind for the murders."

"Why do you think I'm here?" Bran growled impatiently.

"And I thought you came to get your rocks off."

Bran felt his lips curl with rage. "Stay out of my business, MacDonald, or you'll wish you had."

"Is that right?" Rhys snorted, straightening his stance as if he were getting ready for a fight. "While you're here, in *my* club, you'll watch yourself. I'm not going to allow you two to interfere with my livelihood. No cops, no magick, and no trouble, you got that? You might be king back there," he gritted out as he pointed to the wooden door that led to the Cave of Cruachan, "but in my club, *I'm* the boss."

"I'm only here thanks to *your* great-great-grandfather. If

he hadn't left our world to fuck a human, believe me, neither would I."

MacDonald stiffened at the affront, his violet eyes narrowing dangerously. He was mostly mortal, true, but Bran knew he could fight like the devil, and just as dirty, too.

"As I wasn't around a hundred and seventy years ago, I'm not taking responsibility for your curse. It's not my problem Daegan found the women of my species more pleasing than the Sidhe. I know what brings you here, Raven. Now get your fix and do your investigating, but keep a low profile. There're a couple of undercovers here tonight, so watch what you're doing and who you're screwing."

There had never been anything but bad blood between Bran and his mortal relations, but this little prick was the one who had gotten under his skin the most. Probably because Bran saw so much of himself in the immovable, arrogant man's face.

"Oh, yeah," Rhys drawled, stepping closer so that they were nearly nose to nose. "I have a message for you from Keir."

Bran glanced at the DJ, who was still playing music. "What does he want?"

"Stay the fuck away from the one named Rowan."

"And which one is she?"

"The blonde."

Bran was instantly relieved. "Tell your *friend* that the one named Rowan holds no interest for me. It is the other I want."

Rhys slowly backed away. "I'll be watching you, Raven. One wrong move and you'll be back in Annwyn without your energy fix. You got that?"

Bran watched the mortal leave, hating him, loathing his

own miserable circumstances. He despised being weak, hated being without the powers of Annwyn.

With a snarl, he headed for the women.

"*Put on your happy face,*" Sayer ordered him, using telepathy so the women wouldn't hear them. "*You're going to scare them off. And try to talk like you belong in the twenty-first century, for God's sake. Fit in, for once.*"

Bran lifted his lips in a smile, hoping it was the sort that would make the woman's panties wet. He never had been very good at foreplay. He was more a take-what-he-wanted guy, but he knew that just taking this woman wasn't going to get him what he needed: his cock buried deep inside her, all night long.

⚜

The guy looked as if he had a case of severe gastrointestinal upset. Never had Mairi seen a more pitiful excuse for a smile than this one.

"Hey," he said, extending his hand to her. Obviously he wasn't one of those smooth talker types. Taking his hand in hers, she smiled.

"This is my friend, Bran," the golden god murmured. "And I'm Sayer."

"Mairi," she replied, pulling her hand free. "And you already know Rowan."

Sayer's eyes seemed to glow as he looked over her friend. "Not nearly enough, I think."

Mairi heard her friend's breath catch. She was going to have to watch this Sayer character. He was just the sort of smooth operator that got women to do whatever he wished.

And she'd seen many of those women rolled into the ER raped and bloodied after a night out dancing and drinking.

Rowan was easy pickings. She was still reeling from the tumor diagnosis and the fiasco with Aaron. Rowan had never had it easy with guys, and Mairi knew without a doubt that Sayer could make her friend forget all about being cautious, even though the frightening events with Aaron were never far from Rowan's—and Mairi's—thoughts. Now she, Mairi thought with pride, wasn't so easily taken in by a handsome face and buff bod. Unlike Rowan, her inability to trust made it easy for her to avoid becoming a victim.

Looking around the club, Mairi found herself feeling very uncomfortable and conspicuous. She didn't know what to say, and the music was so damn loud they wouldn't hear her if she did talk. And the big guy with the short black hair and the tight T-shirt with the fuchsia VELVET HAVEN logo on his chest kept watching them.

Mairi hadn't missed the altercation between the guy and Bran, and she found herself wondering if Bran wasn't a regular shit disturber at the club. If so, she wanted no part of his company. The last thing she wanted in a place like this was trouble.

"How about a drink?" Sayer asked. Laying his hand on the lower part of Rowan's back, he ushered her along, toward the bar and another room where there were chandeliers and velvet couches.

She followed behind, but all along Mairi was conscious of the man who walked beside her. He was at least six feet six with shoulders the width of a house and legs like oak trunks. He was dressed in black leather pants, black Doc Martens, and a long black coat that was cool in a *Matrix* sort of way. His hair was black as well, long, silky. She couldn't see what color his eyes were, only that his lashes were black and thick.

He walked with a pantherlike grace, his stride long and lazy, belying the power she sensed in him. He was scary in a way, yet sexy, too. She'd never been attracted to the long-hair type before, but suddenly she had visions of running her hands through that mane.

The guys she'd dated had always been safe, even boring. But this guy—he had danger tattooed all over him. A total bad boy that Mairi couldn't deny turned her on.

She sensed he possessed the same sexual prowess her dream lover did. And how stupid was that? Her dream babe wasn't real. And this guy . . . well, what the heck would a guy like him be looking at her for? And why did she care, because she was never going to see him again, and she didn't do one-night stands with complete strangers.

Jumping, she squeaked in surprise as she felt a big, warm hand clamp around her elbow. The minute she felt his touch a warm hum infused her blood. Glancing up at him, she saw that he was watching the crowd as though he were looking for someone. Suddenly his grip hardened.

"Ow," she cried, pulling back. He looked down at her and Mairi got lost in his eyes. They were the strangest eyes she'd ever seen. One was gold and the other pewter, and both were thinly rimmed with a violet edge. Contacts. Had to be.

"I did not mean to hurt you," he said, his fingers soothing the sting on her flesh. "My apologies."

He had a faint Scottish accent. His voice was deep and smooth, and she liked the way it seemed to wash over her. He was watching her, expecting her to say something. She could only nod, bereft of speech as she gazed into his eyes. *Completely mute*. A rare condition for her.

"Shall we?"

He waved her ahead, and Mairi was struck by the gentlemanly veneer beneath the leather and long hair. She would never have pegged him as having manners, but he did. Good ones, in fact.

They followed Sayer and Rowan to the back of the room, where it was darker and fewer people congregated. Most people were at the bar; a few were at booths sipping champagne and martinis. Sayer sat them at a high-backed booth upholstered in fuchsia velvet.

"What are you ladies drinking tonight?"

"Water," they said together.

"C'mon. Just one." He winked and smiled, his magnetic personality drawing them in. "Have one on me. I'll bet you've never had a caramel apple martini, have you?"

Rowan's eyes went wide. "No, but you're speaking to my heart."

"I knew I would," he murmured as he gazed at Rowan. Mairi saw his eyes darken and flicker; then something weird happened to his pupil—it flipped and became long, slitlike. But when he turned his attention to her, the pupil was normal. "What about you?"

"I'll have a beer. With the cap left on, please." There was no way in hell she was taking any chances that she'd be slipped some drug. She glanced at Rowan, shooting her a look that told her to do the same.

"On second thought, I'll have a beer, too. Cap on."

Sayer exchanged a glance with his friend, then strolled

over to the bartender. He ordered, then leaned up against the bar, watching them.

"So, Mairi," Bran murmured, his voice deep and gravelly. "This is your first time here."

It was not a question, but a statement. "How do you know?"

He shrugged, then stretched back, resting his arm on the back of the booth. "If I had seen you here before, I definitely would have noted that."

Smooth. Her stomach did a little flop, but she ignored it. "You a regular, then?"

His brows arched as he scanned the group of people who were headed to the empty booth beside them. "I come here when I feel . . . a certain call."

Uh-huh. "You mean a booty call?"

His gaze slid to hers and she fought the urge to squirm beneath his intense stare. "I'm not familiar with that phrase, but the way your voice changed when you said it makes me believe it is something derogatory to your sex."

Is this guy for real?

"You have a lovely voice, you know. Very soft and soothing."

"Are you changing the subject?" she asked.

"No, we're still talking about you."

She laughed and suddenly felt a ton of pressure evaporate. He smiled and brushed a few strands of her hair away from her eyelashes. "You have a lovely smile, too."

Mairi looked away. This guy was definitely smooth. Top notch in the seduction department. She was definitely feeling tempted just by having him sit next to her, not to mention the way his attention was completely focused on her.

"What do you do for a living, Mairi?"

"I'm a nurse at St. Michael's."

"You're a healer."

She glanced up at him and was once again struck mute by his eyes. And that voice. It was so deep and velvety. Like a fine cognac, it was warm and smooth. "Uh—uh," she stuttered. Good lord, one look into his eyes and then down to those big hard shoulders and she had completely lost the thread of the conversation.

Brushing her long hair back from her cheek, he slid his fingertips down over her shoulders and along her arm. He tracked the progression of his hand as it got lost in her thick hair. Suddenly she couldn't breathe. Couldn't think of anything other than having that big hand caressing her back in slow, sweeping motions.

"I can feel it in you, you know, the power to heal."

Her traitorous libido went into overdrive. God, he had the sexiest voice she'd ever heard. When he ran his fingertips along her arm, raising goose bumps, Mairi gathered her scattered thoughts. "I'm just a nurse," she muttered, inching away from him.

It was not good to be this affected by him. He was a stranger, she reminded herself. He outweighed her by at least a hundred pounds and more than a foot of muscle and bulk. She would not be able to fight a man like this off. Better to steer clear of any possible entanglements.

He moved in, following her when she tried to create space between them. "I bet you care for the terminally ill," he murmured next to her ear.

"No, Emergency Room."

His head cocked to the side as his gaze raked over her. "Are you sure you don't help those who are in a hopeless situation?"

She shuddered. What could he know about her? Did abused women and girls count as hopeless situations? There were days when she believed so.

"I just thought . . ." He trailed off and glanced away, watching the crowd.

"You thought what?"

He swung his attention back to her, making her whole body liquefy. "Because of your aura I thought that you were the type to help people through dark times."

"My aura?" she choked. Whoa! *Weird.*

His gaze turned molten and his face tightened up as if he heard her thoughts and was now offended by them.

"Never mind, Mairi," Rowan said, leaning across the table. "You'll never get her to believe in auras or the supernatural. She's a logical, hard-science girl."

"But you believe?"

Rowan shrugged and smiled mischievously. "Maybe."

"Back at last," Sayer said as he placed a couple of beers in front of Rowan and Mairi. He passed a tall glass of something red to Bran.

"What are you drinking?" Mairi asked, eyeing the glass.

"Something called a Trance. Do you want to taste it?"

"No, thanks."

He took a long drink and held it out to her. "Nothing in it. Honest."

Yeah, right. He was so huge, a little bit of GHB or ketamine wouldn't affect him, but her . . . she'd likely fall flat on her back and then . . . She found herself looking at his mouth, and then at his hands. And then . . . she imagined what he'd do with that mouth and those strong fingers.

"Hello, Rowan."

They both glanced up to see the DJ, or Tarot Guy as he was known between them, pull up a chair. He turned it around and straddled it. Mairi couldn't help but admire his thighs in his jeans. And his eyes . . . they looked silver, but were outlined in violet, just like Bran's. Man, did everyone here wear contacts?

"Hi," Rowan murmured with a shy smile before taking a dainty sip of her beer.

"I'm Keir, my apologies for not introducing myself before." He extended his hand, which was covered in unusual tattoos. Not necessarily run-of-the-mill tribal tats, but something similar. The pattern snaked its way up the length of his arm, over his huge muscles, and disappeared beneath the sleeve of his T-shirt.

Rowan, Mairi noticed, did a full-body blush when Keir gripped her hand, then pulled back only to fiddle with the cap of her beer bottle. Mairi saw him frown, then glare at his friend.

"So, Sayer treating you right? Because if he's not, I'll kill him."

Although the tone was civil, Mairi sensed some menace behind it. Even Bran sensed it, because she felt that great big body of his stiffen alongside hers, and she wondered whether the threat really wasn't an idle one.

"Yes, everything's great."

Keir nodded, and Mairi couldn't help but notice how the blue streaks in his hair glowed in the neon lights. "Just checking. Well, I gotta bounce. See ya."

When he stood and swung his chair around, Rowan looked disappointed. She sent Mairi an it's-no-biggie shrug. But Mairi saw the hurt and the disappointment in her eyes.

Sayer, who had been watching Keir blend into the crowd, turned his attention back to Rowan. "Wanna dance?"

Rowan practically leaped up from the table. "I'd love to."

Great, now she had to be alone with Mr. Built and Sexy. Ordinarily she could hold her own with guys, but this one—he wasn't ordinary. He did something to her body that no one else had ever done. It was as if Bran knew how to order her body to ignore her commands. Even as she tried to remind herself he was a stranger, her thighs got hot and her underwear dampened.

She had had a few boyfriends, and she'd always liked sex, but ever since she'd laid eyes on him, all she could *think* about was getting naked and feeling him hot and hard between her thighs. It was so disturbing. These thoughts, these feelings, they weren't normal for her. Especially with a guy she had just met.

He seemed to be aware that she was nervous, sitting all alone next to him, and mercifully he broke the silence.

"There's a show starting in a few minutes. Would you like to see it?"

Mairi thought of the *show* she'd witnessed in the mirrors when she first arrived. "Depends what it is."

"Magic. Do you like magic, Mairi?"

"Not really. It's just illusions."

He chuckled, a deep baritone rumble from his chest. The sound aroused her, but she hid it. "What's wrong with illusions?" he asked, and Mairi felt his fingers touch an errant strand of hair that had fallen against her cheek.

"You can't trust them," she snapped, thinking of Aaron, and how he was nothing at all what he appeared to be. Ever since, Mairi had been skittish around men, fearing that the kind of games Aaron had played with Rowan could happen to her.

"Do you trust me, Mairi?"

The question was asked so softly that Mairi felt her stomach lurch. He was looking at her, she could tell, but she refused to meet his gaze. "No."

He leaned in, angled his head so he lips were pressed close to her. "Why not?"

His breath tickled her ear and she suppressed a shiver. "Because I know your kind."

He chuckled, deep and seductive. "I don't think so."

"Yeah, I do."

"Some things aren't what they seem, Mairi. Even me."

"Which makes me trust you even less."

"I know your kind, too." She gave him an arch look, and he had the nerve to grin. His gaze lowered to her lips, where her tongue was swiping away a drop of beer. "Should I tell you what I know of you?"

She shouldn't play this game. In all honesty it would probably wind up hurting her self-esteem, but she was helpless to refuse him when he looked at her with that deep, storm cloud gaze of his.

"Well?" he whispered, allowing his fingers to caress her arm. "Do you want to know what I know? What I feel coming off your skin?"

A long, breathy pause weighed heavily between them before it was broken.

"For the lady." A waitress dressed in fishnets and shiny PVC sauntered up to the table with a martini glass. "From the guy at the corner table."

Finally breaking Bran's gaze, Mairi tried to collect herself. "What is it?" Mairi asked, looking at the brown liquid.

"An angel's kiss."

Mairi glanced toward the corner. In the dark, illuminated only by a candle on the table, sat a guy who was the definition of gorgeous. He was beautiful, with shoulder-length brown hair. His eyes appeared dark, and when he smiled, Mairi felt compelled to smile back.

Raising his glass, the man saluted her.

"Don't drink it."

"Hey," Mairi cried as Bran reached for the glass and dumped the contents into a plant that was beside him.

"Suriel is bad news."

"And you're not?" she shot back.

"Compared to him, I'm the least of your worries. Trust me."

Strangely, she did. Even as she glanced once more at the man named Suriel. A little frisson swept up her back. She felt as if she had seen the man before, but could not place him. There was something there in his eyes, a shared familiarity.

"Do not invite him in, Mairi," Bran warned.

"In where?" she asked, suddenly growing languid.

"Inside you."

The words were soft, deep, like a velvet caress. Swallowing hard, Mairi tried to fight the way her body seemed to grow hot and achy. Damn Bran. Every word was an invitation to sex. What the hell was wrong with her?

"What do you mean?" she asked, glancing furtively between the man and Bran. "Inside me?"

"Do not . . . invoke him."

Invoke him? What a thing to say. Demons and evil spirits were invoked, but this guy . . . he had the face of an angel. *A dark angel*, she thought, suddenly bemused. His beauty was not effeminate, but masculine and virile. *Fallen* . . . the word suddenly tripped through her mind and she snapped her head to the left only to come face–to–face with Bran. His fingers trailed down her cheek, his gaze holding hers steadily as he pressed in closer to whisper against her ear.

"Do not allow him inside you."

"I . . . I wasn't planning on it," she gulped. "I'm not that kind of girl." *Liar.*

She met Bran's gaze, saw it glimmer in the candlelight. "There are more ways than sex to allow a man in."

Oh, God. She would let him in any way he wanted.

She should have been scared of the intense vibes he was putting out. But the truth was she was immensely, recklessly, attracted to Bran.

Standing up, she nearly knocked over the little table holding their drinks. "I'll be right back," she said, struggling to get away from Bran and the crazy thoughts she was having.

She didn't even know this guy, for crying out loud! How could she be entertaining the idea of sleeping with him? He could rape her. Kill her. Or worse, he could do the same sort of things that Lauren's killer had done to her.

"You will not go alone. I will escort you."

"No, really, I'm good—"

"I am taking you to wherever it is you want to go. You will not wander the club alone."

His fingers wrapped around her elbow and tugged her gently forward. Then his palm slid down her arm till it reached her wrist. It was like an electric shock, that touch. Her wrist felt as though it were on fire, and she was certain her entire body jolted.

"Mairi?" Bran's voice sounded so distant, like it was part of a dream, even as his face appeared to be coming closer to her.

She glanced over her shoulder at the man named Suriel. He watched her, his eyes dark and mesmerizing. *Unreadable.*

Suddenly, she felt very weak, as if Suriel's gaze had somehow stolen all her strength from her. She wavered and reached for Bran's arm for support.

Shaking her head, which was now foggy and muddled, a horrible feeling of consuming emptiness engulfed her. Suddenly, she was feeling desperate—*terrified*—a helplessness was pulling her down. She looked down at her exposed wrist, at the white scars that ran horizontally across her skin. She had felt like this once before. This frightening emptiness. Loss. And still Suriel watched her, his gaze penetrating.

"Do not fear me."

Mairi heard the voice whisper through her mind, the same voice that had occasionally spoken to her in dreams as a young child. Instead of soothing her, the voice frightened her, made her want to run.

"I would never harm you, Mairi. You know that. You know me."

She shook her head, as much to clear her thoughts as

to deny the truth of the words. Yes. She had heard that voice before.

"I know your secret. I was there; remember?"

Mairi staggered back, still clutching on to Bran's thick forearm. "I need the bathroom," she said in a rush, stumbling away, needing to get away from everyone and everything.

"Have you drunk too much?" he asked, concern flashing in his eyes. His gaze, she noticed, slipped to her drink, then back to Sayer, who was dancing with Rowan. Fear spiked in her heart. Was it possible she had been drugged? If so, she needed to get away from him before she couldn't move. Before she could no longer protect herself. And yet she knew that she had not been drugged.

"I just need . . ." She paused, shook her head, trying to clear it of the heavy fog that seemed to be encroaching. She gazed once more at Suriel, who was sipping his drink and looking out over the dance floor. She was no longer the fixture of his attention, yet something warned her that she was still the focus of his interest.

"I just need a minute," she mumbled, stumbling away toward the bathroom. She felt Bran's eyes on her, but she didn't look back. She headed for the washroom, threw open the door, and entered the first unoccupied stall. Sitting down on the toilet, she closed her eyes and put her head to her knees. The room was spinning and she felt sleepy, languid. As if she were going to black out. Behind her closed lids she saw red pulsations, like beating blood vessels. Then she heard the thumping of a heart, the rhythm slowing . . . slowing, until she held her breath, waiting to hear the next beat, fearing she wouldn't.

Oh, God, was it her heart she was hearing?

Opening her eyes, she looked down at her trembling hands, saw the scars staring back up at her, mocking her; then the oppressive feeling of hurt and anger pulled at her, sucking her into a black yawning void that she feared, but could not step away from.

No, not again. What happened last time would not happen again. She would not allow it.

Jumping up, she lost her balance, forgetting she was wearing stilettos, and banged into the wall of the stall. Righting herself, she managed to unlock the door, despite her blurring vision.

"Hey, watch it!" a woman snapped as Mairi lost her balance and fell into her. Red lipstick was smeared from the corner of the woman's lip to her cheek. Mairi met the woman's gaze in the mirror and was startled by her own reflection. She did not recognize the person staring back at her, even though it was her face. Her eyes were wild and glassy, her cheeks deathly pale.

"Sorry 'bout that," Mairi slurred, trying to focus. "I'm not feeling well."

"Obviously," the woman sniffed.

Feeling along the wall, Mairi finally found the door and let herself out. The hallway was dark. The music was loud, pumping, banging around her head. The air was stale with the smell of spilled alcohol and cigarettes. The combination only made her head feel worse, and still the black yawning emptiness washed over her.

"Come to me, Mairi. Come . . ."

Oh, shit, those were the same words she heard the last

time. And they beckoned her, just as much as they had when she'd first heard them.

"Step over and come to me."

No, she wouldn't do that. She knew what it was to step over. She knew where that led, and she wasn't going there. Not again.

CHAPTER FIVE

Suriel pretended interest in his drink as he watched Mairi disappear around the corner with Bran. He had not meant to frighten her. He sought only to remind her of his presence. It had been a long time since he had made his presence known to her; perhaps that was why she had run away.

Sipping at the drink, his gaze skipped from immortal to immortal, taking in their actions and wondering what purpose drove them to Velvet Haven tonight. He knew why the Raven was here. Sex. It was the only thing that compelled him to mix with mortals. The Sidhe preferred his own world, and Suriel liked him better when he was there.

After nearly a century, Suriel knew enough about the king of Annwyn to distrust him—especially with Mairi.

Mairi was special. Mairi was *his*. They had a bond closer than lovers. Within her small, human body, Mairi MacAuley carried a part of him.

It was that part that had called to him tonight, whispering to him that he needed to follow her. Theirs was a connection that could not be severed. He would not allow it. Not when he knew her power. Not when she could help him.

He needed to find her. To steady her. To keep her safe from Annwyn, and the purpose the goddess intended for her.

Cailleach had robbed him once before. She wouldn't again.

Suriel rose from his chair with one intention. To take Mairi away from the raven.

"Mairi, talk to me."

Her eyes were open, but Bran knew she didn't see him standing before her. Her stare was vacant, her brown eyes clouded. Pressing against her, Bran steadied her with his thighs as he cupped her chin, tilting her head up so he could see more of her in the dim light.

What had happened? One minute he'd sensed her arousal and her softening to him, and the next she was gone, looking as though she were possessed. Something still held her hostage. He saw it in her eyes, felt it in the fine trembles that shivered through her curvaceous body. *Fucking Suriel.* She'd been fine, even turned on, until the angel had somehow forced her attention away from him.

Fallen angel, Bran mentally corrected, and a son of a bitch pain in the ass. Bran didn't understand how, or why, but he felt it in his gut; Suriel had done something, had planted a seed in her mind that was suddenly taking over.

"Mairi, it's all right. I'm here. You're safe."

She looked at him, her eyes now misty, her lips quivering. He wanted to take away her fear with his arms, his mouth.

Damn it, he shouldn't even be thinking this, but he gave words to the thoughts anyway. She was lovely, gazing at him like this. *Perfect.*

The thought stopped him cold. He had never looked at a mortal for more than sex. He never thought of them as beautiful. Never felt any measure of warmth, or care. But he did now. All he could think about was chasing away the panic that racked her body, turning her fear into passion, making her big, wide eyes molten with desire.

"Mairi?" he repeated, unable to hide the worry in his voice. She closed her eyes, cradling her cheek in his palm.

"Thank you," she whispered with a sad smile. "I . . . I can't explain what happened, but having you here now it . . . feels . . . right. *Safe.*"

His heart actually lurched. Damn it, he did not want to feel this, this softness that suddenly wrapped around his chest. He was worried about her. Which was ludicrous. He should be concerned about himself. About Carden. He should be finding Morgan and disposing of her. And Annwyn? He'd been a poor king for more than a century, and as a result of his carelessness the dark arts had returned, threatening his home, his people. There was no doubt in his mind what his priority should be. The rational part of him knew this. But the irrational urge to protect this human female continued to war with the logical side, eventually winning out.

"Can you walk?" he asked, glancing at their surroundings. They were private enough, the hall dark, but he wanted her away from there. Away from Suriel.

He could feel the angel's aura surrounding them. In the dark, the angel was watching. Even with his piercing raven eyes, Bran could not find Suriel hidden in the shadows. But he sensed him.

"Bran?" she asked, her eyes once again focusing on her surroundings. The way she looked up at him with an expression of relief and desire, it undid him.

"I'm here, Mairi. Whatever happened, whatever it was, it is done."

She swallowed hard and he followed the fluid movement of her throat with his fingertips. She shivered, and the sigils on his fingers and hand began to glow in the darkness as they greedily absorbed her energy.

Abruptly he dropped his palm from her cheek, not wanting her to see that he was not like other men she had known in the past.

The action confused him. He'd never before cared about such things. If a mortal woman asked about his markings, he told her they were tattoos. If she pressed, he shut her mouth with his lips until she was too far gone with desire to care. But something told him Mairi would not be put off so easily. It was in her eyes. She was intelligent, but more dangerous to him than that was the fact that she was perceptive. If he were thinking with the proper head, he'd turn around now and find another mortal, a vacuous female who was looking for nothing more than a night of pleasure.

It wasn't like he needed Mairi. Any human female would do to satisfy the Legacy Curse. There were only two requirements. First, she must be willing, and second, she must be pleasured. He could not simply take what he needed; he had to *give*. That was what he hated the most. Him, king of the Sidhe, pleasuring women in exchange for energy. It made him a whore, his curse. Magic was his right by birth, but now he had to purchase it with his body.

Humility. Need. Sacrifice. That is what Cailleach had intended to teach him when she'd cursed him. Instead, all he had learned was shame, rage, hate toward the woman who essentially held him by the balls.

And this one. This female who was looking at him, sexual hunger replacing the veil that only seconds ago clouded her eyes. It made his chest ache. He didn't want her this way. Didn't want to pleasure her in exchange for energy. *A fucking transaction.* He wanted it to be mutual. Pleasure for pleasure.

The thought unnerved him.

The arousal singing within him, the need he felt to slip deep inside her, was stronger than ever.

No, it was better to seek out another woman for the night. One he could easily forget.

She blinked, swallowed once more, and Bran resisted the fierce urge to place his lips to her throat.

Leave, he commanded himself. Except he couldn't make his feet move. Couldn't stop his hand from tingling where he had touched her. Couldn't prevent himself from being pulled into her gaze and imagining what it would be like to look into her eyes as she shivered beneath him, his cock deep within her.

He took a step back, intending to walk away, but he couldn't do it. Instead, he reached for her hand and curled his fingers between hers.

"Let's get you some air."

Still unsteady, Mairi allowed Bran to hold her hand and guide her down the hall, then to a curved staircase with an ornately carved banister. On the newel post was the MacDonald clan emblem. Beneath it was the Celtic triscale. Seeing it made her think of Lauren and the crazy dreams she had been having since stealing the manuscript from Our Lady. A feeling of wariness stole over her.

"Where are you taking me?" she asked as she looked up and saw nothing but blackness.

"Upstairs."

Panic set in and she tried to pull her hand away, but he tugged her along. "Trust me, Mairi."

"It's not something I'm good at."

He looked over his shoulder at her. "Then we have something in common, for I don't trust easily, either."

"Yeah, well, in a fair fight I'd say you have nothing to worry about."

The grin he gave made her light-headed, and like a fool, Mairi kept following him up the stairs, which seemed to go on forever. "This is the old mansion," she gasped, looking at the coved ceilings with their detailed cornice work.

"The entire club was at one time the mansion. This part is used by the owner and . . . family," he muttered, pulling her along a darkened hall.

"Family?" she asked as she stumbled over her feet, trying to keep up with his long strides. He grunted, stopped suddenly, and she ran into his back. He steadied her with an arm around her waist before he opened the door and ushered her inside.

"Daegan MacDonald's study," he announced. The door

shut behind him, and Mairi felt her body jump. She waited to hear the click of a lock, but no sound came. Looking around the room, she studied the masculine retreat, the warm woods, the dark leather wingback by the fireplace. In the marble mantelpiece was an etching of a stag.

This was the type of place she could get lost in for hours, with a warm blanket and a good book. It felt homey and rich and very definitely masculine.

"You mentioned family," she said as she studied the portrait of a man and woman over the fireplace. They were dressed in Victorian garb. The man in it looked eerily like Bran.

Bran nodded at the portrait. "Daegan built this place when he left home. He was my uncle."

"Uncle?"

"Several generations removed, of course."

"Of course," she murmured, studying the picture once again. "You look very much like him. And the lady?"

"Isobel. The love of his life. He cherished her. You wouldn't believe what he gave up to have her."

"What did he give up?"

"Everything he was. His home. His identity."

Mairi couldn't imagine someone sacrificing like that for her. "Well, she's very beautiful."

"I suppose," Bran muttered as he stood beside her, looking at the portrait. "I don't really see it."

Mairi wondered what sort of woman could tempt him if the gorgeous woman in the portrait wouldn't have; then she pushed the thought away. There was no way in this world she was prettier than Isobel MacDonald, so why even hope.

"The man you were speaking to downstairs, with the short

black hair?" she asked, finding a safer topic. "He resembles Dae-gan, too."

"He's my cousin. He owns the club." Bran scowled. "Enough of the family tree." He strode to a window where heavy drapes were pulled shut. He flung them open, revealing French doors. He opened one and motioned her through. "Step outside. The fresh air will do you good."

Following him onto a terrace, Mairi crossed her arms over her chest. It was chilly being up this high, and with the wind blowing. A storm was moving in, and the rumble of thunder sounded much too close for comfort.

"Here," he murmured. He shrugged out of his long trench and covered her shoulders. It was warm and inviting. Discreetly she inhaled his scent: masculine with a hint of spice. Her blood instantly heated.

"It's going to storm." She motioned to the sky just as it lit up with lightning.

"I won't let you get wet."

She laughed. "So now you're claiming you can keep the rain away?"

He shrugged and rested his arms on the balustrade. "Perhaps."

She noticed his left arm was covered in vinelike tattoos. In the moonlight they glowed pewter and silver, like his eyes. "Cool tats." She motioned to his arm.

He nodded and slid his right hand over his forearm, hiding them. "Had them forever."

"Neat work. Where did you get it done?"

He frowned as he looked over the terrace, toward the lake. "Scotland."

"I thought I detected a faint accent."

He didn't reply, but continued to watch the waves pound onto the shore. "What is your favorite element, Mairi?"

That stopped her. What a bizarre question. She looked at him, but he appeared to be dead serious as he waited for her answer. He shrugged, then looked away. "Mine is water. It can be both tranquil and fierce. When it's raging it can be the hardest element to control, but when it is calm it can soothe the soul."

Wow. Not only was this guy a total knockout, he was deep and philosophical. Totally not what she expected from his outward appearance.

"If you close your eyes you can hear the waves."

"Not over the wind," she said as she moved closer to the balustrade. "Plus with the thunder—"

"Close your eyes and I promise you you'll hear them."

Mairi did as he asked, and felt his arm move. She was aware of his body, warm and hard beside hers. "Listen, Mairi."

She did, trying not to focus on him and how he made her want to rub up against him. Pressing in, she leaned against him, and he anchored her with a hand on her shoulder. The winds quieted, and she heard the rhythmic crashing of waves hitting the sand.

"It's beautiful," she purred, allowing the sound to wash over her. She stood quietly for a few minutes, listening, feeling herself calm, marveling at the way she could hear the waves as if she were standing right on the beach, her toes buried in the sand.

He bent down and whispered in her ear, "Feel better?"

She was surprised to realize she did. She didn't know if it was the cool air, or the waves, or Bran's calming presence, but there was no denying that she was feeling much better. "I've never thought about the water before, but I like it. The sound is soothing. Not like the wind. The wind can be so . . . haunting."

"Yes, I find it haunting as well, the way it can whisper to you." Suddenly he frowned, his face growing cold, as if he was mad at himself for saying such things.

"Thanks," she said, nudging in beside him. "I feel much better."

He nodded, but seemed uncomfortable. "Do you want to go back in?"

"No."

"Aren't you cold?"

His coat was huge on her, the hem dragging on the ground. She closed it and wrapped her arms around her body. "Not anymore."

His gaze lingered over her face before he once again turned his attention back to the water. "Tell me about yourself, Mairi."

She shrugged. "There's not much to tell. I'm pretty boring."

He turned to her, and leaned his elbow and hip against the balustrade. He tucked her hair behind her ear and watched as the strands slipped through his fingers. "Husband? Lover?"

She shook her head and felt herself flush. "No."

His fingertips skated along the shell of her ear. "Why? When you are so different from all the other women out there?"

That got her attention. When she met his gaze, her heart stopped beating. The way he was looking at her made her want to jump straight into his arms.

"The trust thing. I'm too suspicious and I ruin it. Plus, I'm a geek. Men have to compete with books for my attention."

His eyes glittered in a hypnotic dance that lured her in. She could trust him. She could feel it.

"Ah," he whispered as he wrapped his big palm around her neck and massaged the muscles there. "A book worm. That isn't a bad thing."

"I know what I'm getting with a book," she admitted, opening up to him. "You never know what you're getting with a man."

He pulled her a bit closer, still holding her gaze. "That's so true."

She wondered what he meant by that. Was he hiding something or just stating a fact? She licked her lips and asked, "And you? Do you have a girlfriend?" She couldn't bring herself to say lover. It felt way too intimate.

"No."

Her blood warmed, and a little current of excitement ran along her spine. She saw his nostrils flare, heard him inhale deeply. "I like the way you smell, Mairi."

She moved closer. Tilted her head up, inviting him to bend down and meet her halfway, but he didn't. He just kept looking down into her eyes.

"What of your parents?" he asked.

"Gone." She swallowed, not wanting to talk about her parents, most especially her father. "Yours?"

"They've been gone many years. It seems like centuries."

"Do you have any brothers or sisters?"

"A brother. You?"

"Nope, an only child. It was a pretty lonely childhood." She couldn't help but notice how he was looking at her. When he tilted her face up with his fingers, she shivered. "What?" she asked, bristling under that stare of his.

"I'm just thinking how beautiful you look in the moon-light. How right, as though you were made to walk in the woods beneath it."

She didn't know what to say. This guy was so smooth. So experienced.

"It's not an empty compliment," he murmured, lowering his head. "I don't give compliments, or at least not ones like that." His mouth hovered over hers, and they looked into each other's eyes for the longest moment. Mairi was screaming in-side for him to take her mouth and plunder her lips. He did, but it was not the sort of kiss she expected from someone who looked like Bran.

It was soft. A sweet brushing of his mouth over hers. Slowly. And again. Then he opened his mouth and kissed her, covering her lips with his open ones. It turned a bit hungrier, a bit deeper, and then his tongue was sliding between her lips, and Mairi felt her entire body go limp.

This man could kiss!

She clung to him, her fingers pressing into his thick biceps. He pushed her back a few steps and brought her up against the wall of the mansion. His hands shot out, his palms landing flat against the wall on either side of her. He was breathing hard as he looked down at her. Then, like a hawk, he swooped down and captured her mouth, devouring her in a kiss that was blis-tering hot.

Mairi had never been kissed like this, like she was food and he a starving man. But oh, God, she loved it. The way it made her feel. Her entire body flared to life, her blood heating her, especially her core.

He tore his mouth away and pressed his lips to the pulse

that bounded madly at her throat. "You smell so good," he growled. She heard him inhale, felt him brush his face into her hair.

She clawed at his shoulders, holding him to her neck as he began to suck and nibble at the flesh, working his way down to the V of her T-shirt. He was pulling the fabric aside, revealing the swell of her breast. His tongue, hot and wet, trailed between the cleft of her breasts and she moaned his name.

His hand left the wall and he snaked his arm through his coat, wrapping it around her waist, slamming her up against his body. He was hard, his cock pressing up against her as he ground his pelvis into her, rubbing in small circles, making her feel him. And holy hell, did he feel big and hard. And she wanted it, buried deep inside her.

"Weep for me, Mairi. Let me smell it."

She could barely understand him, she was out of control with lust. She didn't sleep with strangers, but this guy . . . she would *not* give up a chance to experience a night with Bran. She would never have another chance, and he was too amazing to pass up.

"Let's go inside," she begged, giving him an open invitation to strip her bare and plunge into her.

He pulled back as if she had slapped him. "I'm forgetting myself."

"No, oh, no," she gasped, pulling him closer. "It's all right. *Really all right.*"

"This isn't what I had intended when I brought you up here."

"I know," she said, "but I want to." She hated that her voice sounded needy as she tried to entice him back to her. But hell, the orgasm of her life, the one she sensed Bran would give her, was pulling away. Bran was acting as though he didn't want her.

That thought was like a bucket of water overhead, cooling her libido.

"Oh," she said, embarrassed. "I get it." Maybe she was throwing off those needy, clingy vibes that made men nervous. Or maybe he wasn't that interested in her. One thing was for sure: She was confused as hell by his sudden coolness toward her.

His eyes darkened and he reached out to caress her cheek with his fingertips. "I can't do this. You're not that type of woman, Mairi."

Her lips trembled and she nodded, feeling totally humiliated. She got it. It hurt. And she turned away, walking as fast as she could back into the mansion. She refused to look back over her shoulder. She didn't want to see him standing there, watching her.

At the door of the study, she paused to listen for his heavy steps. There was no sound but the waves crashing, hitting the sand and rocks. Thunder rumbled, and a flash of lightning lit the room in a brilliant flash of white.

The storm was back. Where had it gone, she wondered, when she had been writhing in Bran's arms?

CHAPTER SIX

Bran slid down the wall to a crouch, trying to gather himself. He was in extraordinary pain. He couldn't understand it. Yes, he needed sex to beef up his magic stores—he'd used a considerable amount of magic to hold off the thunderstorm and the wind in order to give Mairi that few minutes of solace he'd wanted to give her. But this pain . . . it wasn't from his Legacy Curse. But he knew it had to do with Mairi. His inner voice, which he never ignored, all but shouted it to him.

"Thought I'd find you up here."

Bran stood to his full height and glared down into Rhys MacDonald's violet eyes. "What do you want?"

He didn't like the way Rhys was looking at him, like he was assessing an adversary for a weakness. "I saw the woman running down the stairs. I wanted to find out what's up."

His cock, for sure. The damn thing wouldn't go down. Any thought of Mairi aroused him, not to mention the fact that he still had her scent burning in his nose. *Her aroused scent.* The heady, sensual perfume reminded him of the orchids that grew by the reflecting pool in Annwyn. He'd never look at them again without thinking of her, never see the clear liquid drip from the stamen without imagining Mairi's core weeping in desire.

Christ, what the hell was wrong with him? She was a mortal, and he was getting way too fucking poetic.

"Raven?"

"Everything's fine," he growled, shouldering past Rhys.

"Did you hurt her?"

"No, damn it."

"She told me to give you this." Rhys tossed his coat to him. When he caught it in his hand, Mairi's scent perfumed the air.

This was the last damn thing he needed. He was so aroused now, he'd do any mortal and enjoy it, just to relieve the ache in his groin. *But I'd be thinking of Mairi.*

"You're in a bad way, Raven."

Bran stuffed his arms into the sleeves and wrapped himself in Mairi's scent and the lingering heat of her body. Below the cuff, the sigils on his left hand glowed, surprising him.

How could it be that he'd received any energy from her? They'd only kissed. Rhys caught it as well and snickered. "Looks like she treated you right."

"You will not talk about her that way," Bran warned. "She's not like the others."

"She's mortal, isn't she?"

"Shut up, halfling."

Rhys snorted, then threw something at him, making him fumble to catch it. It was a phone. "She was crying," Rhys snarled, "and I don't like customers crying as they leave my club. Call her."

"And say what?" he growled, glaring at the blasted thing in his hand. What did he know of using these mortal devices?

"How the hell should I know? Only you and she know what went down up here."

"I did not hurt her," he said through clenched teeth.

"Well, not in the physical sense. Number's already plugged in. Just press send."

Bran watched Rhys leave, then hit the silver button. It rang and rang, till a machine came on with Mairi's voice. A beep sounded and he cleared his throat.

"It's me. Bran. I, ah . . ." He looked back out over the terrace and focused on the waves, trying to find his calming center. "I want to see you again. Tomorrow night. I, ah . . ." He didn't know what to say, couldn't find the right words, the words a human male would say to her.

The wind kicked up, whipping his coat, stirring up her scent, and he closed his eyes and rested his head against the bricks. "I just really . . . need to see you again. Soon."

⁂

Mairi tossed her keys onto the coffee table and gave her dog, Clancy, a rub between his ears. He greeted her with a lolling tongue and big wet licks. "Bad night, Clance," she whispered as she rested her head against his. "Men. Why are they such assholes?"

The wolfhound looked into her eyes and gave her a lick up her cheek. "Except you, huh?"

She went into the bathroom, changed into her comfortable cotton robe, and washed off the little bit of makeup she'd worn and the track marks of her tears. Where had they come from? she wondered.

Weird. Just thinking about Bran turning down her blatant offer made them spring once more to her eyes. The first time she makes a move on a guy and she's shot down. What guy turns down a no-strings night of sex?

Bran, apparently.

Poor Rowan had been subjected to Mairi's rancor on the drive home and tried to make her feel better. But Mairi was nowhere near feeling better. She was angry and hurt, and still aroused.

Damn him.

Tossing the towel onto the vanity, she decided she'd done enough wallowing in her thoughts. In the morning, she'd call Rowan and apologize for ruining her night. Rowan and Sayer had been getting along well. Her friend was actually laughing when Mairi had found her. Just because Mairi hadn't scored with Bran didn't mean Rowan had to leave when she did. Mairi had cheated Rowan of a night of pleasure, and it wasn't fair.

Back in the living room, she went to the bookshelf that housed her phone and answering machine. There was one message, and when the dark, velvety voice came over the speaker, she nearly dropped to the ground. Bran.

How the hell had he gotten her number? Then she remembered signing the VIP clipboard. Obviously he was interested enough to search that out. Or maybe he just felt bad.

Great. Pity was such a turn on.

"I want to see you . . . Soon." Mairi replayed the message. He had definitely said he wanted—no, *needed*—to see her again. She played it three more times before the entire message had soaked through her brain, which seemed to fill with lust at just the sound of his voice.

He'd left a number, and she sat on the couch chewing her nail, wondering if she could call it. How desperate would it look? She glanced at the clock. It was after midnight. But he would still be up, something told her, still at the club. Beside her, Clancy panted and watched her with his head cocked.

"I know, I'm being stupid, aren't I?"

She picked up the phone anyway, and started to dial the number she'd written down. Then hung up. She did it three more times before getting the courage up to let it ring. Two rings, and his baritone rumble was washing over her.

"Mairi?"

Was he expecting her call? *Waiting* for it? Her stomach churned and she lay back on the couch before she fell off.

"Yeah, it's me."

"Your voice . . . it sounds different."

Closing her eyes, she imagined him on the other end of the phone. His voice sounded different too. If it was possible, it was even sexier.

"You are upset with me. You left tonight because you thought I didn't desire you."

She pressed her eyes shut, mortified that he knew. She felt her defenses fly up, and she was about to speak when he went on, his voice low and urgent.

"But I wanted you, Mairi. I *still* want you."

"Oh," she whispered.

"I would have taken what you were offering, but you're not that type of girl. I've had easy lays before, and I didn't want that. Not with you."

A perverse sense of pleasure washed through her. He had wanted her. Still wanted her. Suddenly she felt like giving him her address and inviting him over to prove it.

"Mairi?"

"Yes."

"I'd like to get to know you."

"What do you mean?"

There was a pause that seemed to go on forever before he spoke. "Outside of sex. I'd like to know you as a person."

Like a date? He definitely didn't seem like the dating type.

"I like you, Mairi."

"I like you, too," she replied.

"So will you let me?"

"Sure."

"When?"

She struggled to think, but couldn't. She swore she heard a noise, like metal on metal. Zipper . . . that was definitely a zipper.

"Mairi?"

"I'm, ah, I have this weekend off."

"Good," he murmured, his voice thickening. "Where are you?"

She swallowed. "At home. On the couch. What about you?"

"In a bedroom at the club. Alone."

"Oh." Her heart was beating too fast. She obviously wasn't getting enough blood to her brain, because she was going to pass out at just the thought of him lounging in bed with his leather pants unzipped.

She heard the bed creak, and imagined it was his large frame settling onto the mattress. Her fingers were shaking as she held the phone up to her ear. Clancy jumped off the couch and went to his bed, his nails clicking on the floor.

"Who is there?" Bran demanded.

"No one. It was my dog."

She heard the exhale of breath. "What are you wearing?"

"My favorite robe."

"What's beneath it?"

She froze. Were they going to have kinky phone sex? She'd seen it in the movies, heard about it from her friends at work. But she had never done anything like this. She didn't know how to do it, or if she could.

"Are you naked, Mairi, beneath that robe?"

"Yes."

He sighed and she heard something, like the creak of leather. "What are you wearing?" she asked.

"My coat, which still smells of you."

"And?"

"My pants."

She swallowed, licked her lips, trying to get up the nerve. "Did you . . . unzip them?"

"Yes."

She closed her eyes, imagining it all. "Why?"

"So I can touch myself while listening to your voice."

Oh, God, we are really going to do this!

Mairi took a deep breath, wincing as she heard how breathless her voice sounded. "Are you touching yourself now?"

"Not yet. Are you?"

Her hand flew away from the tie securing her robe, as if he'd caught her red-handed. "No," she answered, trying to sound as though she did this sort of thing all the time.

"Ah," he whispered, his voice dropping to a husky growl. "You want to be seduced first."

She squeezed her eyes shut, then her thighs. "Maybe." She heard movement and asked, "What are you doing now?"

"*Now* I'm touching my cock."

Mairi almost choked, but maintained her dignity—*barely*.

"I'm imagining it's your hand. Soft, supple"—he made a little noise that sounded like a groan—"clever fingers circling the head, then teasing around the shaft. Then squeezing, just enough pressure to build up my desire, but not enough to spill into your hand."

She swallowed hard and allowed her fingers, which were trembling, to untie the sash of her robe. It parted and fell open, her nipples already puckered.

"I'm wondering what you'll think when you see my cock," he whispered darkly, "when you feel it deep inside you."

He must be huge, she silently thought as her fingertips caressed the tip of her nipple. The rest of him certainly was.

"I'd like to lie back and watch you take my cock in your mouth. I'd like to have my orgasm with your mouth, feel my climax crash over me, just like those waves pounding onto the beach." Her fingertips stilled as she waited to hear more.

"Would you do that, Mairi, take me in your mouth and make me come?"

She'd not done that a lot, but for Bran, she would.

"Mairi?"

"Yes," she admitted before she could stop herself. She heard his breath catch, the sound of the mattress creak, as if he were settling deeper into the bed.

"Christ, I'm so close, just imagining you kneeling between my thighs, my cock filling your mouth, your hair spread over my body."

She heard his voice drop away; then it was followed by a husky demand. "Tell me what you're imagining, Mairi."

She bit her lip and tugged at her nipple, her face flaming with excitement and nervousness. "You, how you must look touching yourself."

She imagined him spread out, his cock in his hand as he slowly moved his palm up and down. He would look devastatingly masculine. That much she knew.

"Is that all?"

"Yes," she lied.

"Then I haven't done enough to seduce you, have I?"

Oh, yes, she silently admitted, but he spoke, interrupting her thoughts.

"I can imagine what you look like, your pink nipples hard—they are pink, aren't they, Mairi?"

She glanced down at her chest. "Yes."

"And your breasts are big, big enough to spill out of my hands. I'd want to take them into my mouth, knead them, caress them—*fuck them*."

She gasped, and felt her body spasm as her hand trailed down her belly.

"Would you let me, Mairi?"

"Yes," she breathed as her fingertips grazed her pubic hair. "I . . . I would like that."

"And would you let me taste you, Mairi? Everywhere? Every patch of skin, every curve on your body?"

"Yes," she whispered, her voice hoarse with desire. "Do you like my curves?" she asked as she skimmed her hand along her body.

"Yes."

"Which curve?" she asked, growing bold.

"I couldn't pick just one, Mairi. I'm greedy. I love your breasts and your ass. And your hair," he murmured. "I love your hair—the length of it, the way it slides through my fingers. I'd like to grab handfuls of it and clutch it as I pin you to the bed, filling you full of me."

Gooseflesh covered her body and she shuddered as the image of Bran on top of her, pounding into her, took root.

"I like your hair, too." It made him look dangerous and sexy. A bad boy. Never had she been drawn to that sort of man, but one glimpse of Bran and she was a convert.

"I know what you're thinking, Mairi."

"What?"

"You want to run your hands through my hair and clutch my head, shoving my mouth down on you. You want me to taste there, don't you?"

She was breathing fast, her lips were dry, and she couldn't talk. But Bran went on. "Can you see me going down on you, spreading you, tonguing you?"

She nodded, as if he could see her. Lord, she could imagine it all, and how damn sexy it would be to look between her spread thighs and find Bran there.

"I'd inhale your scent first, Mairi. I love your scent; the

perfume of your aroused sex ignites me. I'd stay there for as long as I wanted, making you wait."

Oh, God, she was wet. And aroused. Her legs were sliding up and down on the cushion, searching for relief. She didn't dare touch herself, knowing she'd go off like a firecracker at the first touch. Besides, the sound of Bran's voice and the descriptions of what he wanted to do with her were too good not to hear.

"Do you want that, Mairi, my tongue on your pussy?"

"Yes," she gasped.

"Then part your legs."

She did as he asked, struggling to hear his voice over the blood pounding in her ears.

"Close your eyes. Run your fingers between your folds, pretending it's my hand."

Mairi hesitated. But in the end, she did as he asked, and the shock that raced through her body made her breath catch. "Bran?" she asked, feeling totally out of control. "Are you ... you know ..."

"Masturbating?"

She stroked herself, lured by his voice and the feel of her fingers as she pretended it was him touching her.

"Yes," he hissed, "and thinking of the next time I see you."

She swirled her fingertip around her clitoris and moaned.

"Picture me sliding between your legs, Mairi. My fingers biting into your thighs, spreading them. Feel me shouldering my way between your legs. Then the warmth of my breath against your core."

Vividly she saw what Bran was describing.

"One swipe of my tongue, parting your swollen lips. One

more, finding your clitoris. You're thick with desire, coating my tongue. I need another taste, Mairi. My mouth on you, covering you."

Yes! She mentally screamed as she found her clit and rubbed it.

"I'll build you up slowly, making you writhe and squirm. I'll want your moans, my name on your lips, as you come."

She was close . . . so close . . .

"I want to hear you, breathing as you are now, searching for release, begging to come. Come for me, Mairi," he whispered. It sounded like a purr, she thought as she got lost in the sensations of her body. "Let me hear your sounds."

She was so aroused, it took no time for her to shatter and cry out. When the storm passed, Bran was breathing hard on the other end.

"Did you come?" she asked.

"Yes."

"While imagining my mouth sucking you?"

"No," he murmured, "I came while picturing myself pleasuring your pussy."

This guy was a sex god! He knew all the right things to say.

"When, Mairi?" he asked. "When will you let me see you again?"

"I don't know."

"Come to the club tomorrow night. For dinner?"

"All right," she murmured.

"Mairi?"

"Yeah?"

"Sleep well."

"Mmm." She heard the sound of waves in the back of her mind, and she remembered what it was like to have him pressing her up against the wall, his cock grinding into her pelvis.

"I can smell your perfume," he whispered. "It'll tide me over till I can taste you."

The phone went dead, and Mairi grudgingly placed hers on the coffee table. She couldn't believe what they'd done, and how easily she'd gotten off. Embarrassing, she thought as she snuggled deep into the cushions. But it had been so good, and so sexy. What she wouldn't give for the sight of Bran stroking himself.

With a smile, she closed her eyes, drifting off to sleep.

Hours later, the morning sun crept in through the patio door, blinding her. She stretched, realizing she had spent the night on the couch. The phone rang, and she practically fell off, trying to reach it.

One word came to mind. Bran.

"Hello?"

"Well, aren't you breathless?"

"Oh, hi, Rowan, just waking up."

"Just? Girl, it's noon."

Mairi glanced out the patio door and squinted from the sunlight. "Really? I feel like I just got to sleep."

"Well, I have something that's going to wake you up."

"What's that?"

"A special delivery that arrived at the shop, not more than five minutes ago."

Mairi sat up. "From Sayer?"

"Well, he was the delivery man, but the delivery is for you."

"What is it?"

She heard Rowan sniffing at the other end of the phone before she spoke. "The most erotic, sensual, *unusual* flowers I have ever seen. And they smell like . . . heck, I don't know what, but one sniff is enough to make your head swim. They look like orchids, but I've never seen, or smelled, any orchid like this."

"Is there a card?"

She heard some paper rustling. "Sure is. Want me to read it?"

"Yes."

Rowan's voice wavered. "I think I'll let you see for yourself."

An hour later, the doorbell rang. The teenager Rowan employed to run errands on the weekends was standing at the door holding an enormous bouquet of flowers.

"Thanks," Mairi murmured, taking them. Rowan was right. She'd never seen flowers like these. Resting them on the table, she reached for the folded piece of paper that was tucked between a few blooms.

Thought of you as I picked them. Waiting for tonight, wanting you to open for me like these flowers—Bran.

Mairi gazed at the pure white blooms with their pale pink center. Running her finger gently along one flower, she watched in amazement as the folds opened, glistening with wetness.

She read his note once more, and felt her body begin to liquefy, blooming just like that damn flower. Bran was definitely a bad, bad boy. She shivered. She'd never been interested in that sort of man, but Bran was all she could think about. Last night she had dreamed of him as well. In her dream she had allowed him to do some very wicked things to her body.

She hoped like crazy that tonight he'd do them for real.

CHAPTER SEVEN

Bran contemplated Mairi over the candlelight and a glass of wine. She was nervous. It was coming off her in waves. He didn't know what to do, what to say to make her at ease. How could he, since he didn't know why she felt this way?

He knew she didn't sleep around. Knew instinctively that she did not altogether understand the sensual hunger that burned deep within her. Bran saw it in her, felt it on her skin. She'd given him energy last night from only a kiss. Remarkable. Mairi had no damn idea how unique she was. How much he wanted to get to know her.

"I want to thank you again for the flowers," she said. "They're really gorgeous."

Their gazes met, and she dropped her fork on the plate and sat back in her chair. She'd only picked at her food. He had the sudden urge to feed her.

"You're welcome." He cut into the chocolate torte and swirled the bite in the whipped cream. Then he lifted it to her mouth. "Have another bite. You barely ate your dinner."

"I'm full."

He arched his brow, challenging her. "No, you're not."

She gave in and took the bite between her teeth. He sat back, watching her, feeling his body grow hot and aroused beneath his leather pants.

He had not dressed for this . . . date, as Rhys had called it. He was what he was. He couldn't change that. No suit and tie would cover up what he was—an immortal, hungering for a mortal. "I've been wondering," she asked, as she toyed with her fork. "Where did you find such exquisite flowers? I've never seen the likes before."

He smiled. No, she wouldn't have. "They grow wild." That was the truth. They grew only in Annwyn, and only by the reflecting pool. The water nymphs were fiercely protective of them. He had paid a high price for the posy he had picked for Mairi. He had allowed a nymph to leave the pool, to change her shape into that which she yearned for—a mortal.

It had gone against his better judgment to grant such a wish. He was king, and as king he had a duty to keep Annwyn and its inhabitants safe, free of all mortal vices. But he had wanted those flowers. Had wanted to smell them and touch them. He had wanted a connection with Mairi. And it scared the hell out of him.

Cailleach would be furious with him. Nymphs were dwindling, unable to breed since their males had died off. Letting one go would be seen as treachery. But he could deal with Cailleach. She wasn't the problem. Mairi was.

She met his gaze over the flickering candle; then she flushed and looked away, and suddenly he knew. She was remembering their conversation last night. Recalled what they had done. Their eyes met again, except he caught her gaze, held it, forced her to not look away, and like the nymph's flowers, she bloomed, revealing her intoxicating scent.

"I don't mean to make you nervous."

She smiled, lowered her head as she brushed her hair behind her ear. "It's . . . awkward."

He reached for her hand, entwined his fingers with hers. "I don't mean to make it that way."

Her eyelashes flickered, her gaze lifted to his. "I'm really not good with this sort of thing."

"I know. It's what I like about you, Mairi."

He had taken a lot of women to his bed, both immortal and mortal. They had all been experienced, well versed in a variety of pleasures. And while Mairi was not a virgin, she had little experience with the sort of pleasure he was aching to show her. He wanted to be the one to open her up to that world of sensuality. He wanted to be her first in true pleasure.

"I wonder what Rowan is up to," she asked as she gazed around the room. "It was nice of Sayer to invite her tonight. Rowan needs to get out."

Bran shrugged. "He wanted to see her again."

She nodded and folded her hands in her lap.

"Do you want to find your friend? I believe she and Sayer were heading to the bar. He's performing in the magic show tonight. Perhaps you would like to see it?"

She nodded, stood, and smoothed her hands down her jeans. Her luscious body called to his, but he tamped down the urge to pull her to him.

Trust. He wanted hers.

They left the dining room, and he guided her down the hall to the ballroom.

With his hand on her back, he steered her through the door. The room was packed, standing room only. He motioned to the back wall, and he stood beside her, holding her hand. She felt so small beside his height and bulk, and he felt oddly protective of her, as if she were his.

Sayer was on an elevated stage, dressed in a hooded robe, as he mesmerized the crowd. With his hands he raised a circular sphere that writhed and moved like a bubble. Like a bubble, the sphere was transparent, except for the odd flashing of muted color, which was illuminated by the pot lights in the ceiling. Inside the sphere, images began to take shape.

The image of a man appeared, followed next by two women who went to their knees before the man's spread legs. A woman sitting at a table near them gasped and slapped the man she was with. The second woman in the sphere was sitting alone at the table beside theirs.

Bran smiled, wondering how many men here were thinking of being pleasured by two women. They had better hope Sayer didn't catch wind of their fantasies or else they'd be sleeping on the couch tonight like this poor bastard.

The sphere cleared, churned. Mist rolled over the undulating globe, and Sayer's hands rose higher in the air. The mist turned to fog, the tendrils writhing and twisting, like the tails of incense smoke. They twined together, forming a couple locked in an embrace. A tendril of fog became a hand, which moved lower, between the thighs of the smoke figure.

"Every guy here wants to finger a pussy," Sayer mentally

whispered to him. *"These mortals really have got to work on their imaginations."*

Bran hid his smile. This was the show that everyone came to see. Sayer, enchanting the audience, pulling from them their darkest desires, their closest secrets. No mind was safe from Sayer's incredible ability. Not even his, he feared, as he saw Mairi's shape begin to appear in the sphere.

"Don't even try it."

Bran saw Sayer grin beneath the hood. *"Ah, c'mon, show these mortals a little Sidhe fantasy. It'll make these bores sit up and take notice."*

"Forget it, Sayer."

"You're really going to force me to perform another blow job image?"

"Give the mortals what they want."

"Why? When I can show them what you want? Your desires are the strongest in the room."

"I said drop it."

"It's dropped. I'm on to more . . . willing prey."

"Sayer . . ." Bran growled in warning.

"Don't tell me you wouldn't like to see the naughty little images flickering through your mortal's mind."

Bran glanced at Mairi. She was mesmerized by the illumination, the hypnotizing motion of the fog and the atmospheric music that played. A mortal's mind was easy for Sayer to seduce, and Mairi, it seemed, had succumbed with alarming swiftness.

"Let her go," Bran mentally commanded him, even as he watched a new image take shape, that of a woman whose hand clasped her breasts, before one hand snaked between her thighs.

"You want to see what she's thinking. Admit it."

The shadowy image took form in the sphere as it moved and undulated, breaking free of the bubble. The crowd gasped as the life-sized image of a woman appeared, her hair long, floating around her shoulders. The image was opaque, her features muted. But Bran knew it was Mairi.

The figure split in two, and a second shape appeared. This one of a man.

"Sayer, stop."

But Sayer was done communicating now that he was deeply inside Mairi's mind, picking through her thoughts, enchanting her so that she would show Sayer what he wanted.

Bran moved against her, shielding her from the sphere, which hypnotized the mortals. He heard Sayer laugh, the sound echoing in his mind.

He looked down at Mairi and he saw her eyes widen. He followed her line of sight, and saw Suriel sitting at a table all alone. He was watching them. Awareness flooded her, and Bran felt her body trembling.

"Let's go," he murmured, wanting to take her away, to keep her safe.

She nodded and allowed him to lead her out of the room. As he closed the door, he met Suriel's gaze. There was challenge in the bastard's dark eyes. A challenge he was ready to meet—for Mairi's sake.

"Wow, that was strange," she whispered, rubbing her arms.

"The magic show?"

"No, the guy. Suriel. I'm sure I've seen him somewhere before."

Probably in her nightmares. Suriel liked to haunt. He found pleasure in the most perverse amusements. Bran wouldn't allow Mairi to amuse Suriel. For some reason, this mortal had begun to matter to him.

Mairi swallowed, unable to look away from Bran. God, he was the most gorgeous thing she had ever seen, and she wanted him. She just didn't know how to get past the awkwardness she felt.

"Mairi, are you all right?"

She nodded. She'd be even better if he would kiss her like he did last night. But so far, he'd given her no clues that he desired her. He'd been nothing but gentlemanly, making conversation, asking her about herself and her hobbies. Nothing like last night on the phone when he seduced her.

He moved closer, the wall of his massive chest brushing the curve of her breast, and she closed her eyes, wanting to feel more. But how did she ask? Did she just take? And what would he do? What would he think if she did?

"You're feeling awkward about last night."

She blew out her held breath and nodded.

"Don't."

"It's just . . ." She looked around, struggling to find the strength to pull him to her and command him to take her.

"Mairi?" he murmured as he brought her up against the wall and brushed her ear with his mouth. "Are you wondering what it would be like to have my hands on you? Wondering what my naked body would feel like on yours, what my mouth is capable of doing as I spread your thighs?"

God, yes. This was what she wanted. She wanted to admit it to him, to clutch him to her, but that was too desperate. Not at all sexy and confident. So she shook her head, denying it all.

"I can feel it within you. Sexual need. Hunger for pleasure. You're starved for it, Mairi, and I want to be the one to feed it to you."

She was robbed of breath. How did he know? Mairi was aware of the mad pulsing of her heartbeat in her throat. One word came to mind. *Now.* She needed him, and what he could give her now.

"Will you take your pleasure from me? Let me nourish you with my body."

The guy was totally out of this world, and every word he was saying was making her womb clench and her panties dampen. Every cell in her body was screaming out for her to trust, to try it just this once and take what Bran was offering her. His words alone had her so wound up that one touch of those long fingers would send her sliding over the edge.

She wanted to touch him, to make sure he was real and not just another dream guy. She couldn't handle that, waking up to discover that Bran was nothing but a dream.

She wanted the feel of his hands on her body, opening her, touching her. She thought of the flowers he'd given her—*picked* for her. She wanted to be that flower, blooming.

"Bran," she whispered, reaching out to him. Giving in to what she wanted . . .

Mairi's hand came up to his face. He watched her reach for him. He saw right away the two scars that slashed across her wrist. Intrigued, he reached for her hand, pinning her arm above her head.

"No," she pleaded, trying to pull away. The sensuality he saw in her eyes quickly evaporated.

His thumb moved over the jagged flesh. Her pulse leaped against the pad of his thumb as he traced the jagged marks. On the surface it was an old wound, but he'd bet all his magic that the pain ran much deeper than the surface of her pale skin.

Their gazes collided and he felt his body being pulled into her shamed expression.

"Please don't ask," she murmured, her lips quivering.

Mairi had secrets. Fascinating secrets for one whose aura was supposedly in perfect balance. He should let her keep them. He had his own secrets to worry about. But for some damn reason he couldn't let her move away from him.

She started to tremble, and he stepped closer, his nose nuzzling the soft patch of skin behind her ear. She smelled good—*familiar*—he thought as he breathed deeply of her skin. The animal in him wanted to suckle that soft flesh, and he let that part guide him. When he brushed her throat with his lips he heard the rush of breath whisper past her partially opened mouth. When he began to suck her, he felt her fingers curl into a claw before they threaded through his and squeezed tight.

Their bodies brushed together in an enticing undulation and her aroma wafted between them, the scent of the wetness he knew was trickling between her thighs. Inhaling, he imagined what it would be like to taste her, to feel her essence on his tongue.

She whimpered in a mixture of fear and desire. She didn't know what to make of her longing. She was not a woman who slept around indiscriminately. He knew that. Couldn't help but be turned on by that and this new, secret side to Mairi.

"I won't hurt you, Mairi," he murmured, licking the tiny bruise he'd given her. He trailed the fingertips of his free hand, the one with his Sidhe sigils, down her throat and into the valley of her breasts.

He inhaled her skin again, drunk on her smell. She smelled so damn good to him.

She arched against him as his fingers found the hem of her shirt. Beneath the fabric her skin was warm and silken. Her harsh rasping breaths aroused him, and he pressed his pelvis into hers, making her feel how hard he was for her.

"I wanted you from the moment I first saw you, Mairi. And I want you now. Feel how much."

In a slow, sensual circle he ground his cock against her. Her eyes went round and her tongue came out once more, but he caught it with his lips and sucked at its tip. She fell into him and he let go of her wrist, wanting her hands on his shoulders, his back, clutching at his hair.

As if she knew what he desired, she pulled him close, rubbing her breasts against his chest as his tongue crept between her lips, tasting her. Beneath her shirt, his palm slid up over her ribs to the edge of her bra. He could have pushed the satin cup up, revealing her breast, but he pulled it down, allowing her breast to spill out over her bra into his hand. She was big and full, her nipple hard, scraping against his palm. He tugged at it, and she moaned into his mouth as she raked her nails through his hair.

It was Mairi who deepened the kiss, taking his tongue against hers as she rubbed the front of her jeans against his cock. It was her sexual perfume that clouded the air, and his thoughts. She wanted him. And he wanted her tasting his passion, feeding her pleasure.

Tearing his mouth from hers, he kissed a path along her throat and neck over to her ear. She shivered, her nipples hard stabbing points that he could feel through his clothes. "I want to feel you tremble like that when I thrust into you."

He realized how big he was compared to her, standing short and small against him. He didn't want her desire mixing with fear. He wanted her free, uninhibited to take what she wanted from him.

Sliding down the wall, he reached for her, taking her with him. She balked, but he held her hand in his until she was sitting on his lap and they were looking into each other's eyes. He was her size now, and the wariness in her eyes slowly ebbed.

"Do not fear me."

"How did you know?"

"I could smell when your arousal turned to fear."

She looked at him oddly, and he knew then he had slipped up. No mortal man could sense, let alone smell, such a thing.

She moved as if she were trying to get away. "I don't want you to go without tasting you." Cupping her cheeks, he kissed her, felt her come into him as their tongues tangled, their mouths angling and moving against each other.

Mairi wiggled on his lap and Bran gritted his teeth. He was hard. He didn't understand it, but he actually *wanted* this woman. It was more than the Legacy Curse. He wanted to touch her. To strip her naked and look at her. He wanted her breasts in his hands, his mouth. He wanted to taste her, to feel the silk of her pussy on his tongue. And after, he wanted to lie with her and watch her sleeping in his arms. He wanted to kiss her awake and talk with her. Learn everything about her, in and out of bed.

He grew longer and thicker as she shifted her weight, aware of his cock, which was growing against the cleft of her sex. He wanted to tie her up and keep her with him all night long. He wanted those chocolate brown eyes on him as he went down on her, and he wanted her nails in his shoulders and her screams in his ear.

He wanted her awakened to him and the kind of pleasure he could give her.

Closing his eyes, Bran eased his body against hers. He wouldn't mind sliding into her this way, with his face in her hair, the long silky strands cocooning him as he slowly thrust his cock into her. He'd enjoy the slow slide as he whispered sex words and took her with his hard body. He imagined it, sliding his thick length into her, opening the petals of her sex as he thrust in. He'd fill his big hands with her breasts and watch as her lips parted on a moan.

He imagined the sounds she'd make as he shoved up into her; the way her breath would escape as she shuddered atop him. He saw her head thrown back as she let herself go, let herself be taken by him, and the image had him in knots—and leaking. The tip of his cock was wet and a drop of pre-come dribbled down his shaft.

"Are you wet, Mairi?" She gulped, and he slid his finger down the column of her throat. "Are you thinking of us together?"

She blinked rapidly, but didn't answer.

"Are you thinking of my fingers inside you? My tongue?"

"I know I shouldn't," she murmured even as he watched her nipples bead beneath her top.

"But can you resist? Can you leave tonight not knowing what it is like to be pleasured by me? To be fucked by me?"

She gasped as his palms slid up her thighs to the zipper of her jeans, where he brushed his fingers over the metal in an unmistakable invitation.

"We may still be strangers, Mairi, but we won't be when we're done. We'll be as intimate as any man and woman could be. Let me be the first stranger you have, Mairi."

He saw the struggle in her eyes, the will to deny what she was feeling. Brushing his fingers along her denim-clad sex, he said, "Tell me you don't want me. That you're not already wet and aching, and I'll leave you."

"I wish I could. But the truth is . . . I want to feel you inside me. *Deep inside.*"

"Is that a yes, Mairi?"

She smiled and ran her fingers through his hair. "That's a you'd-better-hurry-up-before-I-change-my-mind yes."

CHAPTER EIGHT

They stood before a mirror. The room Bran had taken her to was dark, lit only with black candles. In the reflection of the glass, Bran stood behind her, watching her, his gaze skating over her body. She couldn't believe she was here with him, prepared to have sex with him. It was so out of character for her, but she could not have denied him for anything. She was simply dying to feel him naked on top of her, his cock in her hand and between her thighs.

It might bring disaster, but right now nothing in the world seemed more right than to be here with Bran, giving in to the sexual fantasy that had ruled her dreams for weeks. With him she had forgotten about the voice from last night and the fear that had overwhelmed her. She'd forgotten about seeing Suriel again tonight. With the first touch of his hands on her she had felt healed. Safe.

"Is it still yes, Mairi?"

Her gaze flew to his in the mirror. He was asking her, giving her another chance. With a nod, she answered him.

She watched the descent of his stare in the mirror, saw his hand leave his side as he reached for her hair and pushed it back over her shoulder. God, she had never felt this hot, this reckless before. She was literally trembling and he hadn't even touched her yet.

Her eyes closed as his fingers trailed along her neck. The hum she felt when he touched her made her skin hot and tight.

His finger left her throat and trailed down her shirt, where it traced the darkened circle of her areola. The nipple puckered, begging for his touch.

The hum in his body took over hers. She couldn't stand it any longer. She wanted him touching her, his hands all over her skin. She wanted him above her, taking her hard. She should be afraid of this, of these foreign emotions inside her, yet somehow she knew that Bran would not hurt her.

"I want to make you feel pleasure, *bliss*," he whispered as he brushed his lips along her collarbone.

He pulled her shirt and bra up and over her head, dropping them on the floor. Then he cupped her breasts as he stood behind her. Pressing them together, he kneaded, watching her expression in the mirror. He knew she liked it, and he teased her by skimming his fingertips over her nipples, making them harder. She wanted to beg for his mouth on them, but then he released her and moved his hand down between the valley of her breasts, his skin so dark against hers. His palm slipped lower, to the buttons of her jeans. Deftly he undid them and pulled them down, along with her panties. She stood before him completely naked, watching in the mirror as he looked her over, and yearned for his hands to travel along her body.

Without a word he hooked her thigh up over his, exposing her fully to the reflection of the mirror. Her breasts bounced and he caught one in his hand. Sliding the flat of his palm along her nipple, he teased her until she was arching up and digging her nails into his leather-clad thighs. With his other hand, he spread her sex. Wetness glistened between the pink folds, reminding her of the orchids. And suddenly, she knew exactly what he had meant by them.

"You're beautiful, Mairi. And I want you. Everything that's begging for release inside you, I want it."

Mairi suddenly found herself lying on the bed. Above her was Bran, his long, dark hair cocooning them, and his mismatched eyes glowing in the dim candlelight. A five-o'clock shadow crested his chin and upper lip, making him look dangerous . . . and desirable. Her gaze strayed lower, from his full, hard lips, down his neck and the thick cording of his throat, to the twining lines tattooed there, gold and pewter with touches of green. She traced them to where they disappeared beneath his shirt.

He overwhelmed her a bit with his intensity, with his hard body, with the tattoos and leather. Yet she had never been more turned on. She wanted him, and in ways that she had never wanted her other boyfriends. But most important, she trusted him.

He traced her mouth with the tip of his calloused finger, the roughness arousing. Mairi watched as his gaze followed the path of his finger down her body. His eyes, fathomless in their depths, left no part of her unstudied. She squirmed beneath that gaze, fearing every aspect of her was being scrutinized and judged.

"Easy," he whispered, his thumb brushing her bottom lip in a fluttery sweep. "Let me commit you to memory."

"Why?" she asked breathlessly.

"Because I want to remember you this way for eternity."

God, he was perfect. Not even her dreams were this hot. She could actually feel the moist heat growing thick between her legs.

"It would be a beautiful thing to see the moonlight illuminate your body as you lie naked beside me. You'd look so right in the forest, beneath the trees . . ."

Mairi was completely undone by what she saw shining in his eyes.

"Let me give to you. Take from you," he whispered darkly. His mouth covered hers and he kissed her, nipping at her lips as his hand cupped the side of her neck. Gently he eased her back against the pillow and slipped his tongue inside her mouth, licking, caressing, teasing, but his desire was banked. Mairi felt the tension in him as she slid her hands up his arms and over his back. The black cotton of his shirt shifted and stretched over the thick muscles. She felt their shifting beneath her palms and found herself wishing she could be caged by him and his strength. She wanted him to let go, to unleash all that raw power she sensed in him. Instead, he was holding back.

Why?

He continued to kiss her until she could no longer think. Over and over his mouth moved atop hers as his hand slowly slid down her neck, till his palm came to rest against her heart. Lower still, sliding over the crest of her breast until it lay flat over her nipple. She caught her breath as the heat from his hand swamped her. The vibration in his body hummed, pitching higher and higher, and she arched into his hand, her nipple tightening as he ran his thumb over it. He plucked at it, taking it between his thumb and forefinger, alternating between rolling it and pulling it. She moaned, and he swallowed the sound, growling, the vibration in him getting stronger as he stole her breath.

Mairi had never been kissed like this—so deeply, so thoroughly. Her lungs burned and she broke off the kiss, panting, arching her neck as she ran her trembling fingers through his long hair. His lips brushed her chin, then her neck. She felt the warm, wet tip of his tongue as he trailed it along the column of her throat, then flicked the fluttering pulse at the base, sending goose bumps slithering along her spine. Restlessly her legs slid along the slippery sheets as he began to suckle her throat, making her hips roll and lift in greedy anticipation.

"That's it." He rocked his pelvis into her belly, making her feel how hard and long he was beneath his pants. "Show me where you want me to go, how you want me to take you there."

She saw through hooded eyelids that he was watching to see how her body responded to his touch. He rocked against her once more, swiveling his hips, pushing his erection into the softness of her belly. That strange current in him flowed, and her body took it in. It was like having an orgasm, feeling those extraordinary vibrations beneath his skin. It was a delicious feeling and it made her wonder how much more exquisite the sensations would be when he plunged into her.

Mairi felt the warmth of his hand slide up to her breast, as if knowing what she desired. She felt the electric shock of his finger circling the sensitive areola. Her nipple immediately tightened. Her back arched, the vibrations stronger, more rhythmic, despite the slowness of his finger stroking against her.

He pulled at her, pinching then brushing, heightening then soothing. She heard his breath—ragged—felt the heat of his mouth bathing her throat, and she reached for him, raking her nails down his back.

His cock was hard and insistent, and she wanted it inside her, along with those strange vibrations that kept coming in waves off his body. She was delirious with need now. It was the only explanation for the hum she felt.

"I want you—*now*," she demanded, clawing at his back, craving the intensity of the vibrations her body was absorbing.

He dragged his lip across the hard tip, once, twice, then glanced up from her breast. His eyes were glinting like precious metals. In the center, where the pupil should have been, was a dot of liquid silver. It shone like a diamond, twinkling at her.

He captured her gaze and held it while he lowered his chin and dragged his bottom lip once more across her nipple, sending shooting sparks of longing to her core. He bit her gently, teasingly. She scraped her teeth across her bottom lip. The way he watched her totally turned her on.

In truth, she was so close, and when it happened, she was going to come like a bomb. She just knew it, the way her body was lighting up for him. Good Lord, she was panting now, as if she'd run a marathon. She couldn't catch her breath, and every time she looked down, it was to see Bran tonguing her nipple.

He cupped her in his palm, squeezing, watching the flesh spill out of his hand. Then he brought it to his mouth, capturing the nipple gently between his teeth. Mairi held her breath . . .

waiting. He glanced up, caught her gaze, then slipped the aching bud inside, sucking her deep until she moaned and thrashed her legs on the bed.

His fingers ran down her hip and thigh till she felt his broad fingers sliding up the inside of her leg. "I can smell your core. I want to taste it."

Yes! Her legs parted of their own will, allowing him more room to stroke her. He teased her by drawing his finger down her soft hair and tracing the contours of her folds. Then he parted her, drawing his thumb along her, dampening her flesh, spreading the thickening wetness.

"You flow heavy for me, *muirnin*." Then he brought his finger to his mouth and licked. "And you taste so right for me."

No one had ever done anything like that. No one had ever said anything so erotic, so blood-curdlingly sexy. No one had ever looked at her quite the way Bran was looking at her—like he wanted to devour her.

The vibration in him increased, and she looked down between their bodies to find him studying her. She waited, holding her breath as he slowly slid his finger along her plump crease, watching as his finger disappeared between her folds.

"I can hear your heart beating, Mairi, can feel it even here, at your core. It's beating so fast, like the wings of a hummingbird. It's speeding up, isn't it, the longer you wait, the longer you anticipate this?"

She nodded, feeling her heart skip a beat as he pressed closer to her, his mouth grazing her sensitized flesh.

"Do you trust me, Mairi?"

She held his head in her hand, pushing forward, needing his mouth on her. "Yes."

"Do you trust me enough to let go, because that's how I want you, free and wild, writhing as I go down on you."

She could do that. Most definitely. She could be wild. Hell, she was nearly there.

He found her clitoris and flicked it. The motion, combined with the strange vibration in his touch, sent her over the edge. His lips set fire to her, as he spread her wide and licked her all over, leaving no inch of her sex unlapped by his incredibly skilled tongue.

She screamed and arched, holding him to her as she shook beneath his mouth. She probably should have been mortified by how easily she came, but she couldn't think of that. All she could think about were the amazing sensations of her orgasm—then the fleeting disappointment that she hadn't waited to feel more, because she was certain that Bran could definitely have taken her even higher.

She collapsed against the pillows, spent, breathing heavily. He kissed her inner thigh, dragging his tongue up the length of her, before his head fell to her navel. He nuzzled her with his warm lips as his fingers played with her sex.

He was definitely not finished with her. *Thank God!*

"Mairi?"

"Hmm?"

"Undress me. I *need* to be naked with you."

CHAPTER NINE

Banging on the door jolted them both from the sensual haze hovering between them. With a curse, Bran was off of her and striding to the door before she could cover herself with her shirt. With a fierce pull, he inched the door open.

"What do you want?" he snarled with a sound that seemed inhuman.

"We got issues downstairs."

"Not my problem."

A hand shot out and landed on the door, preventing Bran from slamming it shut. "It sure as hell is your problem—it's her friend."

With a sinking feeling, Mairi knew what was happening. "I'm coming," she called as she clutched her shirt to her chest. Rhys MacDonald averted his eyes and turned his back as she got dressed, but he stayed in the hall, his stance telling her that he was pissed off and in a hurry. She should be horrified by how she must appear to him, but she couldn't worry about that now. She had Rowan to be concerned about.

"Is she having a seizure?" Mairi asked as she pulled on her pants.

"No, why? Does she have those?" the man asked, sounding alarmed.

"Yeah. So if she's not seizing, is she stumbling around muttering incoherently?"

"She's walking around like a zombie." The man's gaze slid to where Bran stood, scowling. "Talking about Morgan and hellhounds."

Mairi saw Bran visibly jump. "Let's go," he commanded, all but pulling her from the bed. She was rumpled and her hair was a mess, but at least she was dressed. Bran didn't give her a chance to make herself presentable. He pulled her along the dark hallway, almost dragging her behind him.

"Hurry, before it is too late."

"Too late? Too late for what?" she gasped, pulling away from him. Something dark and scary curled in her belly. "What the hell has Sayer done to her?"

He turned and glared at her. "You said you trusted me."

"I did. Now I'm thinking I might have been wrong. Was it your plan to separate us so that your friend could hurt Rowan and you could do whatever the hell you wanted with me?"

His glare turned glacial; his mismatched eyes actually looked as though they were churning up one hell of a storm. "There was no plan."

He touched her face and his gaze softened. "We'll talk about what happened later. First we have to see to your friend."

Reaching for her hand, Bran tugged her along, down the carpeted steps to the main floor. Skirting the dance floor, they made a left, then another quick left away from the lounges and the bar, and down a dark hall.

A door was suddenly thrown open and Mairi saw Rowan pacing, her jade-colored eyes wide. She was ranting like a madwoman about dogs, fog, and black magick.

"Honey, it's Mairi." But like always, Rowan didn't hear her. "It's okay," she soothed, reaching for Rowan's hands. "I'm here, and I won't leave you."

"A house of mourning, a garden of pain, a path of tears. This is where you will find the first key."

"I know," Mairi whispered, hugging her friend. Rowan always said something about a key, but who or what she was talking about remained a mystery, a vision only she could see. Mairi had tried to put the pieces of the puzzle together, but always came up empty. The only thing they had to go on was a sketch Rowan had drawn during one of her visions. It didn't look like any sort of key either of them had seen. In fact, it didn't look like a key at all.

"Before you arrived, she said hellhounds were coming, coming to tear apart the raven," Sayer murmured to Bran.

"What would a mor—" Bran stopped midsentence, glanced at her. He didn't finish what he had started to say.

"Whatever she's doing, I want her out of my club before the cops come. Understand?" MacDonald thundered. "Use the back door and get her gone."

Mairi tried to find the best way to explain things. "Rowan has these spells a lot. She has . . . a . . . a tumor in her brain," she went on softly, saying the words out loud for the first time. "She goes for surgery next week to have it removed. This"—Mairi

indicated Rowan's trancelike state with a wave of her hand—
"usually happens before a seizure."

A low growl broke the quiet from the other side of the
room. Mairi turned and saw Keir in the shadowed corner. The
look on his face momentarily shook her. The pain she saw in his
eyes didn't make sense.

"What's up with the Shadow Wraith?" Bran mentally asked
Sayer.

Sayer glanced at the Keir. *"I don't know. But he says that she's
not all human."*

Bran's gaze shot back to the woman called Rowan. He
studied how she paced, how she seemed to be in a deep trance,
watching something she only saw in her mind.

*"She described the Wastelands, and the hellhounds that are
coming—three of them. She said Morgan has found a way to free
herself from Cailleach's punishment."*

"How the hell does she know any of this?" he snapped.

"If you two are done with your little tête-à-tête," MacDonald
exploded, looking between Bran and Sayer, "we should get going.
If hellhounds are coming, then we need to prepare. And I'm not
above giving them what they want. If you know what I mean."

What they wanted was him.

"Look, I doubt anyone is coming," Mairi said. "It's the tumor. It gives Rowan . . . I don't know. Visions."

"To disbelieve would be a mistake." The Shadow Wraith's
voice was soft but sure. Bran glared in warning, but Keir met

his glare head-on with his ever-changing eyes, which were now electric blue. "She sees."

Bran thought back to Rowan's aura, the indigo and black melding together. Marked for death, but a seeker as well.

Damn it, he didn't have time to figure out the woman, and how she could see Annwyn. If Morgan was near he needed to act. His powers were weak, and in the mortal realm they were all but nonexistent.

A brilliant flash of white lit up the window of the office. It was followed by an earth-shattering rumble. The growl of the hellhounds.

"Ah, shit," Sayer groaned.

Bran reached for Mairi. "Get down," he hissed in her ear before he shoved her to her knees. "Under the desk. *Now!*"

Sayer reached for Rowan, but Keir already had her. She was in his arms, her eyes closed, her body limp against his chest. "I can walk past them."

True. The lucky son of a bitch. For some reason hellhounds were scared shitless of the bastard.

"I'll get the women out," Keir muttered, "but first, you gotta do your thing."

Bran hoped he had enough magic to do it. Closing his eyes, he concentrated on the thoughts he needed, trying to block out the growling that was growing louder, hungrier. He tried not to hear Mairi's breathing, as fast and harsh as when she had come for him.

A vision of her flashed before his eyes. Thighs spread, waiting for him to taste her. He tried to concentrate on the vision he needed to summon magic, but Mairi was all he could see.

"Oh, for fuck's sake," Sayer cursed, "we'll be here all night if we wait for him." Waving his hand over the room, he wove an enchantment spell from his palm. "Neither woman will remember anything from the time they entered this room. It's not protection magic, but it's the best I can do."

With a flash, Keir was gone with Rowan.

Bran looked helplessly down at Mairi. What did these strange feelings he was having mean?

Bran knew he should be thinking about how he was going to get rid of the hounds, but all he could think about was Mairi and the disappointment he felt at not having been inside her. He wanted her, energy or not. He just wanted to know what it would be like to feel all that passion in her wash over him.

Fucking Morgan. She really knew how to torture him.

"The hounds have reached the Cave of Cruachan," Keir announced as he flashed back into the room. "There's a pack of them guarding the entrance to Annwyn and I smelled them outside as well. I have no idea where they're hiding. But they're out there."

"How did the woman know?" Bran demanded.

Keir's hands went up in the air. "How the hell would I know? From the minute I first saw her, I knew she wasn't completely human. That's why I've been going to her shop every week, to see if I could learn more. I haven't."

"Well, maybe her mortal ancestor got it on with a Sidhe, too," snapped Rhys. "And now she's a half-breed like me."

"Shut it, MacDonald," Bran growled.

"I'll take this one, now."

Bran struggled to show no outward sign that he cared that Mairi was leaving. When the Wraith flashed with her, Bran felt his knees weaken. He needed energy, and soon, but the thought of pleasuring another woman after tasting Mairi made him feel ill.

Striding to the window, he looked out at the parking lot and the little blue car beneath the glow of a streetlight. Something moved, and Bran froze. Two red dots glowed in the dark from the roof of the car.

"On their car," he roared, running for the door. Hell, they'd be torn to pieces by the rabid animals.

"It's a trap," he heard Sayer cry.

Ignoring him, Bran ran to the car, and watched the huge dog jump from the roof to land in a crouch before him. Another one came, growling, showing teeth that were dripping with saliva. Its eyes glowed red and the throaty growl warned that the hound would take great delight in ripping out Bran's throat.

A car engine roared to life, and he watched it reverse out of the parking spot. The red taillights shone over him and he wondered if Mairi noticed him standing there, or if the remnants of Sayer's spell made her mind cloudy.

Most of all, he wondered if he would ever see her again.

The first hound lunged at him, knocking him off balance with its huge paws. Teeth tore into his forearm and the pain was excruciating.

If he had enough power, he could shift into his raven form and fly away, but his magic was too weak for that. It would take everything he had to change, and that would leave him vulnerable. He was in the mortal realm, where his magic was naturally weaker. He couldn't afford to use it all at once. He needed a reserve in case that bitch Morgan came calling.

With a rush of adrenaline, he reached for the hound's head, placing a palm by one of its ears. Despite the fact that its teeth were sunk deep into his arm, so deep its canines scratched against bone, he endured the agony, knowing the dog's bite anchored it to him. With one strong shove, Bran twisted the hound's head, breaking its neck. Its mouth went slack and it dropped to the asphalt.

Panting, he squared off with the hellhound that had been atop Mairi's car. This one was bigger, wiser. The alpha of the pack. And Bran was wounded. Already he could feel the venom of the dog's bite poisoning his blood.

They watched each other, two predators circling, waiting for the other to make a mistake. He was aware of the others watching him from the window of the office. They were as powerless as he in this mortal realm. Outside the walls of Velvet Haven, their magic was weak. His friends could not help him, at least not out here. If he could make his way to the office, he might be able to gather enough strength to conjure the magic he needed to fight off the remaining hounds. Then he needed to get back to Annwyn, where Cailleach could heal him of the poison that was now coursing through his bloodstream. If only he could inch back five steps. But the hellhound knew what he needed, and signaled another of his pack to guard the office door. There was now a rabid animal at his back and his front.

Morgan had trained them well. They knew his weakness and that pissed him off. He despised being weak.

Bleeding, he swiped his brow with his arm, feeling his blood trickle down his temple as he watched the alpha pace back and forth, waiting for his moment to strike. Bran pulled a wiper blade off the windshield of a nearby car. "C'mon," he snarled at the hellhound, "you want me, come get me."

The dog lunged. Bran held out his left hand, allowing his sigils to absorb the power of the moonlight, and the wiper blade turned into a sword. When the hound was in midair, Bran plunged the sword right through the animal's throat. The gurgling snarl and bubbling of blood mingled with the whimper of the hound behind him.

Turning, out of breath and weak, he faced the last hellhound. If he could just take this one he could get back inside the club. Get to Cailleach, who could heal him. He could regain his strength, his magic, and then he could kill Morgan once and for all. But not before he made her tell him where she kept his brother prisoner. Even if he had to torture her.

Vision swimming, Bran took an unsteady step and raised his sword. In truth, he knew he was dying. "Fuck her," he spat. "I won't allow her to win without a fight."

The hound lifted its frothing lips, baring its teeth. Its red eyes glowed as bright as blood; its teeth glinted in the moonlight. It was going to hurt like the burning fires of hell to be torn apart by this creature, but it was more palatable than the thought of being shackled to Morgan for the rest of his days.

Morgan would never be queen of Annwyn. *Never.*

It was all she'd ever wanted, which meant that this hound would not kill him, merely maim him so that he could be taken back to the Wastelands, where Morgan lived in all her misery and evil. She wanted to be queen. She wanted his powers. And it was his belief, his knowledge of Morgan's desire, that told him this hound would not kill him.

But this was an animal, and animals turned. He was part animal himself; he knew that side of him wasn't easy to control. This beast would be no different.

Jabbing the tip of his sword, he taunted the animal as it paced back and forth, showing him its teeth, then clamping them as the sword tip pierced fur and hide.

C'mon, just lunge at me. But the hound knew what he wanted. It paced back and forth, snarling. Bran taunted it some more, jabbing at it, wounding it, and finally he got what he wanted. With a snarl, the hound leaped up, and Bran sliced his sword through the air, but it missed entirely. Lifting the sword again, his arm burning and bloodied, he prepared for another strike.

The beast jumped and shoved him back with all four paws on his chest. Bran fell toward the ground, knowing that in the next instant it would press on him and tear out his throat. He felt himself become weightless. The world blurred and his eyes rolled back in his head.

The next thing he knew he was facedown on asphalt, his nose in a puddle of water.

"Open your eyes, Sidhe."

Bran glanced up at the winged figure towering above him. With a groan, he closed his eyes again. "What do you want, Suriel?"

"How about some thanks for saving your useless ass?"

Suriel never did anything for free, and Bran wasn't willing to pay the debt. He recalled just how Suriel had looked at Mairi and felt a sickening feeling in the pit of his stomach. No way was he making any deals with Suriel.

"I didn't need rescuing," he snarled instead.

"Whatever." Suriel knelt down beside him. Bran opened his eyes to see a pair of green combat boots and the ends of black wings, the feathers dipping into the muddy water.

"The day I need your help is the day you can strip me of my powers and cut my balls off."

Suriel growled as he tugged on a fistful of Bran's long hair and lifted his face from the water. "You have no dominion here, Raven. I rule this place, not you."

True. He was in the mortal realm, and that was the aegis of God and the angels, even this fallen one.

"What do you want? You don't do anything unless there's something in it for you."

Suriel smiled cruelly, his beautiful face contorted with menace. "Ah, but there's something in it for you, too. I know the identity of the human who will kill you."

How does the bastard know of Morgan's curse against me?

Suriel laughed. "This is *my* world and you would do well to ally yourself with me."

"I don't make deals with the devil."

"Fallen Angel," Suriel corrected as he pressed the heel of his boot onto the gaping wound of Bran's arm. "Lucifer was cast out for plotting against God. I didn't plot against Him, I merely got laid."

Grinding the heel of his boot deeper, Suriel inflicted more pain. Bran swallowed back the agony.

"I saved your ass because I want something from you, and I can't get it when you're dead."

"Go to hell. I'm not making any deals with you."

"Look around you, Sidhe—this *is* hell. I've been trapped in this fucking cesspool for nearly a thousand years all because

I got my dick wet." Suriel lifted his boot. "Now listen to me. I know the identity of the one prophesized to kill you. I know of a way to find your brother. All I need is your help to find one small book."

"I wouldn't make a deal with you if my last breath depended on it."

Suriel laughed and stepped on his arm harder, making him scream inside. "So much pride," he said. He clicked his tongue as if he were chiding a child. "It'll be your downfall, you know. You're not in Annwyn, *King.* You're among mortals. And you know what mortals love? They love knowledge, science. They hunger for it. And wouldn't you make a nice little science project for the doctors at the hospital." He jerked his thumb over his shoulder. "Imagine what they would say once they started examining you, system by system."

In the distance Bran could see the big blue square with the large white *H.* "You blackmailing son of a bitch!"

"It's an even exchange, my friend. I need you, and you need me. So, what is your answer, Sidhe? Join me in my quest, or join the mortals at the hospital."

"Fuck you."

Suriel yanked on Bran's hair, pulling his head up to face his. "That wasn't one of the options."

"I'd rather die than help you."

Suriel let go, and in his weakened condition, Bran couldn't hold up his head. His forehead smashed to the rough asphalt, making him see stars.

"Then die, King."

Bran fought to remain conscious as he watched Suriel's boots splash away through the puddles. The hellhound venom was poisoning him, and he was weak from blood loss. He had one of two options left. Die as a man, or die as a bird.

It wasn't a difficult choice. There was no way in hell he was going to be dissected by mortals. Dead or not, he had his pride.

Using the very last of his strength, he reached inside the neck of his shirt and pulled out the fire opal pendant. Brushing his thumb across the smooth surface, he felt one last jolt of stored magic. With a flash, he was the raven, lying with wings spread, waiting to die in the middle of the road.

And wasn't this a glamorous fucking death for the king of the Night Sidhe and the protector of Annwyn? He wasn't dying as a warrior. He was roadkill.

CHAPTER TEN

❧

"So, that Dr. Sanchez is a wet dream, isn't he?"

Mairi turned the wipers on high as rain pounded the windshield. "Still trying to play matchmaker, Rowan?"

Her friend laughed, but it sounded weak and exhausted. "You know me, an eternal romantic."

That she was. Not to mention the strongest woman Mairi knew. Glancing in the rearview mirror, she saw Rowan sitting in the backseat wrapped up in a blanket. Her head was pressed back and her eyes were closed. She looked pale—too pale. She probably should have stayed the night at St. Mike's, but Rowan being Rowan, she flatly refused. Her seizure hadn't lasted as long as some of the other ones she'd endured. That fact, coupled with Rowan's surliness, had provoked Sanchez to discharge her into Mairi's care.

"I made a deal with Pretty Boy Sanchez, you know," Rowan murmured sleepily. "He let me go only because I promised I'd convince you to go out with him."

Mairi smiled and shook her head. "You see me with a doctor?"

"Actually no, I don't, but he's desperate, and I didn't want to spend a night in the hospital, so I figured the deal was the way to go."

Mairi turned her econo-compact onto Sanctuary Street. The street sign made her recall it was the spot where Lauren's murderer had dumped her body. She couldn't let the image of the girl's mutilated body go. The symbols were always there in the back of her mind, haunting her, just like the memories of her dream lover. Somehow the two were linked. She felt it in her gut. Years of listening to that sixth sense had served her well in her nursing career. But Mairi didn't know what to make of this crazy night.

"Wow, this is some good shit," Rowan grumbled. "What'd they give me this time?"

"A little Valium and lorazepam cocktail. You'll sleep well."

"Sorry for interrupting your evening with Mr. Hottie."

Mairi pressed her eyes shut. She purposely hadn't allowed herself to think of Bran or his amazingly skilled mouth. "Don't sweat it. We were just talking."

She thought she heard Rowan snort. "Convo interruptus. It was damn bad timing on my part, wasn't it? I can't tell you how bad I feel."

Mairi laughed. "Seriously, don't."

"Never know where that conversation could have led you." Rowan yawned, then followed with a deep sigh. "I really appreciate you letting me crash at your place tonight, Mairi. I owe you."

"You don't owe me anything. That's what friends are for, right?"

She glanced back to see Rowan nod. "Better than friends. We're family."

Mairi swallowed hard and dropped her gaze to the road. She'd never been one for praying, but she'd begun the night Rowan had told her of her tumor. Every night since she'd prayed and bartered with God to save her best friend. They *were* family. Mairi's mother was gone, and her dad, well, who the hell knew where he was?

"I saw you in the vision tonight."

"Yeah?" she replied, mindlessly rubbing her wrist. It still tingled from when Bran had closed his fingers around it.

"Uh-huh. It was strange because I never see you in my visions. It's always people I don't know, in a place that's mystical and . . . different. I don't think it's Earth."

Mairi was afraid to ask exactly where Rowan was transported during her visions. She didn't think she could bear it if it was heaven.

"I think it's the afterworld, you know? It's so beautiful and green. Lush. Peaceful. But you were there, standing in a wooded grove. I saw you with Mr. Hottie. What's his name?" she asked sleepily.

"*Bran?*"

"Yeah. You were together. I couldn't figure it out, how you were there in the afterlife."

"Maybe it was because we were in the club and you were thinking about me?"

Rowan shrugged, her head lolling to the side. "He was protecting you from something, but I don't know what."

"It was just an aura, Rowan. It wasn't real."

"So they tell me. Mairi?"

"Hmm?"

"Do you know that in the Druid religion, the name Bran means raven? The Celts believed that the raven ruled the Otherworld."

"Really?" Rowan was a walking encyclopedia of pagan knowledge. How she remembered it all baffled Mairi. For as long as Mairi had known Rowan she'd been into the occult.

Mairi smiled to herself, remembering the day they had met in the library at Our Lady of Perpetual Sorrow. They'd been eight and Rowan had been reading a book, her little legs swinging back and forth, too short to touch the ground. She'd looked up and her green eyes had been glowing.

"I've been waiting for you," she'd said as if she'd known all along that they were fated to meet.

They'd been the best of friends ever since. Rowan had been a ward of the school, abandoned on the steps at age five by her mother. Mairi had used the school as a sanctuary from her abusive, alcoholic father.

"In my vision, Bran was standing beside you, and he had . . . wings. Black wings, like a raven."

"What the hell?" Mairi slammed on the brakes as a black shape appeared in the middle of the road. The car came to a lurching halt. Through the swishing wiper blades and the steady stream of rain, Mairi squinted and saw some kind of animal lying in the middle of her lane.

"What happened?"

"Something's on the road."

"Oh," she heard Rowan mumble. Glancing in the mirror, she saw her friend draw the blanket up around her shoulders. Her head rested against the window and her breathing was slow and deep. The drugs were finally working.

Glancing back out the windshield, Mairi saw that the shape was that of a large bird. She couldn't drive over it, nor could she leave it there. She'd always had a soft spot for animals, and the way the black feathers blew in the wind reminded her of the feather that had skimmed down her arm outside Velvet Haven.

She thought back to Rowan's bizarre vision. For a fleeting second she believed her friend, before hard logic smashed the thought. Tumors could provoke all kinds of crazy ideations and visions that didn't make any sense. Still, though, there was no denying that something strange was in the air. Unbuckling her seat belt, Mairi reached for a towel that she'd swiped from St. Mike's and opened the door. She ran to the bird and bent down on the cold, wet road. She saw chest movement, rapid and shallow, and realized the bird was still alive, although its wing was badly mangled. Picking it up as gently as she could, she felt its beak pierce her hand. There was still fight in the thing if it was able to bite her.

"Stop that," she said gruffly as she handled the bird more carefully. "I'm only trying to stop you from becoming tire splat."

The bird stopped and she felt it stiffen in her hands as if rigor had just settled in. Then it cocked its head and looked up at her, as if it was listening. Toweling off the excess wetness from its feathers, she was careful to avoid its wing.

Brushing her hand through the feathers to make sure most of the water was gone and her upholstery was going to stay relatively dry, Mairi noticed the silver stripe that ran along its back. It had been partially buried beneath wet feathers, but now that they were all unruffled, the stripe was clearly visible.

Oh, shit! It was the bird from the club.

"Why are you out here by the hospital?" she asked, as if speaking to a bird were perfectly normal. "You're blocks away from the club."

The bird didn't answer. Not that she expected it to. Cradling it to her chest, she ran back to the car and carefully placed it on the passenger seat. She thought about taking it to an animal shelter, but she knew they'd only put it out of its misery. For some reason, she couldn't stand the prospect. There was something about this bird that she liked. It made her feel calm.

She thought back to what Rowan had said, and an image of Bran looming over her, licking her sex, fired up in her brain. "Stupid," she muttered as she buckled her seat belt and pulled the gear shifter into drive.

So he gave her a hell of an orgasm; it didn't mean he was keeper material. Hell, he was nowhere to be found when she had left the club with Rowan. For all she knew, he'd gotten what he wanted out of her and taken off without a backward glance. Damn, she wished she could remember the events after that blinding orgasm.

What the hell had happened to make her forget?

She looked down at the bird as she drove, studying the gray mark. "I don't know anything about birds," she grumbled. "How the hell am I gonna fix your wing?"

"You'll think of something. And I will repay you with my life."

Mairi looked at the bird. God, now she was hearing things.

"Mairi?"

She startled at the sound of Rowan's voice. "Yeah?"

"Do you believe in fate?"

"No."

"You should, because yours is staring at you right now."

From the shadows of a building, Suriel watched Mairi head back to her car. The raven was in her hands, just as he had planned. He watched her carefully place the bird on the seat. A softness in him warmed his usually cold insides.

He had intended for her to find the Sidhe king. It was their fate.

He knew that now. Although he'd wanted desperately to keep Mairi from the Sidhe, it was not to be. His purpose in her life was ending.

A hollowness filled him as he finally accepted the truth. Unknown to her, he had been at her side since birth, watching over her, guiding her. He hadn't always understood his purpose in her life, just that He had willed it so. And now He had shown Suriel the path her life would take, and the part he would play in it. A damn millennium here on Earth, with no fucking contact from anyone from above, and tonight he gets a message that Mairi's path lay with the raven, and not him.

He still didn't want to accept that his precious human was meant for Sidhe scum. They all believed him responsible for the ills that had befallen Annwyn. But it wasn't as though he'd barged through the veil and slaughtered everyone in sight. He hadn't brought locusts and plague. He'd had sex with a goddess. And *she* had seduced *him*. Yet the raven despised him as though Suriel alone were responsible.

He hated Annwyn and all its inhabitants. He hated the goddesses the most. He blamed them for his fall. He'd had over a millennium to reconcile himself to his actions. Yet a thousand years later he was still embittered.

Except for when it came to Mairi. She was the key to his redemption. She was what was left of the good in him. She was the healer that the raven would need to save himself from Morgan's curse. He had a role to play in both their lives, if only the raven would not be such a pigheaded ass as he usually was.

He wanted out. *Needed out.* He was tired of this existence. And at last he had found a way.

Mairi had the book of the prophecy. She could interpret it, the Scribe's coded message. A flame and an amulet and a divine trinity, which would lead the way to both artifacts.

He didn't give a shit about the amulet. He wanted the flame. Which meant, of course, that once he delivered Mairi over to the raven, his connection to the Sidhe king was not over. To find redemption, Suriel knew, meant discovering the identity of the Destroyer and obliterating him from both Annwyn and Earth.

But first he must unite with the king of Annwyn, meshing both their worlds to one single purpose: uncover the identity of the Dark Mage, and destroy his apprentice.

Only then would God welcome him back home.

❧

After tucking Rowan into her bed, Mairi went in search of her dog's old crate. She needed *something* to put the bird in.

"That's enough," Mairi snapped, tugging on Clancy's collar. "You don't have to show your teeth; believe me, the birdie knows who's boss."

Her huge Irish wolfhound gave a throaty snarl, his long canines bared, staring at the bird, who was standing on her kitchen counter proudly, as if egging Clancy on.

"You must have a death wish," she muttered, scooting the bird farther back on the counter. "He can reach up here, you know. Just look away and show him you know he's in charge and he'll go lie down."

The bird cocked its head to the side and studied her. His eyes actually looked as though they narrowed at the insinuation that Clancy was top dog.

"Fine, then, become the midnight snack," she griped as she left them to duke it out.

She found the old crate in a closet and wandered back to the kitchen with it. The metal box crashed to the floor, clanging on the ceramic tiles, as she took in the scene before her. Clancy was sitting on his haunches, ears back almost flat against his head. One paw was extended as he whimpered in supplication at the bird's feet.

What the hell?

The bird watched Clancy, its head high, its gaze fixed on her dog as if it were trying to teach it some manners. Whatever was going on, Clancy was suddenly as submissive as a lamb.

The bird cawed quietly and Clancy dropped his paw before slinking out of the kitchen, tail between his legs.

Picking up the crate, Mairi set it down beside the kitchen table. Then she reached for a bowl, filled it with some tepid water and an ounce of rubbing alcohol, and reached for a cloth.

As she gently wiped away the dried blood on the bird's wing, Clancy whimpered behind her. *Nothing* cowed Clancy! The bird must have pecked at his eyes! Glancing over her shoulder, she watched as Clancy whimpered once more, then slowly lowered his big body onto the kitchen floor.

"Wow, what's up with you tonight?" she teased. But the dog didn't cock his head while she talked to him as he usually did, but instead stayed totally focused on the bird.

"Don't worry, Clance, he's not going to be a permanent fixture around the place."

The bird was stoic as she worked. It watched quietly as she carefully cleaned the wound with the warm water and rubbing alcohol. It didn't even try to pull away as she poured the solution over its wound, despite the fact she knew it must sting. It was as if it knew she was trying to help, not hurt.

Winding the white gauze around the mauled appendage, she suddenly noticed the glistening swirl of silver and gold on the fine feathers of its head. "What's this?" she asked aloud, stroking her fingertip along the marks. "Did you get into some paint?"

The raven's eyes closed as she stroked him once more. For a wild bird it certainly was calm. She half expected to have her hand pecked as she tried to bind the wing. But it had stood still and quiet, letting her work.

"There," she said, pulling away. "Now in the crate you go."

It squawked, trying to fly away from her, but she resisted the flapping good wing and shoved him into the crate. "Sorry, but it'll have to do for tonight."

The door slammed shut and Mairi clicked the latch into place. She had no idea what else to do for the creature. Was it hungry? All she had was canned dog food and Milk-Bones, neither of which she thought the raven would enjoy.

"Tomorrow I'll get you some seed. Sleep tight," she whispered, gazing into the crate. Man, she was beat. When she bent down to look at the bird she actually thought it had Bran's mismatched eyes.

Yep. Exhausted. It was time for bed.

She shut off the kitchen light, leaving the light on above the oven, then padded across the living room floor to the couch. She stripped out of her shirt and jeans, silently laughing at the bird, who seemed to be spying on her through the metal bars of the dog crate. As she reached for the tank top she'd laid out she had the sudden feeling someone was watching her.

Whirling in a circle, Mairi hissed, "Who's there?"

Silence. Even the bird stood still as a statue, its head cocked to the side as if listening with her. She was definitely spooked. Even the fine hairs on her arms were raised.

Mairi searched the apartment but found nothing other than the bedroom window she'd forgotten to close before leaving for the club. Maybe it was the brush of the curtain against the wall she'd heard? After checking on Rowan one last time, Mairi quietly tiptoed back into the living room, where she dropped onto the couch and covered herself with a light blanket.

It was hot in the apartment, despite the fact it was only May. The heat made her skin prickle against the worn fabric of the couch. It felt abrasive, like steel wool, and she flopped onto her back, trying to find relief.

Above her, the ceiling fan quietly turned, giving her momentary periods of relief from the heat. While her body was fatigued, her mind was active. She couldn't stop thinking about

Bran, about what he had done to her in that room. Reliving that orgasm was all she wanted to do. Dreaming of what else he might have done to her quickly followed. Soon she was fidgety, her body alive and craving his touch. Damn him, she had wanted more—*needed more.*

Her last thought was of him, looming over her, his mismatched eyes glowing with excitement, his heavy cock lying against her thigh . . . when he lowered his head to her breasts she saw the side of his face, heard the deep, velvety rumble of his voice against her skin and realized, as the moment of sleep washed over her, that her dream lover had at last arrived . . .

CHAPTER ELEVEN

Slipping through the holes of the crate, Bran hobbled to the edge of the counter and jumped down. He was too weak to shift into a man, his wing too damaged and his magical stores depleted. Thank the goddess Mairi hadn't possessed an iron cage, otherwise he'd be confined for the night. Iron was deadly to the Sidhe, and he wouldn't have been able to risk touching it.

Mairi . . . He glanced at her restless body sprawled out on the couch. How had she found him? He couldn't fathom it, and finally didn't try to understand. A part of him already knew why she had.

They shared something. Something he had never once before experienced, and it wasn't only sexual attraction. He couldn't explain it, but felt it coursing along his body. Even as she had tended his wing he'd felt her energy pulsing through his feathers, down the bone and into his blood. Her careful caresses had been the furthest thing from sexual, yet he'd felt his body come to life as though he were taking her inside him. His people had a term for that kind of magical bond: *Chosen Fate*.

A lover, a *destiny*, that the universe had created solely for one person. Bran had only ever known one person lucky enough to have found his Chosen Fate, and that was Daegan.

But Mairi couldn't be his. His curse wouldn't allow it. Which made him wonder, if she wasn't to be his in that way, what was she?

He decided not to think about that, and instead chose to make his own search of the apartment. Someone had been here. He smelled it, a different scent from Rowan and Mairi. Yet the dog, Clancy, had not perceived the intruder. Which made Bran wonder if he was dealing with something immortal. But who?

Suriel. The bastard's name was cropping up all over tonight.

With a glance, Bran summoned the dog. Clancy dragged himself up from his arthritic haunches, his nails clicking on the tiles. Lowering his head, he allowed Bran to climb on, then down his back.

"Show me around," he ordered and Clancy obeyed. It hadn't been easy to get the beast to come to heel. He'd been highly protective of Mairi, and while Bran respected that, even welcomed it, he could not allow the dog any sort of dominance while he was in his raven's form. Especially a raven with a mangled wing.

In the end they had come to an understanding. Bran would not hurt Mairi and Clancy would not eat him.

Meandering around the apartment atop Clancy's back allowed Bran to look out every window and ensure they were all locked. He could see everything, every dust mote and cobweb. Nothing had been disturbed. But the strange scent still lingered.

"Take me to the bedroom." The clicking of nails on hardwood made Mairi stir. Clancy stilled, looking over his shoulder at his mistress. When she didn't wake, he continued on into Mairi's bedroom.

Hopping off Clancy's back, Bran landed on the soft mattress. The sheets were cool and crisp and smelled of Mairi's shampoo and her supple skin. He couldn't resist smelling them, remembering the feel of her soft thigh grazing his chin, the scent of her deep in his nose. He had only just begun with her when Rhys had interrupted them.

Damn Morgan and her fucking hellhounds!

Bran hopped quietly forward. Rowan was sleeping heavily, dressed in a white T-shirt. Sweat stains ran down from her neck and between her breasts, plastering the cotton to her drenched skin.

Pressing forward, he ran the tip of his good wing over her brow and closed his eyes. His hand sigils, which were hidden beneath the feathers of his wing, absorbed the salt and minerals. He felt her illness penetrate through his body, and knew it was as Mairi had said. Rowan was ill. Deathly ill, and tonight she had a fever.

He came closer to her, studying her, wondering how she could know of the hellhounds. He thought of what she had said, wondering what key she could mean. Most important, he recalled Keir saying Rowan was not completely human. That more than anything had shaken him. If she was not mortal, then what was she?

As king of Annwyn he had a duty to protect its inhabitants, and if, like Rhys, Rowan was at least part immortal, then it was up to him to make certain she was safe. He needed to identify her other half; maybe then he could heal her. There were many species living in Annwyn, many healers who might be able to help.

She stirred and he smelled the scent of sandalwood and musk mingle with the air from her body. He inhaled it, recognizing Sayer's scent. He had enchanted her. Damn the Selkie, he would cause nothing but problems claiming this one. But Sayer being Sayer, he felt he was entitled to any female, of *any* species.

Leaving Rowan to sleep, Bran climbed once more atop Clancy, who walked him to the living room and stood beside the couch. Bran perched himself on the arm and stood guard at Mairi's head.

She was still agitated, her legs tangling in the blanket, which had fallen to her knees. She was wearing white panties and a pink tank top that had ridden up to her navel. Her skin glowed in the pale light from the window, revealing milk white skin and taut nipples.

Ordering Clancy to the foot of Rowan's bed, Bran settled over Mairi, watching her sleep, sweeping the tip of his good wing through her hair. His sigils tingled, liking the energy he felt, craving more. Over and over, he stroked her, running his wing tip over her brow and down her nose. In a fleeting sweep, he brushed her mouth, watching her lips part beneath the black feathers.

For all of his three hundred years he had felt betrayed by his shifter half. He had wanted to be magnificent and strong—a mountain lion or a wild horse or an imposing white hart like his uncle Daegan. Instead he had been born a bird. All that seemed to fade now as he thought of Mairi naked, pressed against him, his wings beneath her, around her, their fluttering softness caressing her flesh, arousing her, protecting her. He thought of what it would be like to take her as his wings cocooned them both. She would be utterly surrounded by him, and the image made him feel possessive.

For once he gave thanks for his wings.

"Mairi," he whispered, brushing her mouth once more, "I wish I'd had more time tonight to pleasure you."

Those words came from a very dark place within him. He had never known this feeling with a mortal. He did wish he could have pleasured her. He wanted to know what it was like to sink deep into her, stretching her full of his cock. He wanted to learn her sounds, her movements beneath him. He wanted to know *her*, not the feel of the energy she would give or the magic she would create within him. He wanted to know her and he wanted her to know him.

"Bran?"

Her voice was husky with sleep and desire. He stilled, his wing hovering over her throat. The temptation to touch her was overwhelming. Her hand, fragile and pale, skimmed down her belly to where it slid beneath the waist of her panties. He could smell the perfume of her core. With her other hand she raised her top, revealing a perfect breast, the nipple hard. She tugged, rolling it between her thumb and forefinger in time to her hand, which was hidden beneath white cotton.

She purred—*his name*—and he stilled, wishing he could shift into a man and awaken her as he wanted, with his cock stroking in and out of her slick cunt.

Giving in to temptation, he stroked the tip of her beaded nipple with his wing. She moaned, pressed upward for more.

He traced her shape, the sides of her breasts, then beneath, before circling her nipple and watching as she bit her lip and sunk her hand deeper beneath the waist of her underwear.

He teased her nipple with his wing, liking the image of his black feathers against her pure, pale flesh. He usually went for mortals who resembled Sidhe women. Tall, toned, small-breasted. But Mairi's curves and her generous breasts captivated him. He couldn't stop looking or touching, or envisioning those breasts cradling his cock.

Teasing her with brushing strokes of his feathers, he watched her writhe and felt her desire coalesce into energy, which his sigils absorbed. The power slowly ebbed into his veins, heating his blood. Yet he hadn't touched her to make magic, but only for the sake of feeling her against him.

The scent of mutual desire coated the air and he inhaled it, bringing the scent deep into his lungs. Eyes shut, he concentrated on the sound of her breathing—rapid, harsh, nearing orgasm. Surrounding him was that alluring caress, the one that strengthened him, yet weakened him simultaneously.

Suddenly he was back in Nemed, his sacred grove. The image of his death vision rushed back, pulling him in. He felt his heart stop, his breath cease, and then there was complete and utter blackness . . .

"*Mmmm,*" Mairi purred, feeling her dream lover's chin against her cheek. His jaw was covered in scruff, abrading her throat as his lips kissed a path down her neck. Beneath her hands the thick muscles of his shoulders rolled and bunched. His hair, long and black, slid over her breasts, rubbing against her nipples. His breathing was hard, just like the cock that brushed against her sex.

"Let me in," he commanded, nipping her earlobe.

"Not yet," she moaned, smiling at the sound of torment that ripped from his throat. God, she loved this, the power she had over him, the control to keep him at bay as he pleasured her. His big hand slid down between their sweat-slicked bodies, brushing her belly before sliding down the soft rise to the slick folds of her pussy.

She was wet, drenched with liquid desire. He tasted it on his fingers as he pushed against her with his erection.

His hand dropped to her thigh, his fingers squeezing as he spread her. "Fuck me," he commanded.

"No."

She pushed him back so that he kneeled before her, his cock thick and full. He reached for it, stroking it, making it grow until Mairi looked away, gathering her control. She wanted to cradle him in her hand, feel the fierce strength in him, bring her mouth to him and shatter his willpower. Yet she refused to give in to her body's needs.

She didn't understand it, why she felt this need to keep him at arm's length. But it was there, a feeling that she *must* do this. For her own good. For her protection.

Slowly she looked him up and down, from the muscled thighs to the chiseled abdomen, which quivered with pent-up need. Up farther to the bounding pulse in his thick neck, to lips that still glistened with the slickness of her sex. And then she met his eyes, one pewter, one gold, and stilled, frozen in a dream she had experienced so many times yet now was so very different.

Bran?

She was asleep, she knew that, dreaming of the man who

had come to her these past weeks. Yet she had never seen his face, till now.

"Mairi?"

He was in his male form, kneeling, naked on his bed, his cock in his hand, pumping up and down. He was not dead, but alive and in Mairi's dream. She was lying on the bed, the sheets rumpled in a mound beneath her as she balanced her upper body on her elbows. Her long dark hair was draped back over her shoulders, leaving her fully open to his gaze.

With hungry eyes he devoured her lush form, which was illuminated against the white sheets. He reached for her ankle and turned it so that her thigh opened, showing him her core. She had pubic hair, and he stroked his fingers through the wet curls. Sidhe women were hairless there, but he liked Mairi's dark curls, liked seeing his hand in them.

She watched him, her eyes wide. With one hard tug he pulled her to him. She fell back, flat against the bed, her breasts bouncing, her thighs wrapped around his waist, his cock poised to penetrate her in one hard thrust.

"Mairi," he whispered as he pressed forward onto her. But then something caught his eye, at the corner of the bed—*iron*.

"Ah, Mairi," he whispered painfully, realizing that this dream was part of his death premonition. That *she* was. "Have you saved me tonight so that you can kill me later?"

CHAPTER TWELVE

Rowan smiled as she snuggled deeply into the sofa cushions and Mairi covered her with a blanket.

"How you feeling, Ro?" Mairi asked as she gave her friend a big hug.

"Like I got hit with a truck."

"Well, you needed a whack of lorazepam and Valium to stop the seizure. You'll be feeling dopey for hours yet."

Yawning, Rowan nodded. "I can't seem to keep my eyes open."

"Sleep as long as you like. You don't have to keep me company."

"I got a mean craving for Chinese food," Rowan mumbled. "Let's order some for lunch, okay?"

"Your vision," Mairi murmured as she looked at the raven in the crate. "What do you remember?"

"Rabid dogs, and you, a weird place."

"Nothing else?"

"Nope."

Mairi hoped the tumor wasn't growing. She didn't think she could stand it if she was to lose Rowan.

Rowan fell asleep and Mairi walked over to the cage to rebandage the bird's wing. This morning, when she had checked the bandage, she had spent more time studying the bird. The silver stripe on his back was most curious. Clancy chose that time to clomp over to her. He rested his head on the table and whimpered. Mairi glanced at the clock and realized it was past time for the dog's meds.

Clancy was old and his hips were bad, but Mairi couldn't even think of putting him down. So she just kept popping him full of aspirin and dog treats and as much love and affection as she could.

"Almost done, Clance," she murmured, as she tied a knot in the bandage, securing it.

He was facing the bird cage and watching the raven like a hawk. Nothing had changed since last night, Mairi realized. They were still staring at each other, but the struggle for power was over. The bird was in charge. It was so strange how they had stared each other down before Clancy just backed off.

As she went to the cupboard and reached for the aspirin bottle, she thought of Bran, for no reason other than the onyx raven reminded her of his hair. It had been so black and silky. God, she was pathetic.

Really pathetic.

But she found herself wondering what he was doing. Who he was with. If he had even thought of her after he'd left her naked.

"Hey, Mairi," Rowan called from the living room. "I'm hungry. What about you?"

"Starved," she answered back.

"I'm fantasizing here about an order of jumbo shrimp."

"I'm on it," she said, reaching for the phone book and searching for the number of her favorite Chinese restaurant.

"Mairi? How's your friend doing today?"

She glanced up from the phone book and looked at the bird, who was watching her with a look of rapt attention in its strange eyes. He was truly beautiful, though it was so damn weird of her to think so. He's just a dumb bird, she reminded herself, but she couldn't resist looking at him once more.

Rowan sat up on the couch, catching Mairi's attention. She saw Rowan studying the cage. "Feed your raven," she murmured. "He needs energy."

"How do you know?"

Rowan sank back on the pillows, closing her eyes. "I saw it in a dream last night."

"Really?"

"Yeah, some guy named Suriel told me to tell you to feed and care for that bird."

The phone book dropped, and Mairi, white with fear, faced Rowan.

"What did you say?"

"He'll save you, that bird. But first you've got to feed it."

"No, the other part, about Suriel."

"Oh. Yeah. He thought he was in your dream, but then he realized he wasn't."

"I beg your pardon?"

Rowan sighed and closed her eyes. "Honest mistake, Mairi. I was in your bed, after all."

And then she heard a familiar voice. A voice from her

childhood, the one she used to hear when she hid beneath her bed when her father was drunk and destroying the house.

"There's nothing to fear, Mairi. I'm watching over you."

"Here, try this."

Bran watched as Mairi took a crust of white bread from Rowan and rubbed it between her palms, littering the bottom of his cage with bread crumbs.

"What bird doesn't like bread crumbs?" Mairi asked her friend.

This one, he thought.

"He'll eat. Sooner or later."

Mairi stepped away and stretched up on tiptoe to reach into her cupboard. She pulled out a blue box with white lettering. "Frosted Mini-Wheats?"

"Can't hurt to try it."

Again she crumbled up the cereal, which rained down over the bread crumbs.

Why did she insist on crushing everything?

"Go on," Mairi said gently, prodding him with her hand. "You'll like it."

Not likely. He'd much prefer a steak, or some of that food in the white containers. It smelled delicious. Chinese food, they had called it. He'd never had it, but the aroma filled the small apartment. Grudgingly he admitted that he had come to like human food. As a Sidhe who commanded the elements, he did not need food for nourishment. His magic was his food source. But years of mingling with mortals had taught him to eat, and crave, certain culinary delights. And bread crusts and cereal weren't going to cut it.

"Maybe he wants some egg roll?" Rowan asked while she scraped the leftovers from her plate into the wastebasket. "He's big enough to down one whole."

Mairi grimaced. "You don't think he eats mice, do you? Or garbage?"

Bran flapped his good wing and fluttered about the cage. If she stuck a mouse in here, he was going to be pissed.

"Fussy-assed crow," Mairi grumbled as she shoved another Mini-Wheat into his crate.

"I don't think he likes to be referred to as a crow."

He cocked his head and thanked the goddess for Rowan. Despite his strange, and alarming, sexual connection to Mairi, it was Rowan who seemed to understand him in his animal form.

She bent forward and reached her finger into the cage, touching him. "He has lovely markings. I wonder how he got them."

"I'm worried he won't eat."

His heart softened as he saw the concern on Mairi's face.

"He'll eat. Eventually."

Mairi nodded and brushed her hands on her pants. "You look exhausted."

"I am," Rowan murmured. "I called Dillon to come pick me up. He'll be here any minute."

"You didn't have to do that. I would have taken you home."

Bran looked between the two women, wondering who the hell Dillon was. No doubt Sayer already knew, since he'd been in Rowan's mind, enchanting her.

"That's what I pay him for," Rowan said with a tired smile.

"Besides, who knows how long I'm going to be out for, and he needs the money for school."

"Well, tell him to be careful. He drives that flashy little Nissan way too fast."

"Yes, Mom," Rowan said with a laugh. "I'm going to wait outside for him, clear my head with the fresh air. I'll call you later."

Mairi watched the door close behind her friend. In that moment, Bran felt the pain and anguish she was feeling, and he vowed, as he watched her, as he wished he could go to her and hold her in his arms, that he would do what he could to understand Rowan's lineage and get her the help she needed.

If she was not all mortal, then maybe the magic of Annwyn was what she needed to rid herself of whatever disease was making her ill.

The phone rang and Mairi picked it up.

"Hello?" She grimaced when she heard the voice on the other end.

Bran could hear a male voice, and he saw red knowing that Mairi might have interest in another man. For some absurd reason, he thought of her as his. Especially now that she had healed him.

"I can't tonight, Sanchez. What about tomorrow night?"

The man mumbled something and she nodded, said goodbye, then hung up.

"Oh my God," Mairi groaned into Clancy's upturned face. "If I didn't love Rowan so much, I'd kill her for making that deal with Dr. Sanchez. Can you believe it, Clancy? Sanchez only released Rowan from the hospital after she begged and she agreed to get him a date with me."

The dog stared up at her blankly, but the vessels behind Bran's eyes began to pulsate. Mairi with another man? No. *Never.* But then he stopped and realized how foolish his thinking was.

She couldn't be his. He shouldn't be anywhere near her. If what he'd seen in her dream last night was true, she was the mortal who would destroy him.

But she had healed him, the voice inside him whispered. For what purpose if only to destroy him later?

He watched Mairi pace the small living room, lost in thought. Finally she sat on the couch and rubbed Clancy behind his ears. "What am I gonna do?" she whispered to the dog. "I don't want to go out with Sanchez. I don't want . . ." She trailed off and smiled. "That's a lie. I do want someone, but I'll never see him again."

Bran stilled. Was it him she wanted? Half of him longed for it to be true, the other half feared it, knowing she sought only his destruction.

"And what am I doing spilling my heart to you, huh?" With a laugh, she ruffled the dog's ears, then jumped up from the couch and headed to the bookshelf. She picked up a small book bound in leather. On the front cover was the symbol of Annwyn.

Ah hell, he thought to himself. This was the book that Cailleach wanted. Damn it, he didn't like the way their paths weaved. The book. This death vision. Everything led back to Mairi and he didn't understand it. Couldn't figure it out.

How had she gotten the book? And how the hell had she been able to pull him into her dream?

He watched her for a long time as she flipped through

the pages, carefully separating the thin vellum. She sat up and reached for the notepad and pen that sat on the end table and scribbled something down, then returned to the book.

He wondered what language it was written in, the Gaelic tongue of Annwyn, or English. He wondered what secrets the book contained. Secrets Cailleach had not told him.

Did Cailleach know about Mairi?

She stood up, stretched, and he watched her walk across the apartment to the bookcase. Curiously, she hid the book behind her stereo, then disappeared inside the bathroom. Bran heard the taps turn on and the old water pipes groan, followed by the spray of water hitting tiles. From his perch he saw the silhouette of Mairi pulling off her top, then bending at the waist, tugging off her jeans.

Thunder rumbled in the distance, and a black cloud hung heavy over the roof of Mairi's building, making the apartment dark. Steam from the hot water spilled into the living room from the open door, carrying with it Mairi's scent.

Knowing he was a fool, Bran slipped between the wires of the cage. Cursing himself, he hobbled over to the bathroom. With some maneuvering, and a good deal of pain, he managed to get himself up on the bathroom counter, where he could see into the shower.

His breath caught. Mairi was a dream, standing beneath the spray, her long hair hanging in clumps, the water sluicing and running down her curves. She was soaping her body, and he felt his blood heat as her hands roamed over her breasts, then down between her thighs.

He had no idea what she would think once she opened the shower door to see a big black bird standing there watching her, but he didn't care. He wanted every second he had left to be with her. Near her. Beside her. But most of all, *in* her.

Deviant that he was, he managed to get himself to the windowsill. To his delight he could look down upon Mairi and all her naked glory.

❧

Mairi never took baths. Not since the age of sixteen. It would have been lovely to have one now. To soak in hot water with scented bubbles. She would have liked to have lit some candles, poured herself a glass of wine, and lounged in the water and thought of her time with Bran. Perhaps she'd even bring in her vibrator and live out the fantasy that still burned in her mind.

She would have loved that. But she couldn't do it.

Against her hip, her wrist burned. When she looked down she saw it was red, chafed, the scars scratched raw.

The last time she'd taken a bath she had awakened to a steady stream of blood flowing from her wrist. The voice she had heard the other night at the club was the same voice she had heard when she was sixteen. The same voice she heard as a child.

She had felt so much pain, so much emptiness as she sank deeper into the water, trying to shut out the voice. But she had not picked up that razor. She had *not* slit her own wrist.

One of the nuns had found her. Thankfully there had been a doctor there, working the infirmary. He'd stitched her wrist hastily while the ambulance was en route. Almost unconscious from the blood loss, Mairi hadn't felt a single thing.

The next day, Sister Catherine had come to visit her and

told her that Rowan had been raped by the creepy caretaker of Our Lady. It had happened at the exact same time Mairi was in the tub. From that moment on, Mairi had been sure that it was Rowan's pain, her emptiness, that she had felt. But how? Why? There was no plausible explanation, so she kept her thoughts to herself and told no one. Not even Rowan.

Neither of them talked about it. Not Mairi, and not Rowan. Rowan hadn't asked about the injury and Mairi had not dared to ask Rowan about the rape. They were both good pretenders, but now it was hard to pretend, what with her scars reddened and itching. Even the skin around the scars was a dark shade of pink that looked irritated. Since Lauren's gruesome death, nothing had been the same, most especially her scars.

And now Suriel. He had come to Rowan, thinking it was her. His appearance paralleled the resurfacing of memories of the voice that guided her, soothed her when she was frightened.

Was it coincidence? No, Mairi knew it wasn't. She had seen things that science couldn't explain. Miracles that happened, but in theory shouldn't have. Suriel's appearance had a purpose. Rowan's dreams had a purpose. These scars . . . Mairi feared what meaning they might hold.

Shoving aside the old memories that still haunted her, Mairi reached for the soap and sponge and poured some vanilla- and honey-scented bubbles on the pink gauze.

Think of something else. Something happy. Something . . . *Bran*. The name slipped into her thoughts and she smiled. For someone who didn't trust easily, she had certainly trusted him.

As she soaped her body, her hands cupping her breasts, she felt her nipples, which were still tender from Bran's mouth.

But along with the tenderness, she felt the lingering sensation of need.

As her fingertip slipped over her nipple, it tightened, making her belly clench in the same needy response. She was wet and horny. She thought of Bran and slipped a hand between her thighs as she rested her foot on the edge of the tub, stroking herself.

She had never touched herself as much before as she had in the two days since she had met Bran. But damn it, she needed this release! She'd dreamed of Bran last night, confusing him with her dream lover. He'd asked her to fuck him, and like a madwoman she had said no. She had awakened this morning hornier than she had ever been, dying to know what it would be like with him.

Slipping her fingers deep inside, she moaned at the instant relief. She closed her eyes and imagined Bran there with her. She thought about what it would have been like to take his cock in her mouth, to feel the satiny smoothness of him on her tongue, his hands in her hair as he angled her head the way he wanted her.

Fingers frantic now, she moved from her pussy to her clitoris, stroking as the visions fueled her rhythm. Bran on top of her, Bran behind her, taking her hard, whispering dirty thoughts into her ear.

Lightning flashed, illuminating the bathroom. She looked up over the top of the shower toward the window and saw the raven perched on the sill. Forked lightning once more lit the sky, silhouetting the bird; then suddenly it was Bran who stood before her, reaching out his hand. She heard his thoughts in her mind.

I like your fantasy. Let me show you mine.

Suddenly she was transported to a wood. It was night and rain fell steadily from the sky. She was lying on a stone slab like a sacrifice on an altar. Spread wide, her sex aching, her body hungry.

And then Bran appeared, crawling atop the stone, then over her.

"Let me finish it, *mo muirnin*," he whispered.

Mairi's own fingers seemed to be replaced by Bran's hot palms. His gentle fingertips traced her body, touching her breasts, her belly, then down her hip. He teased her with his touch, with the brush of his lips against her body. As he moved lower, his hair trailed over her shoulders, down her arms, heightening the arousal, making her sensitized skin even more so.

Open for me, Mairi.

She cried out, clutching at his hair as she drew up her knees. The rain continued to pour down on them and lightning flashed. Mairi looked down to see the forked line of pure energy hit Bran's skin. The tattoos on his neck, chest, and arm glimmered as the lightning ran down the ink like an electrical current. He grabbed her bottom, pulling her up for his mouth. When his tongue swiped against her, she arched, crying out, begging for more.

And he gave more. His fingers deep inside her as his tongue played with her clitoris. She was greedy, taking everything and asking for more. He brought her to the brink of orgasm, then stopped, pulling away from her.

"No!" she cried, clawing at his massive shoulders. "Don't leave me like this again."

He smiled a smile of pure male arrogance. "Leave you hungering?" he whispered. "Leave you empty?"

"Yes," she said, somewhere between a scream and a sob.

His lips brushed the shell of her ear. "Do you want me to fill you up?"

Not waiting for her reply, he plunged his thick cock into her, making her sex stretch to accommodate him. Mairi felt that current, that electricity invade her body, and when Bran made her come it was euphoric. Mairi felt as though a piece of her had died and she was lifted, floating toward heaven. It was beautiful and peaceful. *Magical.* That was the only word to describe it.

There was an exchange, a connection she had never felt before. It was as if their essences flowed into each other, mingling, becoming indistinguishable from each other.

She felt lighter, almost weak, but he turned her over, onto her knees. "Did you think I was done with you?" he asked, as he slid his cock into her.

He felt huge still and Mairi moaned at the invasion. God, he felt good. The slow, lazy rhythm left her panting. The warm rain hitting her skin made his body slide easily against hers.

She was fully covered by him, his chest on her back, his hands filled with her breasts, and his cock gliding in and out of her.

"You like that, Mairi?"

She couldn't speak, but nodded and moaned as his thrusts became harder, more intent. His fingers left her breasts to skim her hip. They kneaded her bottom before he parted her. His fingers traced her opening and she squirmed away from him, shocked by the sensation that she wanted him in *there*.

Mairi accepted his touch, allowed herself to feel the building passion once more. The pleasure rose and she heard Bran growl, felt his strength grow as his arms suddenly caged her.

Now he was fucking her hard and it felt so good, so powerful to take him like this. The pleasure was rising and rising, but he kept her completion just out of reach.

"Please," she begged. His finger found her clitoris and he stroked her in time to his thrusts, finishing her in short, penetrating stabs.

When he came it was explosive. She was filled not only with his essence, but a strange vibration that radiated from her core to her fingertips.

When she opened her eyes, the grove was gone. She was surrounded by white tile.

Collapsing against the wall, Mairi stilled, trying to recover from her orgasms. She couldn't remember ever feeling this good. For a few seconds she believed that she had actually been in that enchanted wood, spread out for Bran's pleasure.

When she had recovered enough, she shoved opened the shower door, only to see the bird standing on the sill, watching her. Lightning flashed once more, a brilliant, blinding flash, and in that instant Mairi swore she saw the image of Bran. Behind him were black wings, and on his hand were those strange marks glowing gold and pewter.

"How?" she asked, amazed the bird had gotten this far from his cage, let alone up on the sill.

The bird didn't answer, and Mairi was left feeling oddly disappointed. She needed to hear Bran's voice. If only one last time.

She looked back after she covered her body with a thick towel. The bird was watching her with his rapacious gaze.

Thank you for feeding me, Mairi, she heard Bran say.

Then, to her amazement, the bandage fell away from its wing and the bird flew from the room.

CHAPTER THIRTEEN

Bran knew he had to leave. Staying in Mairi's home was too dangerous. *She* was dangerous. Yet he felt his newly shored magic weaken at the thought of never seeing her again.

He had stayed in bird form for the rest of the day, content to stay in his cage watching Mairi and allowing his hunger to grow. She tried to feed him again, more bread, but this time from her palm. He didn't have the heart to refuse her, so he had lowered his head and gently fed from her hand, the act as pleasurable as sex. The bond even stronger.

He had not needed food. But how could she know that what he had witnessed in the shower, combined with the lightning he had harnessed, had given him the fuel he needed?

That incredible shower scene. Bran closed his eyes, willing the memory to life. In his mind, he'd taken her to Annwyn, to his Sacred Space, and placed her on his altar. She was spread, ready for him, gentle raindrops pebbling on her skin. It was no surprise that in his fantasy it had been raining; water was his favorite element. What he hadn't known was how damn perfect

Mairi would look in his grove, splayed on his altar. She'd been regal as a queen—his queen. The feelings the thought evoked frightened him, *still* frightened him, he reminded himself. There was no place for Mairi in Annwyn, and no place for him in her world.

Still, considering they were two souls destined to live apart, she was incredibly bewitching and powerful. Watching her bring herself to orgasm in the shower had provided enough energy to fuel his magic. It had never been that way before. Watching had never been enough. It had taken hours and hours of sexual intercourse to gain what he needed. But with Mairi, it was different. His curse was not acting as it usually did.

More reason to fear, to escape.

Nothing was clear. Everything about her was shrouded in mystery. His thoughts were no longer focused. She was dangerous to him, held an unnatural hold over him. A hold he must sever if he was to go forward and find Carden and put an end to the dark magick before it overtook Annwyn. A hold that could very well be his undoing.

His brother and the Dark Mage. That had been his purpose for coming to Velvet Haven and lurking amongst the mortals. It had not been to forge a relationship with a human. A beautiful, lovely human he could no longer deny he wanted to bring back with him to Annwyn.

Sitting on the end of her bed, he watched her sleep, memorizing the gentle rise and fall of her chest, the way the air passed through her lips that he wanted to kiss. Just thinking about what he'd seen in the shower made him hot. Christ, he wanted her. Even more than last night in Velvet Haven when he had yearned to penetrate her, to feel her body hungrily grasp him. He had wanted more than a magical connection with her. *Still wanted it.*

Their shared fantasy had been enough to fill him magically, but physically it had been a tease. His mind was satiated, while his body still hungered.

The connection they shared was unique. To be able to enter her dreams was a new experience for him. To know that they had been dreaming about each other for weeks now was at once arousing yet unnerving. Because even though he wanted her, he knew what she was. His murderer.

Reaching out, he trailed his fingers along her silken cheek. She'd brought him home, protected him, healed him, and in the process she had softened a place inside him, making it her own.

She's a mortal, he reminded himself. Not to be trusted. She was, most likely, the human who was prophesized would kill him. He should be slaying her now, in her bed, letting her blood spill out onto the sheets, never to awaken again—never able to destroy him.

In his heart he knew she was the woman in the death prophecy. His nemesis. His murderer. Yet as he looked at her he could not fathom Mairi taking a blade to him. She was too kind, too sweet to take a life, whether mortal or immortal.

As he watched her sleep, he knew he should be deciding on a plan to thwart her attempt. An attempt that would soon come. Why? How? The questions burned in his mind. But when he touched her cheek, they dissolved like mist. He knew then he didn't want the answers. He was bigger and stronger than she was. When—if—she came to him, he could fight off an attack. There was no reason to end her life now. She had saved his life.

And how would he repay her? Slay her while she was asleep to prevent a future event that might never take place? He couldn't. It went against everything he was. He was honorable. He did not kill his enemies in their sleep like a coward. He did not kill women.

He closed his eyes and prayed to the gods of his world to please not let it be Mairi who had been created to fulfill the spell that Morgan had cast against him.

Beside her, Clancy slept, and he rubbed the dog behind his ears.

"Take care of her," he ordered.

He hated leaving her, especially this way, but he knew if he stayed, he'd risk his very life for a chance to feel her body against his. His body inside hers. She was too much temptation, a weakness in his armor. He had much to think of, and he couldn't do that when she was close to him.

Sighing, she curled into him, snuggling up against his hand. She looked soft and vulnerable. It would be so easy to roll her onto her back and lie down on her, kissing her awake. But Bran knew that it was time for him to leave.

His wounded arm felt heavy at his side as he released Mairi's cheek. The few exchanges he had shared with Mairi had given him enough power to shift into his male form. Tonight he would walk the streets of this realm as a man, not fly as a bird.

And it was all thanks to this one small human he was still alive. Alive and rejuvenated in his magical powers. Bran would forever remember those moments, of tasting her skin and feeling her pleasure pulled into his body. When his Legacy Curse once more beckoned him, he would recall that feeling of desire and he would pretend that the mortal beneath him was Mairi. Everything, he feared, would always come back to her.

Despite knowing her for so short a time, Bran could honestly say that she was like no woman he had ever met—Sidhe or mortal. His life had been lonely, a solitary existence. These past days with Mairi had made him realize that. What a fucking irony, he thought, to realize something so painful, to ache to change it and find companionship, to yearn not only for a physical connection, but a spiritual bond as well. And with the one human who could kill him.

Mairi shifted, her hips sliding against the cool sheets as she stretched. Her foot came to rest against his thigh and he touched it, allowing his fingertips to graze her skin. Every little contact was like a lightning bolt to his body. She had so much power to give, and he wanted it for his own.

Why must he endure this? Was it not enough to have Morgan curse his beloved brother? Why did she have to design a curse that would destroy him?

It was not dying he feared. It was dying at the hands of a woman he wanted. A woman he . . . he could have loved.

Love. Bran closed his eyes. It would never be his. As king of the Sidhe and coruler of Annwyn, his duty was to his people, to their safety. Love did not factor into his life. Yet when he opened his eyes his gaze fell once more on Mairi, and his heart felt as though it had been sliced through with a sword.

She had looked so right on his altar. It had been a fantasy, but he wanted so much to make it a reality.

He must go—*now.* He was falling into a dark pit with

no means of escape. She had merely been an amusement, he reminded himself, a means to an end.

No. He did not care if he ever saw her again. He would not think of her. Would not recall her expression of ecstasy. His dreams *would not* be filled with her.

Standing up, he moved quietly from the bed, never turning back to look at her. Not giving voice to the desire that suddenly welled within him.

Dream of me, Mairi, threatened to spill from his mouth, but he forced it back and left the room.

As he opened the apartment door, his gaze caught the dog's, who had followed him out of her room. "Protect her," he ordered. He turned to leave, when the flashing of the stereo's display caught his attention. Reaching behind the machine, he pulled out Cailleach's book, his thumb stroking over the triscale pressed into the leather. It was time to get back on track—to find this Dark Mage, to save Carden, to destroy Morgan. He had spent too much time with Mairi and not enough time thinking of what he should be doing.

It was fruitless to think of her. To wish for her.

Pocketing the book, Bran shut the door, feeling the heaviness of his heart that would continue to beat for eternity. Alone. Never loved. Cursed.

⚜

Walking the dark streets, Bran scanned the unfamiliar area. He wished his arm was thoroughly healed. He needed to fly, to lift himself above the buildings so he could see. As a bird, his sense of direction was better, his eyes keener. Every second he walked in the mortal realm would weaken his newly stored magic. He needed to get back to Annwyn, or at the very least, Velvet Haven.

Mindlessly he walked the two blocks to the club. From across the street he could hear the music pounding, see the neon lights flashing from inside. He could smell the sex and corruption seeping from the stone walls.

Stepping out of the shadows, he stopped at the sight of a black shape flying from the roof of the club down to the alley beside it. Immediately his pupils enlarged, swallowing up the irises, showing him the portal to Annwyn. In the gray mist, vapors rose and the scent of death stung his nose. He saw a naked female, kneeling, neck and ankles chained to a stone slab. In a circle around her, black candles had been lit. On the floor, an inverted pentagram was drawn in red—*blood.*

Her head shaved, her pale body shivering with cold, she turned her head, which rested on her knees. Her eyes were gone, replaced by black holes. On her body were carvings, symbols of Annwyn combined with angelic script. The blood that had leaked from her wounds had dried, reminding Bran of dried tears. The agony she must feel. *The terror.*

Suddenly she reached out to him, her voice dry and hoarse.

"Help me," she begged. Then something or someone pulled at the chain, silencing her. Yet she still looked at him with those black holes and he heard the world "please" whisper past him.

The vision melted away, consumed by the curled fingers of vapor. He stumbled, disgusted by the image, and wondering who the woman was. Slowly, he gained his breath, trying to burn the memory into his brain so that he could inform Cailleach, but he was robbed of all thought when his left pupil be-

gan to open and the mortal realm swam before him. He saw
Mairi. Asleep. A shadow at the foot of her bed.

Suddenly a female scream echoed in the night, taking the
vision from him. Before he could think what he was doing,
Bran ran across the street to the alley, where he found a woman
unmoving on the ground. He bent and felt the steady pulse at
her throat. She had fainted. But why? He looked up, peering
through the darkness that seemed to grow thicker.

The air in the alley was stagnant with the stench of decay-
ing rubbish, rats, and the metallic tang of blood.

Quietly he rose to his feet, stepping forward, deeper into
the depths of the alley. He stopped and swore when he practically bumped into Suriel, black wings spread, long black leather
trench scraping against the ground.

"What the fuck?" Bran asked in disgust.

"Raven," Suriel murmured without turning to look at him.
"I see you were able to pick yourself up off that road. How's
your wing?"

Bran ignored him and stepped closer. Suriel lifted his
palms and illuminated the scene with his heavenly light. Now
Bran could clearly see the two bodies pinned against the bricks
in a mockery of a crucifixion; one was an angel—a guardian—
his body limp, his white wings spread and pinned—*nailed*—to
the sandy grout between the bricks. In the angel's arms was a
mortal woman who had been stripped bare. One black-heeled
shoe remained on her foot, the other had fallen and landed in a
pile of old newspapers and a grisly pool of her own blood. Her
body had been desecrated by the same symbols that had marred
the youngling Sidhe. Around her neck, Bran noticed a silver
cord that glistened in Suriel's light.

"What the fuck is going on here?"

"I don't know," Suriel whispered. "But it's far more demonic than I have ever seen."

"Did you do this?" *Did you desecrate the body of one of my kind?*

The look Suriel gave him was murderous. "I'm fallen, not a psychotic motherfucker."

Bran had never believed a word Suriel had uttered, but he believed now. The desperation and pain he saw in those dark eyes was more than enough to convince him.

He glanced back at the woman, not knowing why he was going to confide in Suriel, only knowing—feeling—he should. "I had a vision seconds before this happened. A woman—" He swallowed thickly. "It wasn't her I saw."

"There will be more," Suriel murmured. "He's only beginning."

"I didn't recognize her."

"I know who you saw."

A mortal then, if Suriel knew. He thought of Mairi, what his right eye had shown him. "Mairi," he rasped, licking his lips, which were suddenly dry. If that was Mairi he had seen . . . he felt ill, murderous.

"She's safe at home," Suriel replied calmly. The bastard closed his eyes. "I can see her, she's sleeping."

Bran glanced at Suriel, not knowing what to feel. Jealousy flared, and he wanted to strike out and smash the bastard.

"How do you know?"

"I feel her within me."

"How?" he growled, his lips twisting.

Suriel's dark eyes flickered over him. "What is it you call

it in Annwyn?" Suriel's eyes hooded. "Oh, right. I am her *Anam Cara*."

Bran sucked in his breath. Suriel was Mairi's Soul Friend. *Fuck!*

He felt like his chest had been bludgeoned. He didn't know the significance of the bond in the mortal realm, but in Annwyn, the *Anam Cara* was the most binding tie between people. He didn't want Mairi having this connection with Suriel.

"*Jesus Christ*," he muttered, using the mortal curse words. He was jealous—fucking seething that Suriel had this kind of bond with Mairi. A deep, binding tie that Bran so desperately wanted.

"What in the hell is going on here?"

Both of them groaned when they saw Rhys MacDonald and Keir, the Shadow Wraith, at the mouth of the alley.

"*Jesus Christ!*" Rhys came running forward, flashlight in hand. "What the fuck?"

"Do you know her?"

Rhys glanced at Suriel. "Yeah. She's a regular. Her name's Trinity."

"I'm afraid Trinity, along with her guardian angel, have gone to meet their Maker."

"Christ," Rhys spat, studying the bodies. "What kind of person would do this? Her skin, there's no inch of it that hasn't been carved up." He whirled around, shining his flashlight on the wraith, who seemed to glow in the artificial light. "This is your dream, man."

Keir grimaced and glanced away.

"What does he mean?" Suriel demanded of the wraith. "She is mortal. You shouldn't have seen her in any visions."

The look Keir shot Suriel was one of pure malice. "Fuck you, Suriel."

Bran shot out his arm, halting Keir from coming any closer. "Tell me," he ordered.

As a subject of Annwyn, Keir had no choice but to obey his king. With his eyes flashing at Suriel, Keir spoke.

"I saw this in a divination. There is something evil shifting in both worlds. Can you not feel it?" The Shadow Wraith walked toward them, his gaze intent. "I have seen it in the cards, the rise of a powerful being, the strength to control both mortals and immortals. This is his work."

Suriel glanced back at the wall. "Agreed. It is not a mortal we seek but something else. A mortal would never have been able to see, let alone kill, a guardian."

"Unless he had help from one of your brothers," Keir accused. Suriel bared his teeth, and Keir smiled. "Not all of you play the harp and wear halos, Suriel. I know your kind. Don't forget it."

"Enough shit. Shine the light to the left." Rhys handed Bran the flashlight before striding over to the bodies. Bran illuminated the lower left corner of the wall. "Look at this," Rhys called.

Bran held the light steady on the brick where Rhys was pointing. In the middle of it was a pentagram intertwined with the symbol δ.

Bran hissed. Suriel glanced at him, surprised.

"You know the symbol?"

Bran nodded. "It is the symbol for Gwyn, god of the dead, and ruler of the Shadowlands."

"Is that your hell?" Suriel demanded.

Bran nodded.

"Perhaps in your world he is Gwyn, but in mine this is the angelic mark of Uriel. It was he who was sent to Jesus as he prayed in the Garden of Gethsemane the night before his crucifixion, just before Judas betrayed him. My brothers say that it was Uriel himself who planted the seed in Judas' mind."

"And what relevance would this angel have for us? We do not share your religion or your god."

Suriel looked at him, surprised. "Do you not know? Uriel committed sins of the flesh with one of the goddesses of Annwyn."

Bran looked at him skeptically, and Suriel's gaze grew dark. "What? Did you think I was the first with a hard-on for a goddess? No. Uriel beat me to that. He was the Original Sin in Annwyn."

Cailleach. Somehow Bran knew it was her. He couldn't say how; he just felt it.

"He is known as the Dark Angel," Suriel continued, "and was banished to hell for his sins. In the Apocalypse of Peter, he is the avenging angel of atonement, and on the Day of Judgment, it is said he will open the gates of hell and lead all sinners to God, then burn them in an eternal fire. It is also said that he knows the identity of the Destroyer, the person who will rain havoc upon the people of the world, destroying it."

"The story of Gwyn is much the same. Although in Annwyn, he is known as the Soul Stealer."

Suriel's dark eyes glittered in the light. "He is known by the same name among the mortals who dabble in the occult."

"Well, isn't this fucking wonderful?" Rhys snarled. "And outside my club, too."

Suriel glared at Rhys, then dropped to his knees, the ends of his wings dipped in the puddles of the woman's blood.

"Oh, shit," Suriel groaned as his hands worked along the woman's lifeless body. "The bastard has removed her womb." Suriel put his fist to his mouth. For a full minute, he knelt beside the woman, just staring at her lifeless face before he quietly murmured, "It's a message, you know."

Bran swallowed hard. He knew what he had to do. Keir was right. Whatever the hell was going on involved both the mortal and immortal worlds. "This past month saw eight Sidhe males murdered. Then three nights ago a youngling female was brought to me. She was marked as this woman is. Symbols of our faith were carved on her body."

Suriel looked up from the woman. "There have been nine such killings in the city. Eight were men. The ninth was a woman, her flesh torn like this."

"The power of nine," Keir murmured. "He's performing a ritual. Death magick."

"The beginning and ending of all things," Bran whispered. "And it involves both our worlds." And Cailleach. Is that why she wanted the book? A flame and an amulet. Was the amulet hers? Was the flame Uriel's?

Suriel lifted the woman's body, carefully cradling it in his arms. "Her soul is gone, stolen," he clarified. "I will take care of her body. Later we'll discuss what we're going to do to stop him."

Rhys motioned to the scratch marks on the woman's belly. "What does it say?"

Bran narrowed his eyes. "It is written using the Ogham alphabet. It says, 'The war has begun.'"

"So what you're saying," Rhys growled, "is that we're gonna have one hell of a turf war on our hands."

Suriel swung around as his wings spread out, ready to fly away with the body. "You had better fucking believe it, Mac-Donald. The shit winds are blowing and they're coming this way."

CHAPTER FOURTEEN

Mairi was having the most arousing dream. Her lover was back, and she sank into the pillow, letting the dream take over.

A drop, in the shape of a tear, trickled between the shoulders of a tattooed back. Sweat. She inhaled the scent of man as she watched the crystal fluid run between the rippling muscles that quivered and strained.

He was naked, back ripped and sculpted, arms thick and defined, spread out at his sides. His face was covered by black hair that was long and damp, clinging to his brow. His ass was solid—unyielding—the smooth skin stretched taut over contoured muscles. His thighs were thick, powerful, possessing stamina and sheer strength.

His was a body made to master a woman's.

Straddling his hips, she licked away the rivulet of sweat, tasting salt and arousal as she traced the sword tattooed along his spine with the tip of her tongue. A blast of heat wrapped around her despite the dampness between them. He arched, trying to connect once again with her tongue. Beneath her, she felt his ass flex, rising up hard between her thighs to nestle between the folds of her sex.

He moaned as the heat from her core swamped his skin, coating him with her arousal. Tormenting him more, she dragged her nipples along his back, scraping the pointed tips over his skin as her tongue flicked up his spine in teasing, insinuating lashes. He was shackled, his wrists in black manacles, his fingers curled into fists. On his left hand he wore a ring that bore an oval stone, the color of fire. With her lips and teeth she pulled it from his finger, allowing him to feel her mouth wrapped around his finger. She sucked it, teasing him, giving him a glimpse of what she could do with her lips and tongue.

"I am your slave," he said in a voice intoxicated with lust.

Never more did she realize the truth of his words than now. Never had she seen him so aroused, so eager for her. But she wanted him hotter. Harder. She wanted him begging.

Sitting up, she placed his ring on her index finger and admired the glow of the stone. It felt warm from the remnants of his heat, the hint of power contained within the gem.

Reminding her that she had left him aching, he strained beneath her, rocking against her sex. She was wet. She let him feel that wetness before she reached behind her—between his thighs. He groaned and shifted, the manacles straining with his immense strength.

"You are too impatient," she whispered in his ear.

"I would feel you now," he growled, a sound that made her shiver in desire, and the slightest bit of fear.

"All right." Reaching between his thighs, she teased him until he lifted his hips from the bed. He wanted her to reach for his cock. Instead, she reached for something just as hard.

In her hand was a dagger, etched with symbols. She felt that power of the silver as it touched her skin, the tingling that worked its way down her nerve endings. He turned his head and looked up at her, his strange, haunting eyes glaring at her through strands of damp, black hair.

"After all this?" he murmured. "After everything we've done, you would betray me now?"

Her body jolted and Mairi came awake with a scream. With frightened eyes she looked around her dark bedroom. Shadows played on walls, and her curtain blew in and out with the rhythm of the wind. At the foot of the bed, Clancy was sound asleep.

Just a dream, she reminded herself, even as her hands shook uncontrollably. But this time there had been a dagger, which she had taken a strange fixation with.

He had looked at her as though she would destroy him. She, a person who wouldn't hurt any creature. A person who picked up roadkill and tried to fix it.

Sliding to the edge of the bed, she hung her head in her hands and tried to stop shaking. In front of her, a shadow shifted and a man perched like a bird on her dresser jumped to the ground, his heavy combat boots making a loud thud on the hardwood floor.

"Good evening, Mairi."

Suriel. She scooted up her bed until her back met the headboard. "What do you want?"

"For you not to be afraid of me. I won't hurt you, Mairi. But I think you know that." His leather-clad knee was on the edge of her mattress. "You had a dream."

She shivered, still trying to back away from him. "That's none of your business."

He sat down beside her, crowding her with his body. She was breathing heavily, ready to pass out from hyperventilating. "Are you going to kill me?"

"Of course not. I've worked too hard to save you."

Her eyes widened. "What do you mean?"

He moved closer to her, and she kicked at him, but he reached for her ankle and grasped it, holding her still. "I was there the day of your birth, when you were lying on the warmer, unable to breathe. You were blue, nearly beyond the veil. You would have passed through if *I* had not been your first breath. My air is in your lungs, my spirit in your veins. *Me.*"

She struggled against him, but his fingers smoothed against her skin, calming her. "I have been the voice whispering to you as a child. And then when you were sixteen. I was there. Not with you, but with the *other one.* She was going to die. I was ready to take her, but then I saw you. You were bearing *His* seal."

Mairi shook her head, denying everything he was telling her. "What do you want?"

"You have a purpose in this life, and now our purposes are entwined."

"You're not real. You're not real," she chanted over and over again.

"I am," he whispered. "Have faith. Trust."

"Why?"

"Because you're going to need it for what lies ahead. Things will happen, but know that this is the path you are supposed to take. When the time is right, and when I am summoned, I will come to you. Do not fear me when I do."

"What the hell are you?"

Black wings suddenly unfurled from his back, and Mairi gripped the sheet to her chin. Holy shit!

"I won't hurt you, Mairi. Believe that."

He waved his hand before her face, and she slumped down. The last thing she was aware of was a pair of hands gently placing her on the bed before she fell back to sleep without any further dreams to plague her.

The shop bells tinkled as Sayer swung the door wide open and led Bran and Keir into the cramped little shop like he owned the place. He always was a cocky bastard, Bran thought.

The bells chimed again as the door closed behind Bran. As a precaution, he locked the door. The last thing they needed was an interruption.

"Sorry, I'm closed." Rowan looked up from the cardboard box she was filling. "Oh, hi. Sorry, I didn't know it was you guys."

Rowan looked well, her cheeks pink, the gray cast of her illness gone from beneath her eyes. She was lovely, seated in the middle of her store with her turquoise-colored skirt spread out like a fan around her. Her blond hair was cut short and choppy, making the plump apples of her cheeks more prominent. Her green eyes sparkled in the soft glow of the lamplight. Anyone casting a lascivious eye over her full figure would not believe she was dying.

But dying she was. Bran had tasted death on her skin not more than thirty-six hours before. So long, he thought, since he'd been there in the apartment with Rowan and Mairi.

Such had been the last day for him. Thinking of her. Dreaming of her. *Wanting her.* Not even the gruesome discovery of the murdered woman was enough to prevent him from thinking of Mairi. It might even have made him think of her more, hoping she was safe.

Keir stepped forward and carefully helped Rowan up from the floor. The wraith would not be denied. He had demanded to come, despite the fact that Bran needed only Sayer. "Why are you packing up your store?"

She colored. Not the pretty, flirty type of blush, but one that stemmed from embarrassment. "I have to close up shop."

"Why?"

She appeared surprised, and perhaps alarmed, by the demand she heard in Keir's voice. Sayer quickly stepped in and touched her arm, enchanting her so she would answer their questions willingly. That was their purpose here, to discover more about Rowan, who Bran believed was connected to Annwyn.

"Why must you close the store?"

"I'm having surgery in a few days and I don't know how long I'll be away."

"Have you no one to see to the running of it?"

"No."

"No family?"

Rowan shook her head. "Just Mairi, who already has a full-time job."

"What happened to your family?"

"I . . . umm . . ." she stammered. Sayer stroked her arm and she calmed. "I'm an orphan. Dropped off at Our Lady of Perpetual Sorrow when I was five. I never saw my mother after that, and I never knew my dad."

"We need information."

"What kind?" she asked as she brushed dust from her hands.

Keir pulled out a folded sheet of paper from his pocket and passed it to Sayer, who showed it to Rowan.

"What do you want to know?"

"What those symbols mean to mort—"

Bran cut Sayer off before he could say the word "mortals." They did not need this woman's curiosity piqued. Bran could still see her aura, although it had faded from the other night. The black was there, but so was the indigo weaving in and out. A seeker, he reminded himself. She would take it upon herself to learn more about them if they made her suspicious.

Sayer tilted her chin with his fingertips, bringing her face back to his and looking into her eyes.

"Have you seen symbols like this before, Rowan?"

Bran watched as Rowan allowed herself to be pulled back into Sayer's mesmerizing gaze.

"Yes. A few days ago. Mairi brought a drawing, similar to this one. The same symbols were on it."

Bran visibly jumped at the mention of Mairi's name. Sayer glared at him as his enchantment wavered once more. Then he smiled at Rowan and the woman went molten.

"Did Mairi say how she came to know of these symbols?"

"Yes. There was a murder of a young girl a few nights ago. She lived at Our Lady of Perpetual Sorrow. Mairi counseled her there. When the police brought the girl into the hospital, she was dead and her body was carved up and decorated with these symbols. In her purse was Mairi's business card."

Deeply entranced now, Rowan did not witness Bran's tension, or hear his expletive. She was thoroughly hypnotized, her voice even and automatic. She didn't move, didn't blink. Sayer kept up the contact with her, skimming his fingertips along her cheek, brushing them against her throat. He didn't need the physical connection with her any longer to keep her enthralled, but Bran suspected he needed it for an altogether different purpose.

"Ask her what those symbols mean," Bran hissed. "We need to ascertain if they mean the same in her world as in ours."

Bran paced the small store, taking in the statues of fairies and dragons. His fingers slid over a white crystal ball and an ornate chalice and athame. The craftsmanship was lovely and would have looked right at home on his own altar. He wondered where Rowan purchased the items for her shop. Some of the relics looked ancient, and some looked like they might have come from the Otherworld itself.

He picked up a curved knife, inlaid with gems. Engraved on the blade were strange markings. They sort of reminded him of angelic script.

"Where did she get this? Ask her, Sayer."

The Selkie asked, and without a blink she responded. "It was the only thing besides a pair of pajamas that was in the duffle bag I was left with. The nuns found it and put it away. When I moved out, they returned it to me. I have no idea who gave it to me, or what it is. But I think it's pretty, so I keep it."

Bran knew what it was. It was an athame used in his people's sacred Lanamnas ceremony, an eternal vow taken with a soul mate. He turned it over and noted a symbol much like the one Suriel carried on his neck. Beside the symbol was the Celtic Tree of Life, an icon used by the goddesses of Annwyn.

His suspicions were confirmed. Rowan was not all mortal.

She was at least partly of the Otherworld. Perhaps her mother had even been a goddess. He pocketed the knife to bring back to Annwyn.

"I've finished questioning her. Basically the meanings are the same," Sayer announced.

Bran flexed his arms, tension rippling down his back. He didn't like the feeling. Something was not right here. Mairi's name was cropping up more times than it should. And now this information about Rowan. It was all tied together somehow.

"Ask her what she knows of Mairi," Bran ordered, his insides in knots.

"I dream of her," Rowan suddenly whispered, her gaze clouding, unable to focus on either him or Sayer. "I see her in a magical place, standing in a grove. She's wearing a long gown, white, flowing. Her face is covered by a veil, but I know it's her. She's holding out her arm, and a black raven flies to her, landing on her arm."

"What does it mean?" Sayer asked, glancing back at him. "What place is this you see, Rowan?"

"Heaven," she answered.

"No," Bran roared. "She does not die. She *will not*."

"She dies by your hand, Raven. Your refusal to believe is the knife that cuts."

Suddenly Rowan collapsed, and Bran felt as though his world had come crashing down.

"What now?" Sayer asked as he held an unconscious Rowan in his arms. "Shall we bring her to Suriel? For certain she is no simple mortal."

"She will come to Velvet Haven," Keir demanded. "I don't want Suriel near her. I don't trust the bastard."

Bran nodded as he struggled to right his reeling senses. Did he believe in Rowan's dreams? Why shouldn't he? He believed in his own.

What was he going to do? He would not kill Mairi. Despite the fact that she was destined to murder him, he would not—*could not*—lay a hand on her.

"Where now?" Sayer demanded.

With a curse, Bran fisted his hands at his side. "To the place where all our information keeps returning us. To Mairi."

One thing was for certain, Pretty Boy Sanchez sure did look good in tight-fitting jeans and a plain white T-shirt.

"Thanks." Taking the beer from her, he tipped it to his sinfully seductive mouth.

"I have beer glasses if you want."

"Nah, I'm a bottle guy."

Mairi watched him drink and swallowed hard. She must be ovulating, she thought with disgust, because she was like a dog in heat. All she could think of was sex and how she wanted it. Even Sanchez would do. Although she knew she'd be pretending he was Bran.

But who cared? Maybe once she finally had sex she'd get the constant thoughts of Bran out of her head.

She'd dreamed of him last night. She couldn't remember the details, but she knew she had. In her dream, she'd been in control, straddling his hips, making him burn.

"So, I like this," Sanchez murmured. "Having dinner at home."

Mairi shrugged. "I like to cook and don't often get to do it."

"I'm honored."

Inwardly she cringed. She was leading him on, and all so she could get her rocks off. She hadn't wanted to go out tonight. She'd wanted to get down to business. Damn Bran and the feelings he'd awakened in her. She had been perfectly content with her solo sex life until he had entered the picture and made her want.

"Hope you like pasta," she asked over her shoulder as she walked into the kitchen to check the sauce.

"Sure do," he called. "And I'm liking your ass in those jeans."

Mairi bit her lip. She didn't do this sort of thing. She didn't have guys over to sleep with them. But this fever in her blood, it wouldn't go away. Sometimes she actually felt weak with the need, the hunger for sex.

It was crazy. Her whole life was becoming one big hallucination. Ever since she'd taken that book, reality had been skewed and bizarre things had happened. Like Bran.

I wonder what he's doing. She stirred the sauce, tasted it, then added a little more garlic. *Probably back at Velvet Haven getting lucky. Probably with a blonde with artificial boobs. Bet he isn't leaving her naked and alone, like he did to me.*

Damn it, why couldn't she piece together the events of that night? There had been his touch, his tongue on her pussy, a blinding orgasm, and *bam!* Nothing. Not until the moment when she pulled up to the red EMERGENCY sign at St. Mike's.

But she had had plenty of dreams of him . . .

"I brought you something."

Probably a box of condoms, Mairi thought. Then she chastised herself. It was obvious her one-night stand with Bran was just that—one night. He wasn't coming back. Hell, they hadn't even exchanged last names. Would it hurt to be nice to Sanchez?

Putting the lid back on the saucepan, she fixed her hair in the reflection of the microwave oven door and sauntered out to the living room. Sanchez was standing by her end table. The lamp was on and he was holding something up.

"Whatcha got there, Sanchez?"

He turned; then a slow smile crept across his mouth. Mairi found herself stepping back. Her skin felt like tiny bugs were crawling all over her. She shook herself, clearing her thoughts.

"Come here." He motioned her over beside him. "Most women would want flowers and chocolate, but you"—he gave her a lethal wink—"I knew you'd want something much more special."

He reached for a large brown envelope and pulled a black plastic film from it. "I took these from Radiology. Don't tell on me, okay?"

"Rowan's MRI?"

He nodded and held it up to the light. "This is the one from the other night, when she presented with the seizure." He gave it to Mairi to hold and then pulled another film out of the envelope. "This one was taken a month ago."

"The tumor has grown."

"Big-time," Sanchez murmured. "It's gone behind the periocular orbit; that's probably why her vision has been a bit off. Not to mention the frontal headaches and the violent seizures."

But the position didn't explain Rowan's weird visions, which her neurologist described as auras. Auras were things like smelling burned toast or hearing a sound. Not full-fledged hallucinations of other worlds.

"I'm not sure it's going to be operable, Mairi. It's grown so much and it's intertwined with major nerves and blood vessels. I wouldn't be surprised if your friend gets a call with the news her surgery is canceled."

Closing her eyes, Mairi strived for composure. All along she had tried to prepare herself for the worst, but nothing could prepare her for this, this sick, hopeless feeling in her gut. She couldn't lose Rowan. Hell, it was like losing a piece of herself.

Opening her eyes, she looked again at the latest MRI, amazed at the rapid growth the tumor had taken, as well as the shape. Quickly Mairi compared it to the previous scan. The first showed an oval growth, delineated edges, and little encroachment on nerves or blood supply. But in the latest one, it was more of a circle, with a septum in the middle divided into thirds.

Peering closer, Mairi held the film up higher to the lamplight in order to illuminate the tumor. *Jesus!*

The film dropped from her hold. She was going crazy, she had to be.

"Mairi?"

Pushing away from Sanchez, she glanced down at the scan. Even without the light illuminating it, the tumor still resembled the triscale in the book she had taken from the library.

And so shall come the divine trinity . . .

What she was thinking was absurd, but Mairi could not shake it. The Scribe of Annwyn had written the diary. She described a world of trees and sacred groves. Woods where magic prevailed and nature was worshipped. Where the Sidhe ruled by her side.

Rowan had described such a world. A world of peace and enchantment. Had Rowan seen Annwyn? Was Rowan part of this divine trinity, and the prophecy that had been written about it?

"Is there something wrong? You seem . . . shocked."

Mairi shook her head, still staring at the film.

"You know, I really despise liars."

Mairi looked up in time to see Sanchez toss the MRI film onto the carpet.

"Tell me where the book is."

"What book?" she asked, laughing nervously. "Sanchez, you're crazy."

"The prophecy," he sneered. "*That* book."

She refused to allow her gaze to stray to the bookshelf where she'd hidden the book behind her stereo.

"I'll tear this place apart, Mairi, and you'll have a hell of a mess to clean up."

"You've lost it," she muttered, pulling away. "Get out of my house."

He followed her, tracking her down as if she were an animal and he the hunter. "I want the book. Tell me where you've taken it."

"I don't know what book you're talking about."

"The one with the spells, the one that tells of the flame and the amulet and the way to destroy both worlds."

She managed to hold back her fear. Somehow he had known about the book she'd taken. It had to be worth something, and Sanchez, the greedy pig, wanted it.

She turned away, and he grabbed her by her hair and whirled her around. With the back of his hand, he hit her, sent her crashing into the bookshelf, which rocked, dumping a row of novels around her body.

"Well, I suppose I've learned all I will by using the good doctor." He put both hands to his mouth. One hand held his upper jaw; the other, his lower one. With one great pull, he unhinged his jaw, and Mairi screamed as the top of Sanchez' head was slowly peeled back.

Mairi struggled to gain her feet, but Sanchez, or whoever he was, placed his foot on her stomach, stilling her. A limp body dressed in jeans and a white T-shirt fell beside her.

Slowly she looked up the length of the long black-leather-clad legs, past a silver belt with a knife hanging from it, and up to a black T-shirt with an inverted pentagram.

"Hello again, Mairi," the man said as he flicked Sanchez' medical ID badge to the ground. "I hope you don't mind, but lover boy here made me a nice skin suit."

"Aaron," she gasped. The sick bastard who had stalked and terrified Rowan.

He crouched down on his haunches and smiled. Her gaze caught the body of Sanchez, lying boneless on the floor. Her stomach roiled and she fought the urge to faint. "If you've done anything to Rowan," she gasped, fighting the blackness.

"Oh, what I did to Rowan is nothing like what I'm going to do to you, Mairi." He gripped her chin, forcing her to look into his pale blue eyes. "Tell me where you've put the book, and while we're at it, tell me what you've learned of the Oracle and I'll let you keep your entrails where they belong."

CHAPTER FIFTEEN

"I don't know what you're talking about. I've never heard of an Oracle."

The sting of his hand on her cheek burned. Her head reeled back, and he grabbed her by the throat with one hand, hauling her up from the floor.

"Let's try again, shall we?"

The room spun and Mairi felt the warmth of blood trickle from her nose to her lip. The metallic taste on her tongue confirmed it. She was bleeding.

"Speak," he snarled, shaking her. "I want the book *and* the Oracle."

"I—I don't know what it is," she said, her mind fuzzy.

"Do not lie to me," he growled. He lifted her into the air so her feet dangled and the viselike grip of his fingers steadily increased on her throat.

"The book," she gasped, clawing at his hand. "Is the Oracle the book?"

Through the haze of pain and anoxia, Mairi saw Aaron

pause. His eyes widened "Is it?" he asked. "I thought it a person, but maybe . . ."

Clancy was suddenly there, jumping up, his paws digging into Aaron's shoulders. With his arm, Aaron shoved him off. Which only made Clancy snarl and bite Aaron's legs. With a vicious kick, Aaron sent Clancy spiraling across the floor and into the wall, where he lay unconscious.

"Now, if you don't want the same treatment as your canine, start talking."

"Aaron," she choked, struggling for air, "let me go."

"I want the fucking Oracle—now!" he raged, shaking her like a rag doll. "And if the Oracle and the book are *not* one and the same, I want them both. You know what I'm talking about, and don't bother to deny it."

"How?" she choked out, clawing his hands.

He laughed, squeezing tighter. "I knew one of you bitches had to have the book. I figured it was Rowan, being into the occult and all that. She was desperate enough for a fuck; it was easy to get her to let me in. But once I figured out she didn't have it, I knew it was you."

"Why us?"

"Because I was there that day in the library searching for it. And so were the two of you. Now, I want that book—"

There was a thunderous crash behind them and Bran burst through the door. Wood splintered and cracked, flying into the air. Aaron dropped her and she fell at his feet in a heap.

"Well, if it isn't a little birdie."

Mairi could see that Bran looked as shocked as he was angry. "Who are you?" he shouted.

"Wouldn't you like to know?"

Smoke clouded the room, and Mairi swore she saw the mist arise from a wand that Aaron held in his hand. She knew she wasn't in her right mind when Bran lifted the lamp and it became a metal sword slicing through the air.

Aaron dodged it and laughed. "Your magic is weak, Raven. But then the mortal realm is not your natural hunting ground, is it?"

The remote control lifted into the air, changed into an arrow with a vicious-looking serrated tip. It flew across the room, hitting Aaron in the shoulder, making him roar in pain. Bran charged forward, knocking Aaron flat. Together they struggled and pummeled each other, rolling on the ground.

She had to do something to help Bran. She reached for the baseball bat she kept hidden behind her front door, but a flash of light shook the room. Mairi saw the electrical current that seemed to crackle off Bran's arms. Like static electricity, it zapped between the two men. Then Aaron reached out to her, the electricity a long forked line radiating from his arm. The aluminum bat she held in her hand attracted it like a magnet.

The force of the shock sent her flying backward. Her head hit the door and she slid down. The last thing she heard was a terrifying cry, and the world went black. She felt her body twitch, her heart lurch and spasm, the electrical shock shorting out her heart rhythm.

So this is what it's like to die.

Despairing, Bran cradled Mairi in his arms. He had no knowledge of mortals and their bodies. Had no healing abilities. He held her, watching helplessly as she died in his arms.

"Come back, Mairi," he whispered, brushing her hair away from her face. "Come back to me."

It was no use. She was gone. Putting his head to her chest, he listened for the beat of her heart. There was none.

"Jesus, what the hell happened here?"

Bran looked up to see Rhys and Keir enter through the splintered door.

"What do mortals do when they are hurt?" he barked.

Rhys knelt and put two fingers against her throat. "Shit! She's got no pulse. Keir, call 911."

Rhys tried to pull Mairi from his arms, but Bran fought him.

"For fuck's sake, put her down."

For the first time ever, Bran actually listened to Rhys. Then he was sorry, as Rhys tore open her shirt and placed his mouth over hers.

"CPR," Rhys hissed at he pressed both his hands to Mairi's breastbone. "She needs this if she's going to live. But, shit, I think it's too late."

Bran closed his eyes. His hand went to the fire opal pendant Cailleach had given him. It had protected him from the attack, but not Mairi.

"Ambulance is coming," Keir murmured as he got to his knees. "Here, I'll breathe, you compress."

And so it went, cycles of breathing and compressing with no sign of life from Mairi.

When the paramedics arrived they took over. They started

shoving needles into her arms as two men worked on her chest and mouth. They were shouting and saying things that Bran did not understand. He only knew magic. The bounds of his world. It frightened him, this ignorance. It angered him that he could not prevent her death, or help revive her.

"Stop! Where are you taking her?" Bran demanded as the men loaded Mairi up on a stretcher.

"St. Mike's."

"We'll follow," said Rhys, putting a hand on Bran's arm. "Let them do their job," he muttered. "It's not like in Annwyn, where you can wave a wand. Mortals are different."

With a nod, Bran allowed the men to leave with Mairi. When she was gone, he looked around the apartment, which was in shambles.

"I'll follow the trail of blood," Keir said. Aaron had fled once Mairi had fallen. But he was badly wounded. "I'll report back at Velvet Haven."

"Oh, Christ," Rhys said. "Look at this."

Bran went behind the couch and saw the dead body, all hollowed out except for the skin. "That's how he got inside. He used the skin of someone Mairi knew."

"Whose body is it?"

"Dr. M. Sanchez," Bran read from the plastic ID card.

"Who the hell did the skinning?"

"The same person who butchered the woman in the alley."

The thought of Mairi's sweet body carved like that made his blood run cold. If he hadn't arrived when he did, he would surely have her found her that way.

"Well, c'mon, I'll take you to the hospital. I'll send someone from the club to replace the door and secure the apartment just in case . . ." Rhys coughed and looked away.

"She will make it," Bran said quietly. "She will make it," he growled, this time louder and more forceful. "And I have the thing that will ensure she does." Then, crossing the room, he picked up the limp body of Clancy. "Take me to Suriel."

❧

Suriel looked down from the railing he was perched on and laughed at the sight of Bran holding a large dog.

"I need your help, Suriel."

"Allow me to throw your words back in your face. *Fuck you*."

"I know what you are."

"So?" he said with a derisive snort.

"You're the angel of Death and Resurrection." Suriel's black eyes narrowed. "They say that you were there the day they nailed Christ to the cross. You sat at his feet and when it was time, with your left hand, you facilitated his death, and on the third day, you resurrected him with your right."

Suriel jumped down, his wings unfurling as he landed. "Urban legend," he said with a smirk. "Never believe what the crackheads and heroin whores tell you."

"It's true, isn't it?"

Suriel shrugged his shoulders. "What do you care?"

"I need your help. I'm . . . willing to pay for it."

Suriel glanced at the dog. "I don't do animals," he said with a sneer.

"This is important."

"Sorry. Can't stay and chat, I've got a meth overdose to decide what to do with."

Bran watched Suriel's wings furl and disappear beneath the long leather trench he wore. "I'll give you what you want."

That stopped the bastard in his tracks. Bran held his breath. Mairi had saved him from certain death. She'd shared her body with him, giving him energy, giving him his magic. She'd given all of herself to him, and he *would* save her. Even though one day she might fulfill the prophecy and kill him.

Suriel circled around him, watching him with his fathomless black eyes. "If you're bullshitting me, I'll kill you."

"I'm not. I will give you the book you seek in payment for Mairi's life. And the dog's," he added. Mairi loved this dog.

"I also require access to Mairi. She can decipher the prophecy the Scribe has written in it."

"Resurrect the dog and save Mairi, and I will give you this book you seek." Cailleach would strip him of his flesh if she discovered his treason, but it was Mairi he was worrying about now, not his own hide. Cailleach, for all he cared, could battle it out with Suriel herself if she wanted the damn book so bad.

Suriel waved his right hand over the dog, murmuring an incantation as he did so. Slowly, a shimmering vapor rose from Clancy's body and twisted, arching into a sphere before it lowered. With a small whimper, the dog took a breath and looked up at him.

"It's done. Now to the woman."

Stunned, Bran lowered himself to the ground and watched Clancy take a few unsteady steps. "How—"

"No questions," Suriel said, circling him. "You must know that once someone is reincarnated they come back as . . . something different."

Bran narrowed his eyes. "What do you mean?"

"They are not the same as before they died. Are you prepared for that, Sidhe, that your Mairi might be someone totally different?"

"I want her alive," he growled with everything in his heart. "I don't care if she changes, I just want her . . ." *In my life*, he silently whispered.

"Good. Now close your eyes, Sidhe, and let me go to work."

Bran's whole body stiffened in shock. He felt his eyes go wide; his body arched, then froze, his arms stiff at his sides as though he were paralyzed.

"What in the fuck are you doing?" Bran rasped as he felt Suriel's hand grip his neck.

"Look into my eyes. I need to see what you saw."

Suriel made a growling sound, and Bran felt his body grow limp and weak as their gazes locked. Bran felt Suriel probing his mind, pulling at memories. The fight with Mairi's attacker flooded forward, and he saw Suriel's pupils dilate. Then suddenly Suriel's black wings unfurled, caging Bran against the wall. Bran became aware of Suriel's body, the way it seemed to charge; the vibe coming off him was almost electric, but Bran had no time to think further; Suriel had him by the throat, his fingers biting into his skin.

"Go to St. Mike's. And if you don't cough up the book, I'll do more than just fucking kill you, you got that? I'll torture you. You got my vow on that, *Sidhe*. You've made a pact, and I intend to see you fulfill it."

"What did you see?" he demanded as Suriel straightened away from him.

"A brother," he spat, shaking his head. "I don't know which

one. I couldn't see his mark. It's not Uriel, but Christ, it's an angel," Suriel rasped. "But he's not working alone. He can't be."

"How do you know?"

"Because our powers are limited in Annwyn, like yours are limited in this realm. We can't just stride into your world and start commanding magic. We have to be invited. Besides, black magick isn't our specialty—that's your world."

"Well, who the fuck invited him into Annwyn?"

Suriel glared at him. "How the hell should I know? But at least now we've got a lead. There's two forces here, one angelic, one immortal. Power and knowledge from both realms. Powerful beings working together. You do know what that means, don't you?"

Bran pressed his eyes shut. "Looks like I'm stuck with you."

❧

Suriel watched Bran leave the hell he called home. As he rounded the corner, Suriel stepped back into the shadows of a building. An addict, stoned from the needle that jutted out of his arm, looked up at him, his mouth hanging open in shock.

"What the fuck are you looking at?" he growled, pressing against the bricks, melding into them so he could disappear into the spiritual plane.

Closing his eyes, Suriel concentrated not on the addict, or the miserable conditions of his own existence, but on Mairi, whose energy he sensed was fading.

He had foreseen Mairi's fate. Been told to allow it, to let her go. Not in a vision from *Him* this time. It was Gabriel. And he hated that ass-kissing brother. Gabriel was a two-faced son of a bitch, and Suriel had known from the moment his pure white wings touched the filth of the street that he was stirring shit.

So he had waited for Bran to come to him, for Bran to need him. Suriel would much rather cast his lot in with Bran than Gabriel. After all, it was Gabriel who had sentenced him to this fate. And it would be a cold damn day in hell before Suriel did anything to please him.

Now with this new revelation he had seen in Bran's memories, Suriel was more convinced than ever that it was Gabriel who wanted Mairi dead. Not the Boss upstairs. Therefore, Suriel was going to give her life. In the end, everyone was going to get what they wanted. Bran would have Mairi, Mairi would understand her powers, and Suriel would find his redemption.

His body misted, became particles on the wind, and he flew in spirit for the emergency room of St. Michael's hospital.

Dying wasn't anywhere near as painful or terrifying as Mairi expected. It was quiet, dark—peaceful. She hovered, like in that old movie *Coma*, when the patients hung prone, suspended from the ceiling, unmoving, unseeing.

There was no pain, despite knowing that the defibrillator was gearing up yet again, ready to shock her.

"Clear!"

She heard the warning, heard Dr. Bartlett snarl, "C'mon, Mairi, respond! Louise, crank it up to twenty-five joules. *Shit.*" He panted as he pounded on her chest while the defibrillator recharged.

"What do we have? Anything?"

"No, still asystole."

Mairi wanted to tell him it was okay, that she was peaceful, and while she would have preferred to go later, or at least have the chance to say good-bye, she was strangely good with this new state. It was . . . inviting. She heard someone calling to her, and she wanted to discover who it was.

"Clear!"

They said hearing was the last sense to go, and now Mairi had proof. She couldn't feel a damn thing, but she could hear everything.

"Mairi?"

Mairi turned her head to the sound of a dark voice. She wasn't alone. She felt the presence of another hovering close by.

"I'm here," the voice said. It was deep, masculine, hypnotic. Mairi turned her head to the sound and saw the man from last night's dream.

"It's all right, you're safe with me."

"Suriel?" she asked incredulously.

He smiled, then jumped down from the invisible ledge he was crouching on, his long leather trench flapping behind him, his army boots landing silently on an indistinguishable floor.

"Why are you here?"

"I told you I would come to you. And here I am."

"I'm . . . dead," she whispered, and then the tears came.

"Shh." He came and stood beside her. She was lying down on what felt like a feather mattress and she had to crane her neck to look up at him. "Easy."

Reaching for his arm, she let her fingertips rest against the sleeve of his leather trench. He tingled with an aura she had never felt before.

"You feel . . . different. Nice."

His gaze slid from where her fingers rested on his forearm and rose slowly to her face. His dark eyes had taken on a strange glistening. No longer could she see his pupils. His eyes were now just large black circles as he looked down at her.

The energy from him intensified and she closed her eyes, savoring it as though it were a touch from him.

"Are you an angel?" she asked, starting to feel the heaviness in her body take over.

"Something like that."

"You were in my dream last night."

"Yes. But not your dream. I was actually there."

"You don't look like an angel," she said, frowning as she looked up through a gossamer veil that had lowered onto her face. She took in his size, his broad chest and shoulders, not to mention the black leather, and gave a small grin. "You look more like the devil."

"Yeah, I'm that, too."

"Is this real? Or are you just a figment of my mind?" Mairi felt a fluttering against her hand and saw that one long finger was stroking her knuckle. "Are you taking me to heaven or hell?"

"Neither."

"Purgatory, then?"

He laughed and reached for her hand. "He has a use for you. There is another who needs you, too."

Mairi closed her eyes. "Rowan?"

"Bran." His fingers gently traced the scars on her wrist.

"You've suffered, haven't you?" he asked as his thumb brushed along the scars. "You've known a deep darkness. You've known what it is like to be cast out, to be different, to discover what truly lurks inside you."

She tried to wrench free of his hold, but he gripped her tighter. "How did you know—" She stopped herself before she could say more. She'd never spoken of that night. Never told a soul what she'd heard, what she felt.

"You never told anyone because you knew no one would believe you. How could they?" he asked as he continued to brush his thumb along the old wounds. "Did you know what they were, Mairi? Did you know that these marks were stigmata? That you had taken someone else's pain and desperation and saved them from it?"

Mairi looked down at her wrist. She had not inflicted those wounds. They had been someone else's marks, someone else's pain. And yet her own blood had spilled, coloring the bathwater crimson. It had been her flesh that had to be sewn shut. But she had never tried to kill herself. And no one knew that, except now. Except Suriel. Somehow, Suriel had discovered the truth.

"When Rowan . . ." Mairi took a breath. "Were you there that night?"

"Yes."

"Why?"

His mouth curved into a humorless smile. "Because I am the Angel of Death."

She cried out in a strangled voice that was part fear, part pity.

"I was supposed to take her, after that bastard was done with her. But then I saw you, saw you in pain."

"It was *your* voice," Mairi whispered. "I heard it that night. I heard it the night at the club. You told me to . . . cut myself."

"To save your friend. To show you your gift. But you ran from it. You fear it."

"What gift?"

"The gift He had me bestow upon you with my breath. You are a healer, Mairi."

She shook her head, unable to believe. "Why are you telling me this now when I'm dead?"

"You have a great power, Mairi; you've only to understand how to use it."

"I won't have a chance for that, will I?"

Suriel bent over and Mairi found herself being pulled into his dark, bottomless gaze. "You *will* use this power. When the time comes you will know what to do. You will realize how you can use it to your advantage. Remember that, Mairi. It is within you to save those you love."

She felt the warmth of tears spill from her eyes and trickle down her cheeks. "What are you doing now?"

"Saving you."

He leaned over and captured her mouth with his. In a foreign tongue he murmured something over her, then breathed deeply into her mouth. When he pulled away, Mairi felt a strange shuddering flicker along her nerves. Her heart began to pound, slowly, erratically, then quicker, gaining strength.

"Do not forget what you saw in your dream last night. The time is close for your vision to come to fruition. Remember, not everything is as it seems. Think, Mairi, of our powers. Trust. Believe. Have faith."

He turned to leave, and Mairi reached for him, feeling a strange connection to him. Someplace deep inside her, she felt his aura protecting her.

She clutched him. "Don't leave me," she whispered. "I'm scared."

He peered down at her, and Mairi noticed that his eyes had changed. They were no longer black, but white. The iris opened up, like some kind of portal, drawing her in to the bright light. When he spoke, it wasn't with his usual voice. "You don't know what I am."

"Suriel, I don't fear you."

"To touch me, to care about me, is the path to destruction. You wouldn't want to follow me, Mairi. You wouldn't want me to let you inside. What is inside me is beyond your imagining, beyond what you could endure."

Jesus, she couldn't stop looking at those eyes, at the seductive light where his pupil had been. She felt her body being pulled, slowly, as if she had a rope wrapped around her, and he was pulling her in, inch by inch. "You saved me at the moment of my birth. You've saved me now. Stay with me. I . . . I want to know you. To have you as my guide."

Her gaze darted to the left side of his neck. Below his ear, branded into his flesh, was his angelic symbol, Ψ: the symbol for the Angel of Death. She stared at it, and shivered.

"My path is not your path, Mairi." He pressed her fist to his mouth and kissed her knuckles. He closed his eyes and just held her hand to his mouth. His lashes, long and thick, grazed the high bones of his cheeks. "Don't follow me. Please . . ."

"What is your path, Suriel? Why do you walk the Earth alone?"

"My destiny is to live with my memories, my sins. My purpose on this earth is redemption."

Mairi felt her body being lifted, felt her breasts press against his hard chest and that strange tingling tickled her wherever her skin touched his body.

"I will give you now to the one whose path you will follow," he whispered against her ear.

CHAPTER SIXTEEN

Thrusting the curtain back so hard the cloth tore from the metal rings, Bran stepped into the cubicle, his Doc Martens clanging on the terrazzo floor. Female gasps registered in his brain, but he spared them no notice. Every sense he possessed was focused on the limp body of Mairi lying on the stretcher before him. Her jeans and T-shirt had been replaced with a sheet. Her black hair was fanned out on the white pillow. Sooty lashes lay still against her cheek, shielding her incredible dark eyes.

"What the bloody hell is the meaning of this?" snapped the short, balding man holding a clipboard in his meaty fists.

Bran looked in the corner, saw Suriel leaning against the wall, arms crossed over his chest. Suriel was invisible to all except Bran. With a nod, he indicated Mairi.

She was alive. His to take.

"Don't forget our deal," Suriel murmured as he passed him on the way out of the cubicle.

Like a robot set on a mission, Bran ignored the demands

of the doctor and quelled the nurses with a glare as they reached for the red call light button.

Don't even think about it.

Mentally, he forced the wiring to short-circuit, rendering it useless. Shutting off the power to the cardiac monitor, Bran watched as the line tracing her heart rhythm suddenly went flat. With a whine of an alarm the machine shut down, the screen growing blank.

"Security," the physician shouted, thrusting his round body between the stretcher and Bran. Shouldering the man aside, Bran systematically pulled off the cardiac leads. Next came the probe on her finger that was monitoring the oxygen in her blood. After that, he moved on to the IVs. With one steady tug, he had the tape and plastic tube pulled free and the bleeding staunched with the pressure of his thumb.

In a moment of undeniable need, he bent forward, broadening his already massive back as he loomed over Mairi's delicate hand. Shielding his actions from everyone in the cubicle, he removed his thumb from the bleeding wound and set his lips to her skin, dragging his tongue across her flesh, tasting her, drawing her into his body. Inside, his body hummed with pleasure, energy, and gratitude that she was alive.

Next, he carefully pulled at the tapes that anchored the white plastic tube in her mouth. He pulled it slowly, freeing her from the device. A machine alarmed, but he ignored it, watching instead the sudden expansion of Mairi's chest, followed by the slow exhalation of air.

She stirred and moaned, and he closed his eyes in relief. She was alive.

"You can't just take her," the doctor yelled as Bran straightened and lifted her limp body from the gurney. "For the love of God, we've just resuscitated her. She'll die."

Waving his palm over the doctor, he placed the room under a spell. They were frozen, no longer able to interfere. Without a word, Bran turned around in the small space and shifted her weight in his arms, heading for the exit of the emergency room, where he stopped and once more raised his palm, releasing the humans from his magical bond.

"You will remember none of this. Nor will any of you remember Mairi."

Then he left with Mairi in his arms. She was his now. For better or worse, as the humans liked to say.

Bran placed Mairi on his bed and ran his hand through her silky hair so that it lay fanned out on his pillow. He had lit the candles in the room and closed the velvet draperies on the windows. Pulling up a chair, he rested his booted foot on the frame of the mattress, watching the slow rise and fall of her chest beneath the black sheets.

He had brought her back to Velvet Haven. He couldn't leave her alone in her apartment and he was not strong enough to fight in the mortal realm, if the Soul Stealer were to come after her again. If he couldn't be in Annwyn, then Velvet Haven was the next best thing.

He palmed his pec, rubbing his hand back and forth over his heart. There was a god-awful pain there. One he had never felt before. Sighing, he closed his eyes and saw her as he had that first time standing outside the club, her white aura luring him. He remembered how it was between them in the hall. She'd been afraid of him—his size, his eyes. He'd tasted her fear and he'd felt as though his heart had been carved out of his chest. He didn't want her fear. He wanted her warmth. He wanted her body. He wanted *her*. Not just her sex.

He barely knew her, but somehow he felt that he had to have her in his life.

Disrobing, he studied her face in the candlelight, the way her chest rose and fell softly, making certain that every breath she took was easy and painless. She was alive. He still couldn't believe it. Suriel had resurrected her tonight.

Slipping beneath the sheets, Bran pulled her to him, curving her body into his. He played with her hair, grazed his fingertips along her cheek, and hoped like he had never hoped before that she would come to understand him and accept him in her life.

Maybe Sanchez really was more than a hot bod and a dose of male arrogance. The scent of the bacon and eggs he was cooking for her certainly made Mairi think otherwise.

"She's waking."

That was not Sanchez' voice. *Bran.* She stirred, trying to open her lids, which felt swollen and heavy. No one else had such a dark, velvety voice.

"About time," said another. This voice was deep as well, but not nearly as sensual to her ears as Bran's was.

"You do recall what your end of this bargain is, don't you?"

There was a masculine growl and movement on the mattress beside her. "The damn book is there on the nightstand. Take it."

"It means nothing to me until it's been deciphered. The Scribe has written it as a fable of what may come to pass. It's riddled with clues that I don't understand. But Mairi has the ability to understand it."

"I don't care about the book," Bran growled.

"You should. The Soul Stealer is morphing, Raven. Changing into something more dangerous than he was before. The fact that he is also looking for the book is warning enough. We must find that flame and amulet."

"What the hell are you after, Suriel?"

Suriel. His image swam before her and Mairi felt his presence—and a host of conflicts swirling in him.

"The book decoded," she heard him reply. "And I will have it."

The door slammed shut, jarring against the wood frame. Mairi jumped, struggled to sit up, but her body was weak.

"Here, let me help you." Mairi felt big hands on her arms as they tenderly pulled her up. Behind her, she heard pillows being plumped before she was carefully laid back. A warm cloth scented with lavender was placed over her eyes. "This will help with the swelling."

She heard numerous doors opening and closing. Music from the floor below, and the occasional male voice. She was not in her apartment. And this was not Sanchez sitting beside her, holding a cloth to her face.

Grabbing the thick wrist, she forced his hand away and looked up into Bran's mismatched eyes.

"So, Sleeping Beauty awakens," he said with a smile. "And about time, too."

"What day is it?"

"Tuesday. You have lost two days."

"Where am I?"

"Velvet Haven. And you're safe."

His gaze darkened as he looked at the side of her face. Gently, he ran his fingertips along her swollen cheek. The throbbing she had felt suddenly left, leaving nothing but warmth and that familiar hum she always got when he touched her. "I should have killed him for this," he whispered. "I *will* kill this bastard," he vowed fiercely.

"That's very kind of you," she said with a smile, "but I don't think you need to commit a mortal sin on my behalf."

"Nothing is too much for you, Mairi."

Warm fuzzies unfurled in her belly. "You would kill for me?" she asked, not knowing whether she should be scared shitless or extremely flattered.

"I would do anything you asked, except . . ." He looked away, then swung his gaze to hers. "Anything but leave you," he murmured. "I could not do that."

His expression was serious. She eyed him cautiously. What had happened? How had he come to be here—with her? And why was he so possessive? The last time they were together, he'd left her without even a memory of what had happened to him.

Not that she should be complaining, but still, everything was a confusing puzzle.

"Do not trouble yourself trying to fit all the pieces together. We'll talk in a while, when you're healed."

Mairi fought through the fog, trying to make sense of what had happened. "I . . . I think it was you all along in my dreams. I've dreamed of you—for weeks now."

She felt the tension in him coil. "They are not dreams," he said, "but premonitions."

"If you say so." She licked her dry lips, and a cool glass was pressed up against her mouth.

"Drink."

She took a little sip, wincing as she swallowed.

"Rhys says that your throat may hurt because of the tube they shoved down your airway to make you breathe. I hope I did not hurt you when I removed it."

Tube? Airway? Suddenly she remembered what had happened. Aaron, that sick bastard, had somehow hidden himself *inside* Sanchez. He'd beaten her, demanded to know where the Oracle was. And then Bran had come crashing through her door. He'd picked up ordinary objects and turned them into weapons—swords, arrows. Even electricity.

She moaned, her head hurting as she tried to make sense out of something that defied all possibilities. Magic, and madmen . . . and her death. She specifically recalled dying. Yet here she was, alive and—her stomach rumbled loudly—apparently hungry.

"You're thinking too hard, *muirnin*. Just rest and the events of the past days will come when you are ready."

"I died," she rasped, her voice hoarse. "I felt a shroud cover my face and body, and then I felt my soul lift as it left me."

"You did not pass through the veil. You are alive," he said against her mouth; then he kissed her, making her body heat, showing her that indeed, she was very much alive, with *all* senses intact, too.

"Rhys has brought you something to eat. Start slow, and if you're hungry you can eat something else."

"Aaron," she whispered. "I have to warn Rowan."

"I am sorry that Aaron escaped when I turned my attention to you. But do not worry. Your friend is protected." She struggled against his hold, but he held her tight. "She's here," he whispered, gently shoving her back. "Just down the hall. When you are well you can see her."

A whimper from the end of the bed was followed by a rhythmic thump that stopped Mairi cold. Clancy? The dog's head popped up, its muzzle resting on the black coverlet.

"You saved him!"

Clancy came bounding onto the bed, despite Bran's cursing and commands for Clancy to get down. But the great big lummox came forward, licking every inch of her face.

"Disgusting. You would not allow him to do that if you knew what he had just been licking."

Mairi laughed and rubbed Clancy behind his ears. "How can I ever repay you?"

His eyes darkened. "It was I who owed you. We are even now."

Mairi looked at him. His expression had changed, had grown blacker—angry.

"Thank you," she whispered. As she said it, she allowed her fingertips to graze his tattooed arm. He closed his eyes in response.

"Eat now, Mairi."

Bran left the bed and went to the window seat, where a large tray of several covered dishes waited. With a flourish, Bran lifted the lids.

"What's that?" she asked, pointing at a golden-brown triangle next to the bacon and eggs.

He smiled. "It's Scottish, a potato scone. It's fried in bacon fat and you put jam on it. It's delicious."

"And artery clogging, no doubt."

Bran shrugged and placed the tray on her lap. As he did so, he shoved Clancy aside with a brisk command and sat down beside her.

"I do not worry about arteries," he mumbled as he took a knife out of a napkin and dipped it in homemade strawberry jam, "and neither should you." He lifted the scone to her lips. "Eat."

She took a bite and moaned. *So good.* She tried to take it from him, but he insisted that she eat from his hand. It was the left hand, the one with the tats, and every time their skin connected he shuddered and closed his eyes. It was absurd to be thinking this at such a time, but Mairi silently hoped he was as turned on by the act of feeding her as she was.

"When you can, tell me what you remember."

She swallowed and he passed her a teacup and saucer. It was dainty and fragile. An antique. She glanced around the room, noted the expensive antique furniture and huge fireplace. It was like something you'd see in an English manor home. It might have made sense if this was still the MacDonald mansion, but it was Velvet Haven, a Gothic fetish nightclub. Antiques seemed so out of place.

But then she remembered that Bran had mentioned that family lived there. Maybe this was Bran's room in the club.

The tea tasted good and Mairi took another sip, trying to find the fortification to tell Bran everything.

"Start at the beginning. Leave nothing out."

With a nod, she plunged in, telling him about the book she had stolen, Lauren's death, and the strange dreams she'd been having of a man—of him. She left out the sexual details, and the part about her picking up a dagger. She hadn't made sense of that yet, and she didn't want him to think she'd actually follow through with anything in her dream—well, except the vivid sex parts.

She even told him about Suriel, the part he had played in her life. She talked of Rowan, what had happened and what Mairi had done in return. As she spoke, Bran brushed his fingertips along her scarred wrist. When she was done, he bent and kissed it.

"You have seen much in your life," he whispered. "Much pain."

Mairi felt the sensation of his lips on her wrist and instantly the discomfort in her body eased.

Silence hovered between them till he asked, "Where did you come by your hobby of translating illuminated manuscripts?"

She was relieved to be talking about something other than her scars. "I first discovered illuminated manuscripts in the library of Our Lady of Perpetual Sorrow. I used to go there after school to wait for my mom to get done work."

"Why did you not go directly home?" he asked as his fingers idly brushed her wrist.

She didn't want to talk about this. She'd buried her past.

"Mairi?"

She shrugged. "We preferred to go home together, once my mom was done doing dishes and cleaning up. She worked in the kitchen, making meals for the school and the nuns."

"And why could you not go home, Mairi?"

It was times like this that she hated that soft, deep voice of his. The one that could lure and entice. The one that felt like a tender caress.

"My mother didn't want me alone with my father."

She exhaled a big breath. There. She'd said it.

Fingers under her chin, he turned her face to look at him. His eyes were dark, the pupil now big, swallowing up the pewter and gold of his. "Did your father abuse you?"

She blushed. "No, it was nothing like that."

"Then what was it like?"

She pulled away from his hold and looked down at the quilt. "My father used to beat my mother. She didn't want me to be alone with him because she was afraid that he'd take his drunken anger out on me, instead of waiting for her to get home."

His expression was fierce. "My people would have shred him to bits. In my world, a woman only feels the passion in a man's touch. Never his anger."

"Your world?" she said with a nervous laugh. "Aren't you from Earth?"

His expression changed, his gaze narrowing.

"How did you meet your friend Rowan?" he asked.

"In the library at Our Lady. I was looking through books and she was drawing at a table. We've been friends ever since."

He lifted a strip of bacon to her mouth. "Has she no family?"

She took a bite and chewed. "No, none. She was dropped on the doorstep when she was five. She lived there until we went away to college."

"Neither of you has had an easy life."

She squirmed beneath his scrutiny and bristled against the concern she heard. "No worse than a lot of people."

He pulled back, giving her the space she needed. But Mairi still felt his gaze on her, roving her body and finally settling on her face. "We have much to learn about each other."

"And you still have to explain what I saw."

He smiled and raked his knuckles down her cheeks to her throat. "After. You need rest."

"I've been asleep for two days."

"And you will sleep as much as you need."

She laughed, thinking of all the people she had nursed, and now here she found herself on the receiving end. It was very strange to be the helpless one.

"You must take every care, Mairi."

"Why?"

"Because I cannot lose you again." The words fell from his lips, wrapping around them. When their gazes met, she could not detect any regret on his part for speaking so openly. "Somehow our fates were destined to cross, and now our futures are entangled. I know we've only just met, but I swear to you, I need you in my life. I want to know all your secrets, your fears. I want to pleasure you, to protect you."

She looked at him with an expression of awe. "What are you?" she asked. "Where did you come from? Because I've never met a man like you before."

He caressed her skin, but did not answer her questions.

"Who are you?" she asked in a low voice as she studied him, wondering how a man she didn't know could mean so much, could break past her barriers of mistrust and crawl inside her heart.

He pressed forward and brushed his lips below her earlobe. "Tell me who you want me to be. I can be that person."

"Bran," she whispered, allowing herself to just feel the fluttering sweep of his lips against her throat, his incredibly long lashes against her earlobe. "Just Bran."

His big body softened against her. "I love the way you smell here. I love the way you taste."

His words were followed by the slow flicking motion of his tongue. Her belly flipped. Before she knew what she was doing, her hand was resting low over her belly, trying to relieve some of the empty throbbing she felt.

"Do you feel me there?" he asked in a dark whisper. His palm rested on top of hers, then slowly began moving. Her breath left her mouth, her lips brushing his cheek, which was faintly dusted with a five-o'clock shadow.

Lower he pushed her hand till her heel rested on her pubic bone and her fingers were between her thighs.

"Tell me where you need me, Mairi."

Oh, God! Her heart was bounding and her breathing was all erratic. She couldn't tell him what she wanted. Not when she didn't know him, or understand what had happened. What the hell was she thinking?

"I won't hurt you, Mairi. Trust me."

"I . . . I'm trying, but . . ." She lifted her gaze to his face. "I have questions."

"Later," he said, trying to catch her lips with his. "I will answer everything later."

She turned her face away. "I saw what you did in my apartment . . . magical stuff."

"Mairi, let me do this, let me make you come. Let me use my fingers, my tongue, my cock, to make you feel better."

"Bran—"

"It's the only way I know how, Mairi. The only way I know how to be with your kind. Let me . . . heal you."

She was melting. She truly was, but she couldn't allow herself to weaken—especially when he said things like "your kind." But Bran reached for the tray and set it aside. Then he grabbed the hem of his shirt and pulled it over his head, allowing the garment to fall to the carpet.

Mairi looked her fill, from the thick cords in his neck to the broad shoulders, down to the defined pecs and abs, to the fine line of hair that disappeared beneath his pants. On the left side, the tangle of gold and silver tattoos snaked over his shoulder and around his nipple, then over his ribs, disappearing beneath the waistband of his pants, just like that tantalizing trail of hair.

His skin was golden, smooth. She could smell him, as fresh as the woods after a cool spring rain. She felt the heat radiating off him and the sexual aura that seemed to wrap around her, pulling her in deep.

"We both hunger for this," he growled. "So why do we try to resist, pretending we don't?"

She shook her head, and he reached for her palm, sliding it down the tattoos on his chest. "I don't want to resist anymore, Mairi. I don't want to pretend that you're just another woman. I don't want you to treat me like a stranger."

"We are strangers—sexually compatible strangers."

He crawled on top of her as she sank low beneath the covers. "It is not just sex," he whispered in her ear. "There is more here binding us. Can you not feel it?"

She could and it scared her.

"Give me your fears. I'll keep you safe."

Mairi allowed her fingers to run through his hair. "Please. First I need to know how this has come to be."

He avoided her gaze as he lowered his mouth to her lips. "How what has come to be?"

"How did you know where I live?"

He pulled back, his gaze narrowed, the gold and pewter darkening. Mairi sat up, pulling the sheets around her. He growled, heaving himself up off the mattress, but she reached out to him, tracing the twining vines of ink on his arm. His hair was brushed back from his forehead and she saw that the same marks adorned his left temple. As her finger slid over the tattoos, his skin quivered and the design seemed to move, to curl in and out as if the ink were absorbing her touch.

Shoving away from her, he moved from the bed and walked toward the arched window, which was draped with black velvet. He put his arm on the window casing, his hair shifting with his muscles. And there on his back she could now see a long silver tattoo in the shape of a sword running along the length of his spine.

Her breath caught and Mairi knew for certain who he was. He was the man from her dreams, her midnight lover. And he was . . .

"Why don't you tell me how you think I found you?" he asked as he stared out the window.

Taking a deep breath, Mairi couldn't quite bring herself to believe what she was going to say. "I think you knew where I lived because you were the raven I picked up from the road and brought home."

His fingers curled into a fist. "And why would you think I was a bird?"

She paused, trying to understand how she could believe something so unbelievably impossible. It didn't make sense, but neither did this consuming passion she had for Bran.

"Because I felt the same connection to the bird as I do to you. I don't understand it, but it's true. We had a night of . . . of pleasure and now I can't stop thinking of you, or wanting to be with you. And the bird, every time I looked at it, I thought of you."

She slipped from the bed. Her legs were unsteady and she reached for the post of the headboard for support. Before she knew it, Bran was beside her, his thick arm around her waist. He held her, steadied her, and that arousing hum from his body ebbed into her. "Are you going to faint?" he snarled. "Shouldn't you be screaming and running the other way?"

She saw fear in his eyes. The first time the emotion had ever been there. He was right, of course. What he was defied physics, God . . . even the devil himself. She didn't understand it, couldn't grasp it, but somewhere deep inside her, waiting to be acknowledged, was the fact that from the very beginning he had attracted her *because* he was different from other men.

"I don't know how I can think this. How I can bring myself to believe. I—I—" she stammered, licking her dry lips. "I know this is crazy, but I believe you're not a man. You're something else, part raven, part . . . I don't know what."

"Sidhe." He forced her back on the bed and helped her to sit, then looked her in the eye. "I am king of the Night Sidhe."

"A faerie?" she asked incredulously. When he nodded, Mairi felt her eyes widen in shock. "I didn't think they were so huge and—where're your pointed ears?"

He glared at her. "There are many species of faeries. The Night Sidhe resemble humans, only we're bigger."

Mairi looked her fill and had to agree, he was much bigger—in every place that counted. He was looking at her, too, studying her. The pieces suddenly seemed to fit. She remembered Rowan saying that the Celts had believed the raven was the ruler of the Otherworld. That the name Bran was Gaelic for raven.

"Are you from Annwyn?" she asked, needing to confirm her suspicions.

He nodded and smoothed her hair back over her shoulder. The hospital gown she wore slipped down, baring the crest of her breast. His touch slipped down through her hair; then his fingertips caressed her exposed flesh. So many thoughts were now swirling in her head. But they weren't the right thoughts. Like how was it possible he could change his shape and create electricity? How could he be a faerie king and live in a magical world, yet be sitting here beside her? What did he want with her? What did he mean their futures were entwined? Those were the thoughts she needed to concentrate on, not the thought of falling back on the bed and having him cover her with his tall, strong body.

She tried to formulate a question in her mind and not allow herself to become distracted by Bran.

"Is any part of you human?" She closed her eyes, waiting to hear her worst fears confirmed.

"Not in the sense you mean," he said, stroking her creased

eyelid. "I look like a man, but I am a Sidhe, capable of great magic, and a raven."

"Do you ... feel like a ...?" She trailed off, unable to finish her question.

"Do I feel like a man?" he finished for her. "I don't know. Why don't you feel me, Mairi?" He pushed her down on the bed and brushed his long body against hers. He felt like no man she had ever known before. He was incredibly big and strong, and that vibration his body gave off—no man had ever felt like that.

"Well?" he asked silkily. "Do I feel like a man?"

She nodded, afraid to say more. Even now she could feel his erection pressing eagerly at the apex of her thighs.

"Do I have feelings like a man? Do I feel pleasure? Passion? Pain? Yes. Do I feel for you the way a man feels for a lover? Yes. Do I want to part your thighs, sink into you, and crawl up inside you? Yes."

She couldn't breathe. She struggled beneath him, but he caught both her wrists in one of his hands and held them above her head.

"Do I want to get inside you everywhere I can and come, hot and hard, inside you? Yes."

"Stop," she panted, but he used his strength to hold her, pin her to the bed.

"Why, Mairi? Do I not feel like a man to you? Do you not want me like you have wanted other men?" Their gazes collided. "Or can you not bear to be with such a creature?" Silence blanketed them. "Truth. You owe me that much."

"No," she said. "I have never wanted a man like I want you. I have never felt what I feel with you. That's the truth."

"Then allow me into your body, Mairi. It's what I know, how to please, how to pleasure. I want to bring you satisfaction, happiness, but this is the only way I know how. Accept it, accept me."

She wanted to. Oh, God, how she wanted that. "First, tell me what I need to know, Bran. Make me understand you, your world, and what is happening in mine."

He groaned. "But I need you, Mairi. I need you so much. Your skin is so soft," he murmured; then he leaned in and kissed her beneath her collarbone. "You taste so good, like honey and spice. I want to bury myself in you and forget what I am, forget what you are. Pretend that our worlds do not exist outside this door."

"But they do."

"No! There is only one world for us, the one we are creating now."

Her entire body liquefied. He was utterly perfect. "We can't run from the truth, Bran. You are . . ."

"Immortal."

"And I am mortal. What world can there be for us?"

"One of undying pleasure."

This was getting worse. She was ready to forget her questions and open to him. But she couldn't—not yet.

"Tell me about Annwyn."

He began suckling her skin, marking her. "You read the book. You know of my world already."

She pulled in a deep breath as she felt her skin being gently tugged into his mouth. "You're a . . . a . . ." She sighed, tilting her head to give him better access to her throat. The gown was down to her waist, his fingertips gliding down her throat to the crest of her breast. "You're a magician?" She managed to get the words out before he traced the outline of her nipple.

"Yes. In Annwyn," he said, "my power is unmatched. And here in Velvet Haven, the gateway between our worlds, I am strong. But outside, in the mortal realm, I am easily and quickly drained of my powers."

"Really?" The word was a hiss as he cupped her breast. His thumb rubbed the tip of her nipple, in slow, teasing circles.

"I am king of the Sidhe and coruler of Annwyn," he said proudly. "There is only one who is my match, and that is Cailleach."

"Does Cailleach rule with you?"

His touch stilled. He looked up into her eyes; then he lowered his mouth to her breast. "Yes. It is the way of our world: The Sidhe and the goddess rule together."

He licked her slowly, teasingly. Much too light to satisfy. Her legs shifted, sliding against the comforter. Her foot rubbed his calf up and down.

"I like this form of interrogation," he said before he caught her nipple between his teeth. Carefully he bit down, just enough to arouse, not hurt.

"You haven't asked me many questions."

His palm skimmed down her belly, and she felt the heat of it burning her skin. "I don't need to ask questions. I'm being given all the answers by your body."

She shivered, turned on by his words and by the path his hand was taking. "No questions? Are you sure you don't want to know something?"

He glanced up and smiled wickedly as his hand crept lower and lower. "Maybe one."

"And that is?"

"Are you wet for me, Mairi?"

Persistent. She'd give him that. "Why don't you see for yourself?"

His hand slid slowly down, the heel of his palm fitting over the mound of her sex, his fingers slowly parting her folds. "Slick. Hot. Wet."

Her lashes fluttered closed as he delicately touched her, tracing her folds. She tried to concentrate, to learn what she could, to try to make sense of something incomprehensible. "So are you and Cailleach . . . you know . . . together?"

He smiled while his finger continued to play. "No. Not in that way. My turn." Slowly he circled her clitoris with his thumb. "Do you want my mouth on you here, Mairi?"

Her hips arched up, meeting his stroking finger. She'd love nothing more, but if she allowed him that, she'd never have this conversation with him. "Tell me about Cailleach."

"First tell me you want my tongue on your pussy."

"Yes," she said on a husky sigh. "God, yes."

Leaning down, he spread her folds and covered her sex with one slow swipe of his tongue. "She is a goddess. Her element is air. She commands the winds and the Summerlands."

"Is she beautiful?"

He rubbed his cheek against her inner thigh. "Not like you. No one compares to you."

She melted. Truly turned into a puddle at those words. "And you're her . . . what?"

"Consort."

"Do you love her?"

He looked up at her, holding her gaze. "I do not."

She nodded, relieved, and ran her hands over his shoulders. "The sword on your back? It's an amazing tattoo."

He lowered his head, then placed a kiss on her core. "That is not a tattoo."

"What is it, then?"

"It is a brand."

Mairi gasped. "Who branded you?"

"I offered Cailleach a sacrifice so that my uncle could abdicate his throne and be with the mortal woman he loved. The sword is the emblem of her curse upon me."

"Oh, no! That's terrible. What kind of curse?"

"Mmm," he mumbled. "You taste so sweet, Mairi, you don't know how sweet. I need more of you on my tongue."

She pulled his hair as he tried to go down again. "Bran! Tell me."

He groaned. "A mortal-needing curse."

Suddenly Mairi's stomach fell to her feet and she wanted to press her thighs together, but Bran's massive shoulders prevented that. "As in you need mortals how?"

He closed his eyes as if not wanting to look at her. "I need the sex of mortal women so that I can exchange their pleasure with energy to make magic."

Her thighs tried to clamp shut, but his palms stopped her. "Open."

"Why? So I can be your personal lightning rod?"

He glared at her. "So I can pleasure you as you desire."

"So that's what it was all about, then? You needed me the other night to get off so you could strengthen your powers?"

"Mairi," he whispered, "it wasn't like that."

"Really? You mean you saw me and it was love at first

sight? Or was I looking desperate enough that you thought I'd just fall at your feet?"

"You don't understand—"

"I do," she said, shoving him away from her. "Your mortal-needing curse was calling and you saw me, so you decided I'd do. Then you got what you needed and you performed some damn magic spell on me that made me forget nearly everything and then you walked away."

She expected to hear him deny her words. But he didn't. His silence told her everything she needed to know.

"And that's what's happening now, isn't it? That's why those . . . *things* on your body move when I touch you. I'm right, aren't I?"

"No."

"So you're not getting any energy from this . . . exchange?"

"I am not thinking about magic, Mairi. I'm thinking of you, and getting inside you."

"You're using me."

"Perhaps in the beginning I sought to. But I didn't—"

She snorted and shrugged into a pair of jeans and a sweatshirt that had been left on top of the dresser.

"I'm not using you, Mairi, believe me. If I had any brains, I'd leave you be. But I can't."

"And what the hell does that mean?"

"You are more dangerous to me than I am to you."

"Well, we'll never have to find out if you're right."

"Where are you going?" he demanded.

"Home," she snapped.

"No!" She heard the mattress squeak as he got up. Felt the rumble of his heavy boots cross the glistening hardwood. Her back was to him, her hand on the glass doorknob. His arms shot out on either side of her, and his fists shoved the door closed with a fierce bang. His head dropped to her shoulder and she heard him inhale deeply. "You will not leave me."

It was a command, not a plea.

"Don't you understand, Mairi?" he asked as his lips nuzzled her earlobe.

"Yes. I do."

"I don't think you do, otherwise you would be back on that bed, my cock inside you, moaning as you come for me."

"You arrogant bastard!"

"Perhaps, but it doesn't change what you are."

"And what is that?" she demanded.

"Mine." The fierceness of that whispered word terrified her.

"I don't think so." She tried to match his fierceness, but her protest sounded husky and needy.

"You sealed your fate, *muirnin*, when you tended my wing."

She closed her eyes against the warmth that was flooding her belly. He'd used her to feed a curse. She should not want him. Should not even believe in Annwyn, and magic, and immortals. But every instinct believed. Hell, she had died and been brought back to life by an angel. The same angel who confessed to having been at her birth, and present at the life-altering moment in the tub when her lifeblood ran out of her wrist. Anything was possible.

She believed. God help her, she could actually wrap her mind around the impossible, but she could not stand here and allow herself to be used by him—not again.

CHAPTER SEVENTEEN

"Should I find you another one?"

Bran scowled as he looked out over the dockyards and the blue of the lake beyond. The sun was setting and his fucking curse was calling.

"No," he replied, hating to think of any woman other than Mairi beneath him.

"You owe her nothing. She saved your life. And you saved hers. The debt is balanced."

"I do not want another female."

"But your curse—"

"I doubt I could even get it up for another female," Bran spat. "The thought of pleasuring another makes me ill, which is hardly conducive to an exchange of energy, is it?"

Sayer's elliptical pupils dilated. "That sucks."

"Part of Morgan's curse. She has made me want the only woman who can destroy me. I think she cast this damn curse because she knew I would never love her. She wants me to hurt, to love another and feel the betrayal by someone I love."

"Morgan always had a taste for the sadistic."

"Then she is enjoying my misery, because I am utterly ruined for any other female, Sidhe or mortal."

Sayer looked at him with a mixture of shock and sympathy. "You have fallen for her?"

Bran nodded. The truth became easier each time he admitted it.

"What will you do?"

"I don't know."

"She could kill you."

"I know."

"Why not leave and return to Annwyn?"

"I cannot leave Mairi alone while that madman is running loose. He is not only working in Annwyn, but here, amongst mortals as well. He wants Mairi and I cannot let him have her. I *have* to protect her."

"I could enchant her—"

"No!" If she was to desire him, then he wanted it to be of her own choosing, not Sayer's magic binding her to him.

Sayer's eyes softened. "Rhys says you bargained with Suriel for the girl."

Suriel. How he hated to hear that name! This afternoon when he saw Mairi with Suriel, sitting close together, heads bent over Cailleach's book, he felt enraged. Filled with an absurd, dangerous jealousy that made red mist gather at the edges of his eyes. The way Mairi gazed at Suriel made him want to tear the angel apart, limb from sinful limb.

"Is it true, then, that you made a deal with Suriel?"

"I did what I had to do," Bran growled. And in doing so, he'd handed Mairi to Suriel. Now she knew of the bond they shared. A union that was deeper than what he and Mairi shared. Suriel was Mairi's *Anam Cara*, her Soul Friend. Nothing in Annwyn was stronger than that link. What he felt for Mairi was nothing compared to the chain that now bound her to Suriel.

It made him realize that Mairi would never fully belong to him. So he had decided that he would leave her. Would no longer think of her. Would use her only to discover the true identity of the Soul Stealer. When he was caught, when the Dark Times were over, he would release her without a second thought.

Until then, he would remain apart from her. He had to. For his own sanity. "You know, by striking this bargain, you've managed to climb into bed with the devil."

Bran glared at his companion. "You talk too much, Sayer."

"You don't talk enough. I think that's the problem with your human. She needs more than what you're giving her."

"Fuck off, Sayer."

The Selkie laughed. "That is my cue, then, to depart." Sayer flashed him a smile before he slapped him on his back. "Cheer up, Raven, you might find you enjoy snuff sex." Sayer held up his hands when Bran's expression blackened. "I'm leaving."

"Going to check on Rowan again?" Bran taunted.

"Maybe. I like her. And she likes me."

"Don't hurt her. Mairi would be unhappy. You know what will happen to you if Mairi is unhappy."

"You've got it bad," Sayer teased. "A few days ago you were boasting that you would not be brought low by a mere mortal."

"I hadn't met Mairi yet." Hadn't felt her incredible energy, or tasted her sweet arousal. How could he have known what she would do to him? How could he have guessed that a human could be a perfect fit for him?

Silence and the howl of the wind echoed through the terrace. Sayer had left him alone with his thoughts. Thoughts he didn't want.

What was he going to do? He couldn't allow himself to be intimate with her knowing she was part of Morgan's curse. Yet he couldn't walk away from her either. He'd given his heart to her. A heart he didn't even know he had, and love he wasn't aware he could give.

"You bitch," he roared to the heavens, hoping Morgan could hear him in the Wastelands, where she had been exiled for the past hundred and seventy years. "I'll kill you for this."

The wind rose, blowing past him, carrying with it the tinkling of a woman's laughter. "Oh, how I love to see you brought low. So proud, so powerful, brought to your knees by a mere mortal."

"I'll make you pay for this, Morgan."

"Try, Raven, and see what will happen. You do want to find your brother, don't you? Or have you forgotten all about him while you've been fantasizing about your mortal whore?"

He had not forgotten about Carden. There was no doubt, however, that Mairi had become his first priority.

"Time is running out for your brother, King. Submit to me. Marry me, and I will release your brother from his curse."

"I would rather die than marry you."

"Then I am naturally happy to fulfill your wish, my king."

She would use Mairi, of course, he thought with hatred. To destroy him she would use the only woman he wanted.

"I will find Carden," he vowed, "and when I do, I will break both of our curses and send you to the Shadowlands where you belong."

"You will try, but I know your weakness."

Morgan's laughter drifted away on the wind. Bran turned to look for her, but she was not there. In her place was Mairi.

❦

Mairi wrapped the heavy woolen shawl around her shoulders as a gust of wind whipped past her. She saw Bran, standing alone, dressed all in black, looking fierce and gorgeous.

His black hair rippled in the wind. He wore only a T-shirt, leaving his arms bare. It was cold, yet he didn't shiver. He stood perfectly immobile, lost in whatever he was thinking as he studied the tattoos that ran along his forearm. A soft glow flickered from his flesh and she wondered how he had gotten energy to make them glow.

As she got closer to him, she let her gaze travel downward. He had a fabulous ass in his tight-fitting pants. An image came to her of him sitting on the bed beside her. She remembered the way he'd looked naked, all sculpted and hard—and the tattoos—she remembered them, too, and how when she ran her fingers over them she felt his muscles shift and slide beneath her fingertips.

Bran was handsome in a lethal sort of way. And Lord, she wanted him. Despite what he was.

She was standing right behind him when he turned suddenly and faced her.

"Your tattoos—they're glowing."

"They're called sigils."

"Looks like you've gotten some energy." She tried to keep the jealousy from her voice, but she couldn't. Bran was gorgeous. He oozed sex. There were a number of women, both guests and staff, wandering about the club, even at this early hour of the evening. He could have any or all of them.

"I can harness the elements to make magic as well. It's windy tonight. It's helped shore up my flagging stores."

"Oh." She felt small and petty. Especially after she'd thrown him off her and accused him of using her. Why shouldn't he go find someone who would do him right? She'd given up that chance when she'd stormed out of the room, her Scotch temper getting the better of her.

"Did you keep the rain away that night?"

"Yes."

"And the wind?" she asked, stepping closer. "Did you quiet it so I could hear the waves?"

He nodded. "You needed solace. After . . ." He turned his head and looked down onto the beach below. "After you had that initial meeting with Suriel, you needed to calm your thoughts."

"Thank you."

His shoulders stiffened and his voice turned to one of indifference. "It's cold. You should go inside."

Mairi pulled the shawl tighter around her. "I'm okay."

"No, you're not." He shot her a glare, then turned his palms upward toward the sky and closed his eyes. The wind immediately calmed.

"No guy has ever stopped the wind for me."

"Don't get used to it," he muttered.

In silence they stood, looking out over the water. It was

unnerving standing there, wanting to reach out to him, but knowing he was cold and closed off. An invisible perimeter surrounded him and she didn't know how to breach it.

How did one get a conversation started with a Sidhe king? She hadn't a clue, so she used what most people did—the scenery.

"This gargoyle is rather fearsome," she said, touching the frightening head of the demon that overlooked the stone railing.

Bran grunted and nodded to the other side of the stone wall. "That one is uglier, if you ask me."

Mairi glanced at the demonic face with the serpent's tongue sticking out of its mouth. With bulging eyes and fanged teeth it was indeed the stuff of nightmares. "Well, he's definitely not stuffed animal material, but he's kind of cute, in a demonesque way."

"Damn thing is eerie as hell. Always makes me feel like it's watching me," he muttered as he glanced once more at the statue. With a shake of his head, he said, "I've looked at it many times, wondering if he's Carden."

"Carden?"

"My brother."

Mairi felt her eyes bug out. "Your brother is a gargoyle?"

"He is a shape-shifter, like me."

"This is going to take some getting used to," she muttered beneath her breath. He grinned, but looked away, hiding it from her.

"He's been missing for nearly two hundred years, cursed by Morgan to stay in his gargoyle form."

"Why?"

Bran turned and faced her, his beautiful eyes shadowed.

"It's my fault. I was supposed to marry the bitch. I despised her, but Carden adored her. He went in my place, hoping to seduce her. She figured it out and cursed him to stay in his gargoyle form. She cursed me as well."

"How?"

He looked at her in surprise. "You don't know?"

"How would I?"

"Your dreams."

She blushed. "My dreams of you are sexual."

"Nothing else?"

"No." She thought of the dagger that she had been drawn to in her dreams. Wondered if it represented anything. "Bran?"

He closed his eyes, and Mairi marveled at the length of his lashes. She reached out to stroke the crease of his eyelid with her fingertip. He flinched and stepped back, but she whispered softly, staying him.

"Talk to me. I want to understand. Tell me everything."

"Mairi, don't—"

The hum from his body intensified, warming her fingertips. "Just talk to me."

"You can't touch me," he growled, pushing away from her.

"Why? Don't you feel it anymore? This *thing* between us?"

"I feel you too much," he whispered, and Mairi thought she had never heard a voice sound so anguished. "I feel your touch all over my body. I feel it go straight to my heart, my soul."

"Then let me touch you."

Deftly he moved to the right, avoiding any contact with her. "No. What we have—had," he corrected, "cannot last. As you said, we are from different worlds. Worlds that don't mix."

It killed her to hear him repeat what she had said, especially when she now believed she was wrong. She touched his face, and he closed his eyes.

"Why do you make this so much harder?" he asked through gritted teeth.

"I don't mean to."

"Then leave," he growled, turning his back on her.

"I tried that earlier but Rhys was blocking the door. He said it was on your order."

His shoulders stiffened. "For your protection."

"Or is it to keep me with you?"

"I want nothing from you."

"Then why do you keep me and Rowan here?"

"Because I made a bargain with Suriel. He was looking for a book that belongs in Annwyn. I knew you had it, and knew you could decipher the clues behind the story. So that is why I keep you here, because we need your knowledge."

His words were intended to hurt her. To push her away. And they did hurt, but Mairi was done running. She wasn't going to let him win this easily. "What you're doing is denial."

He glared at her. "No. It is not. It's self-preservation."

"This morning you wanted me. I believe you would have done anything to have me."

"That has changed."

"Has it?"

His stance told her he was struggling with his facade, but he held to it, stubborn to the very end. "Everything has changed. My world has been thrust into turmoil. Your world . . . it is the same here. Dark times are coming, and we are caught up in it.

Me, you, your friend. We're to play a part in it all. What has happened, it's merely the beginning."

"Rhys told me about the body you found in the alley. He says that more like it have been discovered in Annwyn, and then there was Lauren. This . . . killer is who you search for."

He nodded. "Until I discover his identity and what he wants, you cannot leave here."

"And that is honestly the only reason you're keeping me here?"

"Yes."

"I don't believe you. I think what you said this morning is closer to the truth."

"I was manipulating you. I needed energy to feed my curse."

"What is it that has suddenly made you turn from me? What is it you fear?"

"Let it go," he demanded.

"Why, because you're too much of a coward to admit what you feel? Are you afraid of me? A mere mortal?"

"What am I afraid of?" he stormed, capturing her shoulders in his big hands. He brought her body up hard to his, forcing her to tilt her head back to look at him. "I'm afraid of loving you and never having you. I'm afraid that you're going to be Suriel's lover and I'll have to sit on the periphery and watch."

"Suriel?" she cried. "He is not . . . that is . . . that's insane."

"He wants you."

"Not in that way! Oh, don't," she gasped, cupping his face in her hands. "Don't keep your hands off me because you think I'm with Suriel. Please, Bran, it isn't at all what you think. It's you I want."

"You don't know what you're asking for."

"I know what I want."

"No, you don't. *Fuck*," he ground out. "Can't you understand that this cannot go any further?"

"Why did you go to Suriel, then, and ask him to save me?"

"Because Annwyn needs that book and I knew you had it. Just like I need your friend Rowan and her visions. I saved you because, simply put, you're useful to me."

Mairi felt her lips tremble, his words sinking home. "You said this morning that you didn't intend to use me."

"I lied."

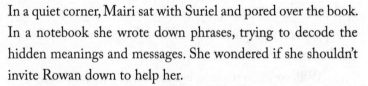

In a quiet corner, Mairi sat with Suriel and pored over the book. In a notebook she wrote down phrases, trying to decode the hidden meanings and messages. She wondered if she shouldn't invite Rowan down to help her.

"You are not yourself tonight," Suriel said, as he watched her break yet another pencil tip against the paper. She threw the pencil down and reached for another one.

"Mairi," he said gently, "what is going on in that mind of yours?"

"I'm trying to get this damn book deciphered so I can get the hell out of here."

He put his hand over hers. "The raven will never allow you to leave."

She snorted. "Yeah, right. He can't wait for me to be done with this."

Squeezing her hand, Suriel forced her gaze to his. "He burns with jealousy because he covets the bond we have."

"Ours is spiritual. I told him that. But the stubborn ass has it in his head that we're together, in the sexual sense," she clarified.

"Only because he fears the bond we have is stronger than yours with him. What he doesn't understand is the mortal heart. Passion, love, it binds much stronger than that of a spirit guide."

"Well, it's not my fault he's a shape-shifting immortal from the wrong world."

Suriel laughed and ran his hand down her hair. "Then it is up to you to show him."

She gazed at him, wondering. "What is in this for you?"

He glanced at the book. "You might be able to help me find that flame. Other than that, my wishes for you are to find your path and your power. I'm walking the path with you, Mairi, but I cannot continue to lead the way."

"Well, we're on it alone, because Bran isn't following."

"He will," Suriel murmured, his gaze flickering over her shoulder. Mairi turned to see Bran walk into the bar. His eyes blazed with anger when he saw Suriel's hand on hers. He turned and left, and suddenly Mairi knew what she needed to do.

❧

Watching Bran in the shower was an invasion of privacy. Mairi knew she shouldn't be doing it, but she couldn't look away. Something drove her to this man—bird—Sidhe.

Whatever he was, she wanted him.

He was beautiful, with the water rushing over his naked shoulder and chest muscles, then running in rivulets down his chiseled six-pack. Her gaze lowered, taking in his navel, studying the way the shower water trickled down the fine black hair on his belly, then lower to where his hands cradled his shaft.

Look away, the modest voice inside her screamed. But the devil lurking inside her lured her on. It wasn't like there was a shower curtain he was hiding behind, the voice told her. He was standing in the open ceramic tile shower, beneath the spray of water, gloriously naked, just begging to be watched.

Six feet six and stacked, Bran's body was model perfect. The sigils that were scattered over his arms and chest were beautiful to her. On the outside he was all rebel bad boy, but on the inside, she'd glimpsed a softness in him. It was that softness, and the promise of another blinding orgasm, that made her take another silent step closer to the shower.

Bran lifted his face to the spray of water and closed his eyes, his long hair hanging down his back, the cords of his neck exposed. *Sexy as hell.* Mairi had never seen anyone as sexy as Bran. And if she had any sense at all, she'd strip down naked and join him in the shower, throwing herself at him and not caring what he thought of her being so damn brazen. She closed her eyes and envisioned him pinning her against the tile wall, the spray of the water caressing their bodies as they moved against each other, just like she had the other day when she'd masturbated in the shower. Except it really *had* been him perched on the windowsill.

Suddenly Mairi felt herself grabbed and brought up against the shower wall. Her flimsy cotton shirt and shorts were drenched in seconds.

"Did you actually think I wouldn't *feel* you standing there, watching me?"

"I didn't know—"

"You didn't know my body lights up whenever you look at me?" he growled. His eyes were glowing silver and gold in the sheen of the water as he loomed over her. There was anger in those eyes, hatred maybe. "Did you think now would be a good time?"

"N-no," she stuttered, unable to find her voice. "What do you mean? A good time for what?"

His body was taut, filled with a tension she didn't understand. "No, I can feel the time has not yet come. I can still do *this*."

He pressed his cock into her belly as he reached for her hands and brought them above her head. His gaze slipped down between their bodies, to her breasts, which were pressing against her shirt. She was braless, and everything she owned was openly displayed for him. His eyes grew darker, the pupils expanding, swallowing up his irises as his gaze fixed on the dark shadow of her nipples.

She was bowed back, her breasts prominently displayed as he pulled her back a fraction more. Then he circled his erection deeper into her belly. He stroked her with his massive erection, circling her belly as if he were buried deep inside her. "Tell me what you're doing here."

She heard the pain in his voice and couldn't understand where it came from. She wanted to ask what she had done, but his cock felt so good against her that only a husky moan made its way past her lips.

"You want me to take you in the shower?" he asked as he pressed his mouth against her ear. "Why, Mairi? Will you wash me away when you're done?"

"I—I didn't mean to disturb you—"

He laughed, the sound dark, menacing.

He freed one hand from her wrists and brought it down between their bodies. She followed his hand and watched as he brought it to his cock. Something glinted in the sheen of the water, and she blinked, her lashes heavy with water. Something silver flashed at her.

"So, do you like it, Mairi? Are the men you bring home for sex always pierced?"

She looked down and saw the tiny silver ball. Oh, God, his cock was pierced. And covered with the same sigils on his arm and temple. Normally tattoos and piercings would have sent her running, but somehow it suited him. It more than suited him; it completed him. And truth be told, she couldn't wait to experience just what kind of bone-melting pleasure he and his pierced shaft could give her.

She looked up at him, blinking through her heavy lashes and her soaked hair. She saw the expression in his eyes, the one he tried so hard to hide behind his tough-guy exterior. And in that moment, she felt far more than just lust coursing through her veins.

"I've never brought a guy back to my apartment for anything, let alone sex. What I want is . . . you."

"I can't seem to get the taste of you out of my head, Mairi, even though I know I shouldn't be thinking of it, or remembering how damn sexy you looked spread wide for me."

"Why shouldn't you?" she asked as he released her wrists. She ran her hands down over his shoulders and between the muscles of his back. He groaned as she ran her fingertips over the two small bumps beneath his flesh.

"Do that again, *muirnin*," he moaned. She repeated the action and he shuddered against her.

In a blinding whirl, he had her turned around, facing the tiled wall. Her T-shirt was thrown aside and his hands were suddenly overflowing with her breasts. He kneaded her from behind as he pressed his cock against her bottom, his breathing harsh against her neck.

"Please," she pleaded as she pressed the side of her face against the warm tiles. From over her shoulder, she watched him, watched the way his palms smoothed down the sides of her breasts to her ribs and down over her belly, where his fingers kneaded her. A rush of arousal seeped out of her, but she was too far gone to care or be embarrassed. He knew how aroused she was, because his gaze flickered up to meet hers, a knowing grin on his lips. He held her steady as his hands slowly caressed her bottom, before ripping off her shorts and gathering the edges of her panties in his fingers.

Pushing the edges of her panties up, he pressed them up into her crease, as his fingers slowly stroked her swollen and slick sex.

Never had she been more turned on in her life. It was as if every cell in her body was just waiting for Bran to pounce on her and take her.

"Bran, I want you so much," she said, throwing her hips back and rubbing her bottom against him. She was drowning in excitement. If he didn't quit teasing her, there was no telling what she was going to do.

"What will you do after I take you, Mairi?" he asked, tracing the shell of her ear with the tip of his tongue as his fingers slid slowly, playfully in her folds.

Probably die of sheer pleasure.

His voice was velvety dark against her ear. "No matter what happens, I'm going to remember this forever, the way you feel, the way your energy invades my body. And I'm going to keep those memories for the rest of my days."

Mairi closed her eyes and let her head rest against the crook of Bran's shoulder. He was hard and hot against her back as he fingered her. His free hand skated down her belly and over her hip. His touch was overflowing with that magical essence that seemed to seep out of him. She felt the hum start to travel up her body, along the nerve pathways, heating her skin, filling her blood, filling her core with him and his magic.

"That's it. Let the energy build inside you. I can feel it drawing me in. It feels so damn good to be pulled into you. It's a gentle tugging—no, a sucking," he rasped. "The same sort of sucking sensation your mouth would give my cock." He brushed his erection up against the cleft of her bottom, letting her feel how hard he was. "I can imagine it, you know, how'd you look tugging me into your mouth, sucking me into your body."

"Bran," she moaned, feeling her body begin to open to him.

"You cannot even imagine what it's like to feel you, to feel all this energy coming into my body. You cannot believe how erotic it is."

"Yes, I can." She arched as his palm rested beneath her breast. "I know what it feels like. I can feel you inside me, too. Your energy. The hum that comes off your body, I can feel it working deep into mine."

His breath hissed and she felt his hips press into her backside. He was hard—unbelievably hard. And that special vibration of his worked up her back and down into her sex, where it languished, teasing her with a glimpse of what it would be like to feel him deep inside her.

"Pull me deeper," he urged, wrapping his body around hers. "Take me inside, *muirnin*, and suck me in deep."

Pressing in, Bran reached for the delicate lace edging, then tore the white cotton in half, letting her panties fall, sopping wet, to the floor of the shower. She was now naked, the full globes of her ass beckoning his hand to rub them.

She whimpered as he grabbed for her hips and took them in his palms, angling her back toward him until he had her positioned in just the right way that her pink sex was visible and shimmering with arousal.

"What are you going to do to me?" she gasped through hurried breaths.

He lowered himself until he was kneeling behind her and looked up to meet her gaze. "What is it you want me to do to you?"

He pressed into her, moving his head to the side, so she could see everything as he let his mouth glide down her rounded bottom, until it reached the curved hollow. With a flick of his tongue, he licked an errant drop of water that had dripped onto his lips.

"C'mon, *muirnin*, tell me what you want me to do to you."

She didn't answer him, just twisted her body in order to watch him at work. He bit her then, a little lover's bite, a bite that aroused her—and him.

"You want my mouth here?" he asked, parting her sex, exposing her. She nodded, as she stood beneath the water raining down from the showerhead, watching him.

"Bran," she moaned. "I want your mouth everywhere."

✌

Jesus! He loved the sound of her voice and the way the water rushed over her body and along her curves, shaping her, in an erotic rhythm that mesmerized him. Her moans burned in his ears, and the way her ass moved in his hands was more than magic.

If it was the last thing he did, he was going to lick her until she cried out his name as she came.

Pressing in, he kissed her there, the pink skin of her pussy, lapping the wetness away from his lips, savoring her taste. Her juices were flowing even more heavily for him than that first night. And the way she was trembling, her fingers scratching at the beige tiles, made him want to stretch this out, made him want her to beg for release.

So he dipped his head in again and dragged his tongue along her slick flesh and watched as her bottom moved, answering the swipe of his tongue.

He was flicking her clitoris when he saw her hand slide down the slick tiles. He moved in, sucked her clit between his lips. She tossed back her head and moaned, deep and long, and his blood sang in his veins, mixing with Mairi's energy.

He couldn't look away from her hand cupping her breast and the way her fingers slid over her wet nipple. She began to knead, to cup them both in her hands and press them together, teasing him with glimpses of pink nipples.

He knew then he had to get in there, between her breasts, to feel her warmth surrounding his pounding cock.

He stood up, roughly gripped her thigh and hooked it over

his. She met his gaze, her lashes wet and heavy with water, her lips full and ready to commit carnal sin. Her breasts were still in her hands, but now she was tugging on her nipples, rolling them as her tongue streaked across her lower lip. He pulled her hips back, her sex already exposed and slick, and slid between her pussy, finding her clitoris with the tip of his erection.

"This is what a pierced cock feels like, *muirnin*. Get ready to scream."

She gasped as the little metal ball at the top of his cock grazed her clit and slid over the taut bud, rolling along it, sensitizing it with alternate strokes of smooth metal and hot male flesh. She felt so fucking good that Bran forgot about the fact that she was supposed to kill him.

Oh my God . . . In her mind, that was all Mairi was able to say. Her clit was on fire, her lips stretched wide with the width of Bran's shaft. The piercing at the end of his cock teased her clitoris, making it hard and erect. She throbbed there, aching for something she didn't know—harder, softer, she couldn't say. She just knew she needed *something*.

In alternating rhythms he stroked her, metal ball, then his velvety tip . . . metal ball, then tip, until she was mindless and rolling her hips for more of his touch. She was so out of control that she was pulling hard at her nipples, increasing her sensation as she moaned.

While he pleasured her with his cock, Mairi felt the glide of his fingers down her spine. Up, then down, following the same path over and over. The skin all over her body was intensely sensitized. Her clitoris throbbed between pleasure and pain and the shattering need for release.

He knew, because this time when he reached the dimples in her back, he did not stop, but went lower, between the crease of her buttocks, and stroked up and down in a teasing line of fire that he kept in time with his cock.

"You're ready to burst, aren't you?" he murmured darkly in her ear. "You'd probably let me in here, wouldn't you?" Gently he pressed his finger into her. "You gonna let me in, *muirnin?*"

Yes, she would let him in. She wanted him in every way.

He slid his finger into her at the same time he stroked her clitoris with the metal ball at the tip of his cock. She fell apart then, and screamed his name. He held her tight, his fingers pressing hard into her thigh as the vibrations in her body spread out among the pathway of her nerves.

She absorbed the vibrations of Bran's body, too, bringing them in deeper. His energy coalesced with hers, making her orgasm even more potent.

She was nearly done when he pulled away from her. "Don't leave," she whispered, reaching for him. But he grasped her and whirled her around so that she was facing him. His cock was huge and purple, the veins distended with need. She wanted his need, wanted to feel the length of him filling her hard as he pinned her to the shower wall with his body. She wanted it . . . but was he going to give her what she wanted?

⚜

Bran thought she had to be the most gorgeous creature her God had ever created. Long hair fell down past her shoulders and her brown eyes had grown darker with passion. Her face was a perfect oval, and her lips were full and ripe. And her body. It was a thing of beauty. Full and lush with heavy pink-tipped breasts and round hips that filled up his palms. A soft little mound of a belly beckoned him, told him she was ready to be taken and explored. And hell, he was ready to take her, even though he knew he should do no such thing. She was his enemy.

"It's okay," she whispered, as if she could sense the turmoil inside him. "Really, I want . . . it's all right. Please, Bran," she moaned, as he shifted the shower head to spray directly over her breasts, bathing them with warm water, making them all glossy and wet and slippery. He turned the ring of the shower head, changing the flow of water from a gentle spray to a hard beat, making sure the water hit her nipples. She gasped and arched.

"Take them in your hands," he said gruffly.

She cupped her breasts, then shoved them tight together, letting the pulsing water hit her nipples. He penetrated her with his fingers, stroked her, felt her grow warmer, wetter . . . hotter.

"You take my breath away, *muirnin*." He tried to stem the words, to hide from the strange new feelings bubbling inside him. But he couldn't. So he said it again with all the desperation he felt.

She nodded and licked the tip of his finger as he brushed it across her lips. Unable to resist the temptation she offered, he lowered his head, nuzzling the valley of scented skin. His cock grew, and he drove it against her belly as he sucked her nipple greedily into his mouth.

Her hand slid down between their molded bodies. Her fingertip found the tip of his cock, and she flicked at the metal ball while she ran her fingers along the sigils that decorated his shaft.

His glans was on fire as she teased the piercing at the tip of his cock. Then her fingers moved down until his heavy length was in her palm. Gripping him, she stroked, softly at first, then more firmly, until she was tossing him off the way he liked it, hard and fast. He was ready to explode, but not in her hand.

Their gaze met over the mounds of her breasts, and he reached for her wrist with one hand before gently tugging her down to her knees. They were kneeling, face-to-face. Their mouths met, hot and wet, kissing hungrily as their tongues swirled and his hands worked her breasts and nipples. He was blind to every thought except that of fulfillment.

She surprised him by breaking off the kiss and leaning forward, taking the tip of her tongue and circling it around his glans, flicking the metal ball. He groaned, then fisted her hair in his hand, drawing her down lower to fill her mouth. He savored it, the sound and feel of Mairi sucking him off.

She took him in, his entire length, and he felt the first rush of arousal seep out of his tip.

"Finish me," he ground out. One more draw of her lips and he was gone, pulling out of her mouth and spilling himself between the cleft of her breasts.

He couldn't catch his breath. He collapsed against her, and she cradled him, brushing her hands over his shoulders as she kissed him tenderly.

Their combined energy melded, drawing them together, and for a few seconds, he let it. Just enjoyed feeling her invading his blood. But then reality came crashing down.

She couldn't be his. And to drop his guard like this could be a lethal mistake.

"Where are you going?" she asked. He shoved aside the confusion and hurt in her voice. He didn't say anything; he just left her crouched down on the shower floor, the warm water washing away the sins of what they'd done.

He didn't look back, knowing that if he did, he'd never give her up.

CHAPTER EIGHTEEN

It had been a long damn time since Mairi had cried herself to sleep, but she'd done just that. The tears she had spilled the first night they had met were nothing like this. She'd balled like a baby after Bran had left her. She'd seen the pain in his eyes and knew what it cost to leave her like that. Why did he need to make her think he didn't want her when his desire was so blatant in his eyes, in his touch? In that special of hum of his?

"Because you are a danger to him."

Mairi was dreaming. She had to be to hear a voice in her head like that. But she couldn't wake up. She didn't like this place in which she suddenly found herself. It was a crypt of sorts, with torches that cast eerie flickering shadows along the stone walls. Drawn on one wall, in red, were the symbols that had been carved on Lauren's body, along with symbols she had never seen before.

"Hello?" she called. "Is anyone here?"

Her voice echoed off the walls and the ceiling. She rubbed

her hands down her arms, attempting to ward off the evil she felt wrapping itself around her.

She walked forward, toward the light that flickered a little way ahead. She heard a quiet sound, like a woman's voice. Then that of a man. Peeking around the corner, she heard another voice.

"Bran?" she asked in a hopeful whisper.

There was no response. She turned, back to the light, to the cavern that was beyond. At an altar of sorts was a hooded figure; on the altar was a man, naked, bound, his head shaved. Black wax dripped from a cup the hooded figure held. The man moaned when the wax hit flesh. Mairi studied the flesh, and saw the familiar vinelike sigils that adorned Bran's body.

"Hello, Mairi."

A woman with long black hair stepped from the shadows. She wore an opaque white gown that displayed her naked body beneath. She walked with the sensuality of a cat, slinking across the floor with an air of supremacy and confidence. Her smile was cruel. Calculating.

Mairi glanced over her shoulder, back at the hooded figure. He was picking up a knife—no, a dagger—similar to the one she had dreamed of. Her gaze returned to the woman, and then Mairi took a step back. "Do I know you?"

The woman's long fingers caressed the velvet-covered slab of stone that separated them. "I think you do."

Mairi glanced down at the altar that lay between them, then back, to the one the man was bound to. They were exactly the same. *This is a dream*, she reminded herself. She could wake up—at any time. Anytime she wanted. The woman moved forward, smiling as if she knew of Mairi's thoughts.

"Do you really think so?" she asked, her gaze flickering down her body.

"Where am I?"

The woman laughed. "Do you not know?"

Mairi glanced around her, trying to look past the symbols and the shadows. Behind the woman's shoulder, Mairi saw a tunnel. "Does that lead to Annwyn?"

"Hardly." With a flick of her hair, the woman considered her with her violet-colored eyes. Was she a Sidhe, too? "This is a Tumulus, and you have, indeed, been here before. This is where I found you as a little girl, playing where you shouldn't have been."

"I've never been here. I've never even heard that word."

The woman's gaze narrowed. "A Tumulus is an underground chamber used as a ritual space. Can you guess, Mairi, what sort of rituals are carried out here?"

The man screamed, and Mairi felt her stomach churn.

"Death magick," the woman said with what could only be excitement. "Sex magick." Her eyes glowed. "Can you imagine who you will bring to this cairn?"

She shook her head and stepped back, but came up against stone.

"Stupid human," the woman admonished. "*Bran*. Bran is the one who you will bring to this chamber."

"No!"

The woman laughed. "You have no choice, Mairi. You were born into my spell. I don't know how it happened, but sometime after I cursed darling Bran to love a mortal who would betray and kill him, you were born."

Mairi kept shaking her head, trying to wake up, but the

woman stepped closer until Mairi was looking into her ruthless eyes. "You have no choice. You will bring him to me. Do you understand? He's mine."

"Morgan," Mairi hissed.

"Not entirely stupid, then. But not smart enough to disentangle yourself from my web. Tomorrow, on the night of the new moon, you will bring Bran to me."

"What do you want with him?"

"What any woman wants, of course."

Mairi bit her lip at the thought of Bran with this . . . creature. "He won't have you."

"I've found a way to have *him*," Morgan snapped.

"His magic is powerful."

"And what makes you think mine isn't?"

True. How the hell did she know what Morgan was capable of? She only knew she had to wake up from this nightmare.

Mairi looked around the chamber for a way out. She needed to keep talking, to try to distract Morgan, to have time to think. "Why do you hate Bran so much?"

"The question is, why don't *you*?" Morgan asked as she walked around the altar. "He's a parasite. He cares nothing for you. He's using you, just as he's used hundreds of other mortal women."

Mairi shoved aside the creeping jealousy she felt. Morgan was manipulating her. "He's not using me."

"You fool! He lives under a mortal-needing curse! He fucks them because he's compelled to, and that makes him hate mortals. He hates *you*."

"That's not true!"

"Such naïveté." Morgan laughed. "I've been on the receiving end of his deceit, mortal. I know the pain. Don't tell me it doesn't hurt to think of him fucking those other women."

"Stop! Don't," Mairi pleaded, deciding to play along. Misery loved company, and she hoped Morgan would feel as though they were kindred spirits. How else was Mairi to outwit a sorceress?

"Do you think he did anything different with you? Felt any different? He used you the same way he did all the others."

"I—I don't believe you," Mairi said, making her voice break.

"In a hundred and seventy years of being cursed, how many do you think there were?" Morgan taunted. "Sometimes he had three a night—three at a time," she continued, relishing the pained expression that crossed Mairi's face. "You mean nothing to him, Mairi. He doesn't care. All he cares about is his next meal. His next energy fix."

"He said he loved me!" Mairi let out a pained sob, and Morgan fell into her hands.

"I know you're in pain. I've been there. And Bran . . . he can be a bastard, can't he?"

Mairi nodded and pretended she was choking back tears. "I—I thought I mattered to him."

"Bran cares for no one. That's the first thing you must know. The second is, he'll never stay with you."

Mairi wrung her hands. "What should I do?"

"Help me. I only want what is rightfully mine, what was promised to me. A husband, and a throne. You understand, don't you?"

"Of course," she lied. "But I don't know why you need me."

Her gaze flickered over Morgan's shoulder, and Mairi saw the hooded figure move around the altar. "I have someone to help me once I get Bran. But I need you to bring him here."

"What are you going to do with him? Are you going to kill him?" Mairi didn't know if it was the right thing to say, but she needed to know just what this witch had in store for Bran.

Morgan smiled. "Only temporarily, sweetie. With no Bran, I can't have the throne. But with death magick, my . . . *friend* and I can reanimate him, make him bend to my wishes. There is such power in the dark arts."

Inwardly, Mairi cried *No!*, but she pretended to consider what Morgan had said. "I don't know. I just want to forget this ever happened."

"Think of what he's done to you. What he's made you feel. You gave him your body, your heart. You love him, don't you? And he's made a fool of you."

Mairi nodded, placating Morgan. "I would dearly like him to pay," she growled, pretending to be angry. Out of any of her emotions, it was the anger that got the most response out of Morgan.

"Yes," she hissed, her eyes glowing. "Make him pay. Make him suffer as you are now, knowing he has preyed on so many women, knowing you are one of countless women whose face and name he will not recall. Let us work together and make him rue the day he ever set eyes on us."

"What do I have to do?"

Morgan smiled, showing white teeth that appeared sharp and cruel. "Take this." She thrust a long silver chain attached to black manacles into Mairi's hands. "The iron will weaken him so that you can bring him here."

Mairi lifted her chin. If Morgan thought they were two of a kind, then Mairi needed to be as cunning as she. "And what do I get in return?"

"Aren't you the little mercenary?" Morgan murmured. "I've underestimated you."

"He lied to me. I want payback."

"Then we are kindred spirits, you and I. Tell me, Mairi, what is it you would like? But do not ask for Bran's life to be spared. I won't grant that."

"I don't give a shit about his life," she spat, hoping she was convincing in her anger. The length of iron rattled in her hand as she pretended to think. "If I can't have Bran," she said thoughtfully, leading Morgan, hopefully, along the right path, "I want someone just as pleasurable. And I want him to be jealous."

"The gargoyle," Morgan said, glee dripping from her voice. "Oh, yes, the raven would loathe that, his brother with you. I accept this bargain."

Morgan's hand reached out and grasped hers. In her hand a dagger appeared, the same one that Mairi had seen in her dream. At last she realized the significance. She was to use it on Bran.

"You will plunge it between Bran's shoulders and kill him. Do you understand? Once he is dead I will be able to bring his body back here."

"Hold on—you said I would only have to bring him here! I can't *stab* someone, even if you are going to . . . to reanimate him."

"Think how wonderful it would feel to have him at your mercy. To show him how strong you are. To make him pay for taking your heart and stomping on it."

Mairi tried to hide the horror in her voice. "All right. But what about Carden?"

"You will find Carden, and then you will return here, where I will torment Bran with the two of you."

"Fine, I'll do it. The bastard deserves it."

"And, Mairi?" Dread filled her as Morgan's lips peeled back in a cruel smile. "You will not double-cross me. And to ensure you don't, I have your friend. Your little ill friend. Her surgery is coming up, isn't it?"

Mairi wanted to scream. Rowan was ill, and this bitch was holding her hostage. It took everything she had to maintain her act. "I understand."

"I knew you would. Now," Morgan instructed, "the moment the tip of the blade goes deep enough to pierce the raven's heart, I will whisper the gargoyle's location to you. You will free him. Return here and your friend will be waiting for you."

Mairi had no choice but to agree with the madwoman. Not only did Bran's life depend on it, so did Rowan's. "All right."

Morgan smirked. "It has been extremely satisfying to do business with you. Till tomorrow night, then."

The clock chimed in the hall, and Mairi came awake with a start. This was the reason Bran was trying to stay away from her, she realized. He must have seen the same visions she had. He truly believed she was going to kill him. *Her.*

"Suriel, I need you," she whispered in the dark.

He appeared beside her. "Hello, Mairi."

She swallowed, slightly unnerved by what she saw gleaming in his eyes.

"I had a dream."

"I know."

"So then you know that Morgan wants me to kill Bran so that she can reanimate him."

Suriel's eyes went wide. "It all makes sense now. Morgan is working with the dark mage. Bran will need to know."

"I don't know the identity of the mage; he was hooded. In the dream I was in some sort of cavern. There were symbols on the wall, and there was a man on an altar. His head was shaved and his body was carved. It was . . ." Mairi swallowed hard. "I think it might have been Bran on the altar."

Suriel looked away. "It was your dream, Mairi."

"Jesus Christ, Suriel," she demanded, "just answer me. It was Bran, wasn't it? That's what Morgan is going to do to him."

"Morgan was showing you what will come to pass. But it can be changed, I promise you. It's not a path that's set. Have you figured it out yet, Mairi? What you need to do?"

"I think so. I can take away the pain of those I love." He watched her with his dark eyes. "I . . . I saved Rowan by shedding my own blood." He smiled. "And now I will die for Bran."

❦

It had not been hard to garner Bran's notice. In the club she had sat at a table with Suriel. They had some drinks, and Mairi had flirted shamelessly with Suriel, trying to invoke Bran's jealousy.

"It's not working," she hissed.

"Patience," Suriel whispered, moving closer to her. He wrapped his arm around her waist and brought her hips next to his. "And don't glare at me. He'll see through the charade."

She smiled and pressed closer to him as Suriel leaned in

to her, nuzzling her unbound hair. "Good," he purred. "I can practically hear him choking on his tongue. Don't look." He chuckled. "Have eyes just for me."

She looked up at him then. "I'm getting a bit nervous. I'm right in believing that I have you in me, don't I?"

He nodded and caressed her cheek. "Yes. Remember that when it comes time to do what you're going to do."

"All right," she whispered.

He kissed her hair and murmured, "I'll be there when you need me most."

"I'm ready to do this. Now if only *he* would cooperate."

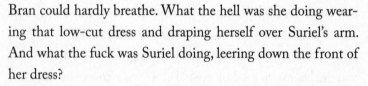

Bran could hardly breathe. What the hell was she doing wearing that low-cut dress and draping herself over Suriel's arm. And what the fuck was Suriel doing, leering down the front of her dress?

He saw Mairi cuddle into the bastard, saw her look up at him and smile, and rage like he had never felt before shot through him like a bolt of lightning. He couldn't stand this, watching her with him, especially now, knowing what it was like to feel her clamping around him, sucking his cock in deep.

In three strides he was at her side, pulling her away from Suriel.

"Come with me," he growled.

She dug the heels of her shoes into the carpet. "I don't think so."

Bran's mood blackened and he picked her up, carrying her out of the room and to the stairs that led to his bedroom.

"Put me down," she yelped, hitting his back with her fists. He did, but then all but dragged her up the stairs before shoving open the bedroom door. He slammed it shut and pressed her against it with his body. He was hot. Hard. And dying for her.

"If you want it so bad," he growled, "I'll give it to you."

Roughly, Bran crushed his mouth against Mairi's, forcing her to accept him, wiping away all traces of Suriel. Moaning, Mairi wrapped her arms around his neck, bringing the mounds of her breasts up against his chest. His body tightened, his cock swelling. Their kiss was unbroken as he crossed the floor and pushed her onto the bed. Her body was restless against his, her fingers clenching in his hair, bringing him closer to her. Bran's kiss turned more carnal, and Mairi returned it with exuberance, matching his rhythm and allowing her tongue to dance with his.

"I want you naked," he said in a gruff voice. He wanted to tear that dress from her body, but he didn't want to spare the time, so he waved his hand and the fabric melted away.

His gaze took her in, and he hungrily devoured her. He couldn't wait to feel her thighs wrapped around him and his cock sinking into the cunt he had been dreaming of all day.

He found her mouth again, ravishing her lips. He cupped her, skimming his thumb along her nipple. She moaned into his mouth and he filled his hands with her breasts, watching the expression of pleasure cross her face. Their gazes met and he very purposely skimmed both thumbs across the taut, pink nipples so that he could watch her eyes widen and her tongue come out to wet her lip.

His body was raging with heat and the urge to take her. To fuck her—*hard*.

He pressed forward, nuzzling the valley of scented skin between her breasts. Then he kissed a path down her abdomen as his fingers set about stroking her calves, working their magic up past her knees to the inner facings of her thighs.

Mairi was panting with lust. She twisted beneath him, but he stopped her with his heavy thigh on hers. "Be still."

Bran's tongue crept out and raked along her flesh. He felt in his own body the stabbing pleasure that snaked through hers. They were connected in a way Bran had never known. His sigils, already glowing, were now a pure white, instead of gold and pewter. Something was happening. The exchange was different, more powerful. *Exciting.*

He returned to her quim, stroking it with his tongue, covering every inch of her. "Watch me between your thighs," he demanded. "I want you to know who is giving you this pleasure."

Mairi studied Bran's dark head moving languorously between her legs. Reverently she raked her fingers through his hair, watching as he slowly made love to her with his lips and tongue, listening to his sighs of pleasure as he brought her closer and closer to orgasm.

Mairi drew her knees up, holding her thighs to Bran's head. He took his time, savoring her; bringing her up, then slowly down, each time building her up higher and higher until she was nearly there, nearly able to grasp the orgasm, only to have it snatched away.

"Oh, God, Bran, *please*," she cried, reaching for him, but he pulled away and sat up, away from her reach.

He looked down at her, and wings suddenly appeared, black and shining, from between his shoulder blades. She gasped in surprise, but they were beautiful, magnificent. They wrapped around her, cocooning her as he grasped her wrists and brought them above her head. She gave a little moan of pleasure, at the strength in his hold, and the erotic play of feathers at her back.

"Have you ever been tied up, Mairi?"

She shook her head, her hips meeting the thrust of his, the folds of her sex opening, rubbing against his cock. A black feather gently brushed the swell of her breast and she moaned, liking the sensation and the tingling.

"Will you let me?"

Trust. It would take so much to allow this. But this was Bran. And inside the span of his wings, she felt safe and secure. "Yes," she breathed.

A feather fell from his wing and stretched into a band of black silk, then wrapped itself around her wrists and tied them to the headboard.

She gasped as it pulled tighter, making her arch till her breasts were at the level of Bran's mouth.

"Very nice," he whispered, touching his tongue to her nipples. His gaze flickered to the feathers that brushed against her hair. They came free and trailed down her body until they pulled at her ankles, spreading her legs as Bran straddled her hips. The feathers became lengths of black silk that tied her to each post on the footboard.

"Your magic comes in rather handy," she panted, trying to lighten the mood.

With his hand, he spread her sex and touched her. Around her all she could see was the black of his wings. Before her was Bran, looking feral and beautiful.

"You're very wet, Mairi, and that's not by magic."

"No, you're right."

He rolled her nipple, pinched it, letting it sting, before soothing it with his touch. His sigils glowed where he touched her, and she watched, mesmerized as they moved, absorbing the pleasure she felt.

"You are very powerful, Mairi. Already I can feel you creeping into my blood. Your energy makes me strong."

"I'm glad," she murmured, wetting her lips. His thigh rode up, pressing against her sex, and she moaned.

"I like you spread like this," he whispered darkly in her ear. "You're dripping wet, Mairi. And it's just for me."

Nodding, she moaned, closed her eyes, and felt the vibration of his body as his chest brushed against hers. She was aching for it, the feel of him, pierced and hard entering her.

She arched more, trying to get his thigh in the right spot, but he moved back and reached for her hips. Lifting her, he thrust into her, firm, hard, and she cried out, feeling the hum in him course through her entire body.

He moaned as well, and thrust again, slow. Intent. She opened her eyes, saw him watching his invasion of her, and grew wetter. He touched her clitoris, flicking it just the way she liked.

"Faster," she begged, twisting in her bonds. The tips of the feathers that lay near the curve of her breasts whispered softly against her nipple. "Bran," she cried, needing the orgasm that was so close.

He stroked her faster, harder, his cock going deep inside her. "*Muirnin*," he whispered as he pressed against her, his mouth finding hers in a hungry kiss.

Rocking against her, he entered, retreated. She felt at his mercy like this, unable to touch him, and she knew that was what he had intended, to have her feeling him surrounding her instead.

He thrust hard, the bed groaning beneath his weight. She took him all, wanted more, until his hands slipped between their bodies and he found her clitoris, finishing her off. He swallowed her sounds, fell atop her. The binds released her and his wings were suddenly gone.

He curled into her, holding her tight, breathing in the scent of her hair as his body trembled atop hers. She held him safe as she ran her hands over his shoulders, kissed his neck.

She loved this man. She had known it all day. There was nothing she wouldn't do for him. *Nothing*.

All he could smell was her, coating his skin, his nose. He felt her touch, stroking him, and he felt himself grow strong, yet weaken. He pulled away and got off the bed, watching her, knowing that this was the moment he had envisioned for weeks. This was his death vision. And all he could think about was how damn much he wanted to sink deep inside Mairi's body and fill her up.

He didn't want to believe that Mairi would kill him. Would take the athame that lay on the nightstand and plunge it between his shoulder blades. Not a mere mortal. Not Mairi, the woman he had fallen in love with.

But if he died tonight, so be it. He was done denying himself.

Mairi dropped her arms and slowly lowered her leg, revealing a thatch of soft black curls and a glistening pink quim. Her scent was thick, evocative. His head swam with it, and his taste buds tingled. Even his sigils flickered, remembering the kind of magical essence Mairi possessed.

"Bran?" she asked, and he reached for her ankle and pulled her to the end of the bed.

His hand fisted in her hair and he sat her up, fitting his cock into her mouth. "Please," he begged, as her tongue flicked over the sigils that ran up his shaft. The energy she created snaked up his cock, making the piercing burn. It felt so damn good.

She looked up at him as she sucked him, and he watched her, loving the way she looked with his cock in her mouth. Her fingers wrapped around the base, stroking up and down, and he groaned, unable to hide the sounds of pleasure that erupted from deep within as she flicked her tongue over his piercing.

"Mairi," he whispered as orgasm threatened him. She wouldn't listen, but sucked him harder. He pulled away, crawled on top of her till she lay flat on her back, her tongue on his cock. His hands found her breast, then her nipple, and he tugged gently, then harder as she increased the suction on his cock.

She was wild beneath him, and he slipped a finger between her folds, making her moan.

"You flow heavy. And it's all for me. Isn't it, Mairi?"

She moaned as he filled her with another finger. He wouldn't last like this, and if this was the last night he was to have with her, Bran didn't want it to end so soon.

Mairi wrapped her thigh around his waist. He rolled with her onto his back so that she straddled him. Her heavy breasts dragged across his chest, and he felt the sharp stabs of her nipples brushing his skin.

"Kiss me." He reached for the back of her head, fisted his hand in her long, tangled hair, and brought her mouth down to his. But she took over, and instead of pressing her lips to his, she flicked her tongue along his lips.

She repeated the movement, but this time she swirled her nipples against the width of his chest. Again her tongue crept out, but he tricked her and met her tongue with the tip of his.

Slowly, erotically, their tongues touched in curling flicks, reminding him of the way her tongue had licked its way up his cock. As he gazed up into her eyes, Bran felt her hips shifting, rocking against his shaft, her pussy trying to find its way to him. He reached down between their bodies and stroked himself, rubbing the head of his erection against her sex, which was hot and wet. The slick head found her clitoris and her eyes flared, deepening to black as he circled the erect nub with his cock.

Now fully ensnared in her trance, he wet his lips and cupped his hand around her head. His fingers tangled in her hair, he brought her forward, crushing his mouth against hers. Like the animal he was, Bran broke the kiss and fitted his hands around her waist, lifting her up, bringing her breasts to his mouth. Hungrily he took from her, suckling her—starving for her.

His hand moved between their bodies, as she writhed atop him, her moans filling the room. He reached for his cock, brought it to her opening. She sank down fast and hard, taking him all the way in her tight cunt, which squeezed him like a choking fist.

He groaned, clasped her hips in his palms, and showed her the rhythm he wanted, a slow, writhing dance of seduction. He wanted to last, didn't want to spill inside her after a handful of strokes. He wanted to be inside her all night.

❧

He was watching her. Mairi knew it, even though her eyes were closed. She could feel the heat of his beautiful gaze traveling along her body as she hovered over him. She was in a shaft of moonlight, and she knew that the silver glow gave a luminescence to her body. She could literally feel his desire coursing along her skin where he touched her.

"You look so good riding my cock, *muirnin*."

Her body hummed. His words were so arousing, just like the incredible vibrations from his big hands, which were roving up her hips. She felt his gaze burning her nipples, and knew then that he was watching the sway and bounce of her breasts. Suddenly he covered them with his hands, and she opened her eyes to see how they spilled out of his palms.

"I like the way you feel, big and strong between my thighs. You make me feel wild." With a smile she tossed back her head and listened to the harshness of his breaths as she leaned back, giving him a full view of her undulating body. She writhed and moaned on top of him. "Harder, Bran. I want to feel you go deeper inside me—so deep," she moaned.

He surged upward, filling her full. "You fuck like a nymph," he said, his voice now a low growl in the dark. "A beautiful seductress, sucking the life out of me. It is a torture I'd willingly die for. But you know that, don't you?"

His words broke her heart. He truly believed that she would take his life. She tried to show him with her body how she felt. Tried to make him see that it was her love for him, and not some curse, that made her desire him.

"You have no need for nymphs," she whispered as she bent to kiss his nipple. "You have me. No one can love this body better than me, Bran. No one can love you, as you are, more than I do."

He moaned, reached for her hips, and thrust deeper into her.

The bed was rocking with his thrusts. Mairi rode her lover harder and harder, and still he wanted more. When she grew tired, and her thighs burned, he helped her, thrusting his hips up, filling her impossibly farther and deeper, unrelenting in his strokes until she was sweating.

And then, knowing she was so close, he found her clitoris and stroked it, pulled at it, until she screamed and stiffened, but he kept thrusting into her, and her body took him, until he stiffened, pulled her roughly down to his damp chest.

"I am your slave," he moaned as he came hot and hard, pulsing heavily inside her. "Do with me what you will."

"I want you to submit to me," she whispered, kissing his mouth.

"Yes, *muirnin*. For you, anything."

Rolling off of him, she pulled out the iron manacles. She couldn't believe he was going to let her do this. She could not look into his beautiful mismatched eyes. She knew if she did, she could never go through with her plan.

"You may use my feathers, Mairi."

Her heart skipped a beat, but she ignored it, knowing she was doing the right thing. "You're so strong. How could I feel like you're at my mercy wrapped in feathers?"

"You don't need chains to have me at your mercy. Can you not feel how weak I am now? I'm yours to do anything you want with."

"This is how I want it. Now roll over."

He turned onto his stomach. She straddled him and he looked up at her unblinkingly.

Her heart felt heavy, and she kissed him. "I love you, Bran. Believe that." With a click, she manacled his wrists.

CHAPTER NINETEEN

Bran was on his belly, his wrists manacled. He was sweating, knowing what would come. He felt Mairi straddle him, her wet core dampening his skin. She licked away the rivulet of sweat, and his body strained, his wrists tugging at his bonds. Her tongue was flicking along the tattoo of the sword on his back, and he felt his curse grip him even tighter.

He wanted her again. Her sweet, wet cunt that was teasing him. She licked him, and he arched, trying to connect once more with her tongue. Beneath her, his ass flexed, rising up hard between her thighs to nestle between the folds of her sex.

He moaned as the heat from her core swamped his skin, coating him with her own arousal. Tormenting him more, she dragged her nipples along his back, scraping the pointed tips over his skin as her tongue flicked up his spine in teasing, insinuating lashes. He was shackled, his wrists in black manacles, his fingers curled into fists. On his left hand he wore a ring that bore an oval stone, the color of fire. It was the seal of the king of Annwyn. With her lips and teeth she pulled it from him, allowing him to feel her mouth wrapped around his finger. She sucked it, torturing him. He wanted that mouth on his cock, sucking him in deep, drinking him down.

"I can't wait," he said in a voice that sounded intoxicated with lust. She didn't answer him, and he growled, pulling at his bonds. "Let me taste you one last time," he begged. Inside him a fever raged. She rocked her sex against his ass. She was wet. He groaned and shifted, the manacles straining with his immense strength.

"Once more. Let me you feel you again."

"You are too impatient," she whispered in his ear.

"I would feel you *now*," he growled, a sound that made her shiver, which he felt all over his body.

"All right." Reaching between his thighs, she teased him until he lifted his hips from the bed. He wanted her to reach for his cock. Instead, she reached for something just as hard. Her breasts scraped against his back and he closed his eyes, tortured by the feel of the hard nipples moving along his flesh. She reached over his shoulder, saw her fingers curl around the hilt of the athame. Her body shifted; the petals of her sex caressed his skin. He inhaled her scent, let it wash over him, just like he had done when he had picked the flowers by the reflecting pool. She lifted the athame high in the air. When he turned his head to look up at her through strands of damp, black hair, he felt his entire life force stop, then hang by a thread.

"After all this?" he murmured. "After everything we've done, you would betray me now? Why, *muirnin*?"

Mairi's grip on the athame faltered. This was her dream. Down to the very last detail.

She was breathing heavily, knowing what would come next. Tears trickled down her face and she squeezed her eyes shut so she wouldn't have to see him.

"Mairi?"

She didn't answer him, but her eyelids flew open and she held his gaze as she plunged the blade of the athame deep between his shoulders. Using all her weight she shoved the blade deeper, feeling it tear through muscle and connective tissue, scraping between two ribs to puncture the tough tissue of his heart.

She heard Morgan's voice whisper in her ear, "In a house of mourning, a garden of pain, a path of tears, you will find him."

"No riddles," Mairi screamed, but Bran's cry of agony deafened her to Morgan's answer.

With a flash it was dark and she felt the familiar veil flutter down, covering her body.

Rain poured down on them and Bran opened his eyes to the sounds of Mairi's scream. They were on the ground, in a grove. In Nemed, his sacred space. Back home. In Annwyn.

Rain fell onto his face, and he wiped his wet hair from his eyes. His wrists. They were freed. Pulling himself up, he saw Mairi lying next to him, writhing in pain. Blood pooled beneath her. There was so much of it that the rain could not wash it away.

"Mairi," he cried, reaching for her, cradling her in his arms. "What have you done?"

"Saved you . . . from Morgan's curse," she said between harsh breaths. "You're free now . . . Your brother is free . . . I know where to find him. He's—"

"Shh," he whispered, holding her closer. "Why did you do this?"

"To break the curse and . . . and save your brother. The thing you want most in this world."

"No," he said, shaking his head as he held her closer, melding her body into his. "You're wrong," he whispered. "You are what I want most in life."

She smiled, a weak one, and raised a shaking hand to his face. "I love you."

His eyes stung, as tears mixed with the rain. "What can I do? How do I fix you?"

"Can't." She gasped as another pain overtook her and her vision dimmed. "Just hold me."

"No!" he said, his voice panicked. "No, there must be something. Mairi, open your eyes, damn you. *Now*—open—"

"It is of no use, Raven."

Cailleach appeared as a misty vision amidst the rain. Her gaze strayed to Mairi, then to him. "Heal her," he demanded, "and I will do whatever it is you want."

"I cannot. My powers are not for her kind. She is mortal. Death is part of her."

"I won't lose her," he cried, burying his face into her neck. She had saved him, not once but twice.

"She was never yours too keep. Surely you understand that."

"No, I don't!" he roared. "I don't understand! Tell me, Cailleach. You know. You're the one who saddled me with this fucking curse! Tell me why I am unworthy of love!"

She raised her chin, her expression one of defiance. "You are the one who decided it was so. You offered an *Adbertos*. You sacrificed your happiness for Daegan."

"So I am never to feel warmth?"

"No."

"I am never to love or be loved?"

"No. Those things are not meant for you and me."

He wept then, unashamed to be doing so in front of Cailleach. "I never got to tell her that I loved her," he whispered as he buried his face in her wet hair.

"Then tell her now, Raven, before she passes beyond the veil. She will not hear you there."

"Damn you! Can you do nothing?"

"No, I cannot. I can only facilitate her death to make it quicker."

"Come back to me," he whispered over and over. "Come back, Mairi, and let me love you. *Please,*" he begged.

"She is in great pain, my king," Cailleach said as she knelt beside him. "Allow me to do this kindness, in repayment for her sacrifice. She saved you. And for that, she has proved herself worthy of you."

He couldn't let her go, but neither could he bear the thought of Mairi suffering.

"The pain, Raven."

With a slight nod, he agreed.

"I will send her to the Summerlands, where, if the Gods are willing, they will reunite you with her."

"Hands off, Cailleach."

The goddess whirled and her silver robe swirled out around her, covering Mairi's naked body. "Suriel," she gasped.

She stepped back as he emerged from the shadowed grove, his black wings huge as they unfurled from his back. "You have no power in Annwyn," she sneered.

"True. But what you have there is a mortal. And that's *my* domain."

Bending on one knee, Suriel brushed aside the hem of Cailleach's cloak and waved his hand over Mairi's face, murmuring something in a language Bran had never heard before.

"How did you manage to come here?"

"The same way I did the first time. I opened the door. And you let me in."

Cailleach looked quickly at Bran. "He lies."

"I am not here to divulge your secrets, Cailleach. They are safe enough with me."

Her gaze turned mutinous. "Then why have you returned?"

"Our worlds are changing. A force neither of us can defeat alone is rising. We need each other, Cailleach."

"I neither need nor want anything from you."

Suriel circled the goddess, even as he kept his eye on Mairi, whose breathing was slow, much too slow.

She was dying and Suriel and Cailleach were fighting like younglings.

"Would you bring disaster upon your world because of your pride, Cailleach?"

"I do not require a *fallen* angel to preach to me."

Suriel reached into his trench and pulled Cailleach's illuminated manuscript from the pocket. "A good-faith gesture," he said. "Now it is time to return the favor."

Cailleach did not retrieve the book that landed at her feet. She did not look at Bran, or Mairi, but kept her gaze on Suriel, her eyes blazing with hatred. The two of them squared off. Cailleach, immune to the rain, radiated her pure white glow. Suriel, with his black feathers and black leather, stood drenched, the rain running down the black like droplets of sinful blood.

"You will allow Mairi to live in this world. You will give your blessing to whatever union they desire. And you will vow to work with me to find the Soul Stealer. The Dark Times, Cailleach, have been brought on by both of our sins."

"You have no authority here. No right to order me to do anything."

"You're right. I have no power. But I have something you need, Cailleach. I know where your amulet is."

Cailleach's slender body vibrated with hatred. "Give it to me."

"Give me your word that you will not interfere with Mairi and Bran."

She nodded. "Very well, the mortal may choose her fate."

Suriel focused his attention on Bran. "She's in your world now. I can do no more for her. She left me when she died for you."

Bran looked down at Mairi, who was lying in his arms. "I . . . I don't know how."

"You've always had the power."

"What do you mean?" he growled at Suriel.

"The first time you touched her, she felt safe. Free. When she heard my voice, she ran to you. When she saw me, she turned to you. It's you, Raven, who can heal her—because she was always intended to be yours. When Morgan needed a mortal for her spell, someone heard her."

Bran looked up through his wet hair. "Your God."

"She was supposed to die at birth, but then I was given new orders. I was told to give her my breath. When I did so, I gave her the ability to be reborn. But she doesn't belong to me. She never did. She is yours. *His* gift to you—to bind our worlds in this cause."

He didn't know what to say, what to think. To think . . . she had been created for him.

"Time is of the essence, Raven. She is still mortal, and she is dying. If she passes through the veil, there will be no return for her. She will not come back to you. And I cannot go there to get her."

"I don't know what to do!"

"You must."

Touch her. Take the pain away, he thought. He could do this. He needed to have faith in that. Damn it, Rowan had said his lack of faith would kill Mairi. He would believe. He would trust.

Closing his eyes, Bran pressed forward, letting his lips touch her brow, then her cheek. *I love you. Don't leave me*, he silently pleaded. He moved lower. She purred and moved closer to him, letting him kiss her and wrap her up in his arms. He felt her energy growing, strengthening, and he worked harder to heal her, drawing her pain away from her body, taking it into his, where it magically dissipated.

His lips found the open wound on Mairi's chest, where the blade would have gone through his heart if Mairi had not taken his pain. "Come back to me," he whispered, "and I will make you happy, Mairi. I'll love you forever."

Mairi came awake in his arms, looking around in shocked wonder. "It worked. I outsmarted Morgan."

"You saved me, *muirnin*," he said on a sob as he clasped her close.

She looked up at him, smiling. "I did, didn't I?"

"And she will be able to do it again," Suriel said quietly. "Over and over. She is the healer in your Sacred Trine. She will protect you and the other eight warriors that you will nominate. The Powers of Nine," Suriel reminded him. "You are their leader, and she will protect you all."

"No," he pleaded. "Do not make her suffer."

"It is her destiny. Her gift. The power you will use. She has the ability to protect you, to take your wounds and steal your pain. Leaving you to fight your enemy unencumbered."

"I don't want her to have this power!" Bran roared.

"It is not up to you. *He* has given her this power. But only you can heal her. You are her Chosen Fate, as she is yours."

Burying his face in her hair, Bran wept. She was his, and nothing was going to take her from him.

CHAPTER TWENTY

Bran lowered Mairi into the tub. Water continued to trickle from the faucet, a slow drip that was the only sound in the room. She sighed, drawing her knees up to her chest, and sat huddled, her body shivering. With pain? Exhaustion? Fear?

"I haven't had a bath since I was sixteen. I've forgotten what it feels like."

"Your scars," he murmured, raking his thumb across her wrist. "You were in a tub when it happened."

She nodded and trembled once more, drawing her knees tighter to her chest.

"*Muirnin?*" he asked, feeling inept and lost. He reached out and smoothed his palm down her naked back. She didn't flinch, but seemed to relax into his touch. "Does this feel good?" She nodded and her hair fell forward, shielding her face from him. "Lie back and rest."

He helped her so that she was resting against the tub. Her arms floated beside her and the bubbles came up to her chin, covering her nakedness. His hand was shaking as he slid his palm along her cool cheek. "Would you like a shower instead?"

She smiled and rubbed her cheek against his hand. "I'm okay. This is . . . good. I want to let go of the past. To face the future without fearing what came before it."

"Why didn't you tell me?" he asked hoarsely. "You should have told me . . ." He choked back the emotion.

"It's okay," she whispered.

Damn it, seeing her in pain, feeling her die in his arms, made him feel murderous. Christ, she'd taken it all . . .

Pulling the washcloth from Mairi's body, he wrung it out and wiped her face with it. She moaned and stirred, causing the bubbles to part, baring the white skin of her breasts. The red welt where the blade had pierced her chest had faded. It was amazing how his mouth had done that, healed the burning pain and given her relief.

"Bran?"

"Hmm?" he murmured, watching the water sluice along her body.

"We have to find Carden."

"You played a dangerous game, *muirnin*, making that bargain with Morgan." He shuddered, thinking of Morgan anywhere near her.

"She double-crossed me, the witch," Mairi grumbled as she sank lower into the water. "Instead of telling me where to find him, she gave me a riddle to solve."

"Morgan is a selfish bitch. She's never been known to fight fair."

"We have to solve the riddle. Rowan can help—"

"Shh," he ordered. "Do not make yourself uneasy. There is

still time to find my brother—and we will. But tonight is about you—and us. Close your eyes, Mairi, and enjoy the sound of the water around you."

"Bran," she said, stirring once more. "That feels really good."

"Good. You just lie back and let me take care of you."

She sank a little lower into the water. He saw her shoulders quiver. "More hot water?"

"Please."

He let the water run, filling the bath nearly to the lip of the tub. "Better?"

"Mmm. I'm so glad that you have tubs in Annwyn. I'm going to need them if you and your friends get yourself into too many scrapes."

He gave her a soft, lingering kiss, then pulled back, watching her relax in the warm water. "I don't want you to have this power, *muirnin*. It's too dangerous."

"I've had this power since well before I met you. I just didn't know how to use it. Or maybe it was because I hadn't met you that I didn't realize it was a power." She shrugged. "Anyway, it's what I came equipped with. I doubt God is giving exchanges, if you know what I mean."

"Be serious."

She opened her eyes, leveling him with her dark brown gaze, which was now free of pain. "I am being serious. I've never been more so in my life. This . . . power," she said, wetting her lips. "It gives my life meaning, and I want it. I want to be useful to you—to Annwyn. I want to help find this Soul Stealer and defeat him."

"By taking on others' pain and suffering? No, I won't let that happen."

Her hand came out of the bubbles and shackled his wrist.

"Let it be, Bran, and be happy that we're going to be together, and that you're the one who can heal me when the pain comes. Think of it as a game," she said, with a teasing smile. "We can play doctor."

"This isn't a game!" he exploded. "This is your life. You're not invincible, Mairi. You're a mortal."

"I know that."

"Then why?" he shouted. "Why would you willingly go through this?"

"Because this is what I was born to do. This is *my* destiny, Bran, not yours."

The air left his lungs, leaving him feeling deflated. "What if I can't get to you in time?"

There it was, out in the open, the crux of his fear and the reason he didn't want her having this power. *What if I can't save you?*

"C'mon, you're a magician. It probably takes you—what?— two seconds to dematerialize."

"In two seconds you could be dead, and then what?"

"I don't know—"

"You could be taken from me, *that's* what!"

"Then we'll have to trust that it's His plan."

"Fuck that!"

"Bran," she whispered, trying to soothe him, but he wouldn't let her. Instead, he tore away from her hold and paced the bathroom floor.

"I won't lose you. I won't."

"I don't think you'll have to."

He wheeled on her. "You nearly died tonight. I couldn't protect you."

She stood up from the foam of bubbles, sloshing out of the tub. She stepped out, her legs wobbling as she reached for him.

"Don't you dare do this!" she begged. "Don't pull away from me again. All I want is to be with you. And you did save me tonight. And furthermore, I trust you to be around when I need you."

He gathered her up in his arms and held on tight. His heart was beating like mad and his eyes were beginning to sting—*again*. Shit, he was becoming a bloody watering pot.

"Can't you just accept me for what I am?"

Her voice was muffled against his chest. He pulled her back and looked down into her face. "Yes. But I don't know if I can live with the idea of you in pain."

"This is all new, Bran—to me, too. I just need to figure out how to control it. Tonight the pain ruled me. I need to find a way to keep it at bay so that I'm not overpowered by it. I *will* find a way, because this is how I am, this is why I was born. I was born to save you, and I was born to love you. None of that is going to change just because you don't want it to be that way. This is how He made me."

"And, damn, he made you perfect, *muirnin*."

She jumped into his arms and wrapped her legs around his waist, holding him tight. She felt so right in his arms. Her energy, that addicting essence of hers, poured into him, and he buried his face in her hair. "Together we'll find a way for you to get through this. *I'll* find a way."

"I trust you, Bran. Now it's your turn to trust me."

"I trust you," he murmured, hugging her tight. "It's your God I'm questioning."

"Don't. Just believe that this is the way it's supposed to be."

Bran closed his eyes and rested his chin on top of her head. Her teeth began to chatter and he realized she was still wet from her bath.

"Warm me up," she ordered, and he carried her to his chamber, where the large stone hearth blazed with light and heat.

He set her on the floor atop a pile of furs and dried her with a soft towel.

"This is very . . . medieval," she said with a smile. "I like Annwyn."

"Our ways are old. We worship the moon, the stars, the trees."

"Like Druids?"

"Who do you think gave the Druids their religion?"

"The Sidhe?"

"Yes." He set aside the towel and lay down behind her, warming her back while the fire heated her front.

"I need some clean clothes."

"'Tis the custom of the queens of Annwyn to go unclothed."

"Really?"

"They are displayed for their king's pleasure."

"You're making that up!"

"Our ways are ancient. And it is one custom this king is not going to change."

Bran let his gaze roam liberally along her body. He took his time studying her, watching as the firelight kissed her flesh. His gaze flickered up to the gentle slope of her shoulder, to the curve of her neck. Reaching out, he trailed his fingers along the indentation of her waist and up and over her hip. Gooseflesh sprang to life beneath his fingers and he felt Mairi sway into him. He liked seeing his fingers against her skin, as if he were marking her for his own.

"*Muirnin?*"

"What does that mean?" she asked sleepily.

"Beloved."

She sighed and snuggled her bottom into his groin. "I like that."

He kissed the top of her head, noticing the brilliance of her aura. Pure white. He understood it now. "Do you remember that first night in Velvet Haven?" he asked her. "When I said you were a healer?"

She laughed. "Yes. I guess you were right."

"I never understood it fully. Your aura is white. It means perfect balance. Now it all makes sense. We balance each other, Mairi. You take my pain, and I heal you."

"Who would have thought it, that a pair of free tickets to a goth club would change my life?"

Resting his chin on the top of her head, he smiled. "I have never been grateful for my Legacy Curse. But I am now. It brought me to you."

"Well, just as long as you realize when you need juice, it's this mortal you're sexing up."

He laughed and kissed the top of her head. "You are the only mortal I need." He kissed her again and brushed his chin against her. "Tomorrow I'm taking you to the reflecting pool. I want to show you where I picked those flowers for you."

"Reflecting pool?"

"Hmm," he murmured. "You'll like the nymphs there."

"Nymphs? Argh, there is so much to learn about your world."

"Shh, this night is only for us. There will be time tomorrow to discuss things."

"I have two questions that you have to answer. They've been burning in the back of my mind for days now."

"What are they?"

"How old are you?"

He frowned, knowing where Mairi was going with this. "I stopped counting at three hundred."

She sat up, bumping his chin with her head. "That old?"

"I'm still considered in my prime."

She smiled and brushed her fingers across his lips. "That's why you sometimes talk . . . old-fashioned."

"Jargon and slang change over the years. I learned quickly not to rely on language to appear mortal. Although I do have a fondness for certain words involving the female anatomy." He leered down at her. "For instance, you have the most beautiful pussy I've ever seen."

She laughed. "Be serious."

"I am."

She sobered. "Will you really live . . . forever?"

He laid her back down with a gentle hand on her shoulder. "I live an extremely long life. But I can choose to end it, and I will. I will go to the Summerlands when you do."

"I'm mortal and I'm thirty."

He kissed the tip of her nose. "And you're a worrywart. Do not be anxious about such things, Mairi. Time moves much slower in Annwyn than it does in your world. We will have many years together. Perhaps more than you want."

"But you can't die."

"I can choose to end my existence and follow my Chosen

Fate." She looked up at him, her huge brown eyes glistening with tears. "And that is what I will do when it is your time. I will follow you to the Summerlands. Now, then, that is your two questions."

"No."

He looked up from her shoulder, which he was kissing. "There is another?"

"Yes." Her eyes were dancing with amusement. "When you're in your bird form, what do you eat?"

He laughed and pinched her bottom. "Not worms or mice or garbage. I assure you."

She laughed with him and nestled deeper into his hold.

"Watch the fire, Mairi," he whispered. Then he closed his eyes and reached out to the flames, harnessing its powers, bending it to his own. She would find this amusing. It was a youngling's trick, but he sought to please—and surprise her.

※

Mairi watched the orange flames begin to dance, to meld into shapes, twisting and twining, then separating. They became distinct. People. A man and a woman. The shapes came closer to each other, a spark reaching out like a hand to grasp what looked like the breast of the woman.

She sighed, watching as the shapes became her and Bran.

"What do you want him to do next?" he asked.

She smiled, liking his magic trick. "What does he want to do?"

The shape of the man pressed forward, kissing the woman. She fell back and the man pushed her knees up, parting them.

Mairi's breath hitched. "You like to do that, don't you?"

"I love your taste on my tongue, my lips."

She rolled onto her back, giving him her arms. "I'm start-ing a new tradition. The queen gets to ask for whatever she wants while she's lying before the fire, and the king must see that she gets it."

"What does my queen want?" he asked.

"The king, buried deep inside. All night."

CHAPTER TWENTY-ONE

"You have made a grave mistake, brother."

Suriel pressed his forehead to the cold stone. He'd been kneeling so long that his knees were numb, his back stiff, his fingers bloody from gripping the stones as he patiently waited for this audience.

Gabriel pulled at his hair, lifting his chin up from the floor. "You should have let the woman die. This is not your war, Suriel."

How he hated the pompous, self-righteous Gabriel. God's messenger, he silently mocked, who always thought himself above *Him*. "Is it His war, Gabriel? Is it yours? If it is, you're not fighting it very well."

A stinging slap across his mouth was made to silence him, but Suriel could no more hold his tongue now than when he resided with his brothers in heaven.

"Truth hurts like a bitch, doesn't it?" he asked as he licked away the black blood from his lips.

"You've grown arrogant in your banishment, Suriel."

Glaring at his brother, Suriel made to stand, but Gabriel put his foot between his shoulders and slammed him down.

"On your knees!" Gabriel shouted. "You're corrupt. Sinful. Fallen. You no longer have the right to look upon me."

Defying Gabriel, Suriel rose slowly to his feet, to stand inches above his brother, who was forced to look up at him. "What brings you to Earth, Gabriel?"

"I have a message."

"Don't you always?"

"You will forsake the mortal Mairi."

Suriel pressed his eyes shut. "No."

"Her fate is preordained and you have interfered. You will not interfere again. You gave her a gift she was never intended to have." Gabriel circled him, taunting him. "Now take it back."

"Why don't you, Gabe? Go get the gift if that is what *He* wants."

"You know what happens when you willfully change the course of a human's life."

"Yeah, *He* gets pissed and tosses us out on our asses."

"You upset the balance, Suriel," Gabriel thundered. "And now you have brought events upon these mortals that they will not understand. That they would not have had to endure if you had not allowed yourself to weaken to the power of a mortal. You interfered in her destiny. She was to die, but you brought her back to life. And not only did you prevent her death, you gifted her with your power to resurrect herself—over and over. Now, *you will* take it back."

He could not agree to this. He had worked too hard to save Mairi. To hide the Oracle from everyone who wanted it. *To give up now . . .*

"You will also vow that you will have nothing more to do with the human. You will leave her, never to see her again, or to enter her dreams. You will not speak to her in her thoughts, and you will never, ever use your powers to prevent her death. Most of all, you *will* retrieve that gift and return it to me."

"And in return I will get what?" Suriel snarled.

Gabriel met his gaze, his eyes glowing with triumph. "He will forgive you your sin and bring you back home."

The breath was sucked out of Suriel. For a thousand years he had begged forgiveness. Had sought redemption so that he might once more soar in the heavens with his brothers. He wanted the burden of his black wings lifted, the stain of the onyx-colored feathers washed away to reveal the pure white beneath, returning them to their glorious state, before his fall from grace.

"Think of it," Gabriel taunted. "A full pardon. Forgiveness. To walk in *His* light once more."

Suriel fell to his knees at Gabriel's feet. He imagined what it would be like to have his honor back. To walk among his brothers, his name unsullied, his sins forgiven.

"Just give up your claim to the mortal," Gabriel whispered in his ear. "That's all you have to do."

Mairi. Her image flashed before his eyes. There was a reason He had wanted her saved as a newborn. A reason she had saved Rowan. She wasn't meant to die. He knew it. Felt it. Giving his power of resurrection had been right. For the first time in a thousand years he had felt his Creator with him, willing him to do what he did.

"She's just a mortal," Gabriel reminded him. "Clay and dirt."

No. If she were just a mortal, Gabriel would not be here, offering him absolution. Suriel had walked the Earth alone for a millennium, begging God's forgiveness. In those thousand years, God had never once acknowledged his prayers. Until now. Until Mairi. There had to be something else going on. Gabriel was too intent, not only on Mairi's death, but on the powers he had given her. Why? What problems did it cause for Gabriel?

"Does He know you're here?"

"Who do you think sent me?"

Suriel tasted the lie, smelled the deceit, and knew then that Gabriel had not been sent. He had come alone, seeking his own motives.

"Have I your word, Gabriel, that my pardon is the truth? That if I forsake her, I will come home?"

"Yes," Gabriel murmured.

Pressing his eyes shut, Suriel nodded.

"Good." Gabriel's white robe swirled on the stone floor as he stepped away. "Is your word of any worth, Suriel?"

"As much worth as it can be, coming from a fallen angel."

Gabriel laughed. "Defiant to the end."

"Tell me, Gabriel, what will you do with the woman?"

"She will be safe."

Suriel looked up to see Gabriel sheathing his sword. "And what of your word, Gabriel? Is it of worth?"

When Gabriel turned to look at him, the archangel's eyes were black. "As much as yours is."

Which meant Gabriel was a fucking liar.

Suriel closed his eyes and prayed to the god who had created and destroyed him. Trying one last time, he spoke the words aloud. "Show me the right path and I will take it."

"You will have a day to return to the woman and regain the gift. I will await you. Once I have it in my possession, I will return with you to the heavens."

"I'll be there."

Gabriel turned, then stopped. "See that you are, Suriel. I don't tolerate fuckups."

❧

It was past twilight and Mairi waited in the grove that Bran had called Nemed. His sacred space. He had wanted her waiting there for him. With her arm outstretched she waited for her raven to appear. She saw him in the distance, soaring high above the trees, the moonlight glinting off his onyx wings. Her heart filled with love at the sight of him.

"Mairi, I must speak with you."

The world skidded to a stop. Mairi turned to see Suriel standing behind her.

"Suriel." Mairi dropped her arm to her side. "What is it?"

"You must listen to me."

"All right."

He paced around her, his gaze never once landing on her. "I need to leave."

"Annwyn?"

"You."

She stopped him with a hand gently laid on his arm. "Why?"

"I am in danger, and because of me, so are you. They will come for me, and if they find you near me, they'll take you. Stay close to the raven. He will protect you."

"Suriel—"

"I've spoken to him already. He knows what this is about. Mairi, I can't delay here with you any longer. I must . . . you must have something from me. You must keep it safe. Give it to no one. Not even your raven."

"All right."

He clutched her face in his hands and lowered his mouth till it hovered over hers. "I wish I didn't have to do this, but you are the only person I trust. This gift, it is all of my power. Everything I am. Everything I know. About the Oracle. And the amulet. Use the knowledge, but be careful. Let no one know. If they come after you, this is what they will want."

He kissed her, his mouth opening over hers; then he breathed into her mouth, filling her lungs. He broke away and she gasped, choking as images swirled before her.

"You will feel me at times. I'll try to speak to you, to help you on our quest until I can join you. Good-bye, Mairi." Suriel clutched her face in his hands, his wings spreading wide.

"Will you come back?" she asked, clutching his hands.

"If it is His will."

"Suriel—"

"Go to your raven."

In a flash of white light, Suriel was gone. She turned, saw her raven hovering above the treetops. He swooped down and landed before her, taking her into his arms.

"Good eve, *muirnin*."

"Hello, my love." She reached up on tiptoe and kissed him. "Were you able to get Rowan?"

"She was with Sayer all along. Morgan never had her; it was a ruse. Now she is ensconced safely at my court. Cailleach will come tomorrow to see her. It is my hope that here in Ann-wyn her illness will progress more slowly, giving us time to find a treatment for her."

"And what did it cost you to bring yet another mortal to live in Annwyn?"

"Do not worry about that. There is another who is most eager to see you again," he murmured, kissing her nose. "Clancy. I told the beast that if it ate one thing that was not put before him in a dish, he would be sent back to live at Velvet Haven with my surly cousin. He already attacked a tree sprite when he first entered. Tree sprites are sacred. I can't have him running amok, hunting as he pleases."

Mairi twined her arms around his neck. "I will repay you for your kindness and indulgence, my king."

"I know, and I've been thinking of how all day."

He took her lips hard, then stilled, breaking away. He looked around the grove and sniffed the air as the breeze stirred. "Your *Anam Cara* was here."

"No. Suriel was. *You're* my *Anam Cara*."

"Ah, Mairi, you undo me. Your Chosen Fate *and* your Soul Friend?"

"Mmm," she murmured as he kissed her.

"Is everything all right?" he asked.

Mairi closed her eyes and felt Suriel's presence settle deep inside her. He was safe—for now. That much she was certain of. "We can talk later. Now I need you."

Bran's mouth skated softly down her neck, then over her cheek to her mouth. Their lips met, and they kissed, bathed in a shaft of moonlight. Slowly at first, then more eagerly, their tongues touched, stroking.

"Mairi," he murmured, "I want a Lanamnas ceremony with you."

"And that is?"

"An eternal vow taken with a Soul Mate. *Muirnin*," he whispered, "you are my heart and soul, and for eternity is how I want you."

"Promise?"

"I want to make this so beautiful for you, *muirnin*. So perfect that you'll cry in my arms from the pleasure."

"It already is perfect, because it's with you."

He smiled, cupped her face in his palm, and dragged his mouth across her cheek. "Not yet. But it will be. Close your eyes."

She did and felt herself being lifted in his arms. "Open them."

Her lashes fluttered. Before her was another altar, draped in dark blue and silver velvet, pillows scattered around the makeshift bed. On top was a fur blanket that would feel decadent and wicked beneath her naked body.

When she looked up at him, she saw that he was watching for her reaction. "It's always been my fantasy to take you here, in my sacred space. Will you give me this fantasy, *muirnin*?"

He set her down and she reached for him, sliding her palm up along his hard abdomen, up higher to his pectorals. "Spread on an altar, sacrificing myself for you, is that what you've dreamed of?" she asked, totally turned on by the image of herself as a sexual goddess. Living out his fantasy was definitely something she was going to enjoy.

He didn't answer, just closed his eyes and swallowed hard. Lovingly she traced the outline of his sigils on his neck, watching as they glowed beneath her fingers. He rested his forehead against hers. "I want this night to be perfect for you."

"Oh, you are," she said, rubbing up against him. "Just like this, this is perfect. This is how I want you. This is how I love you."

He brought their hands up and placed her fingers against his cheek. "Touch me, *muirnin*," he said in a voice that was little more than a broken whisper. "Touch me."

Need had replaced the masterful tone of his voice. With shaking fingers she caressed the arch of his strong brow, down to his cheeks, which were already starting to stubble. The roughness of it grazed her fingertips, heightening her senses. She liked Bran with an evening beard. She liked him looking hard and strong. It made her feel secure and safe in a new world where she felt so out of place.

His breathing was hard when she reached the corner of his mouth. With a gentle glide of her fingers, she brushed them over his lips, startled by their softness. Mairi closed her eyes when she felt him reverently kiss her fingers. His energy, which had been an even hum, spiked at the touch.

"I need you—so much."

His head dropped down and he rested his forehead in the crook of her neck. She felt the tips of his fingers glide down her throat. "Don't stop," he begged. "Don't ever stop."

With her palms she traced the sculpted contours of his shoulders, then slid down to the insertion points of his wings and rubbed. He shuddered and let out a low moan of utter pleasure. The energy increased, humming along his body, flickering along his muscles. It drew her in, made her feel bold, and she pressed her body against his, rubbing the points between his shoulders as she kissed his neck.

"You feel so good," she whispered, running her fingers down his spine to the waistband of his pants. "So strong beneath my hands."

"You make me feel strong."

The longer she touched him, the more the energy seemed to flow between them. It was pouring off him, and Mairi knew that this loving would be like nothing they had ever shared before.

She kissed his shoulder, licked his skin, tasting the salt of him. Her mouth lowered, brushing over his nipple. She flicked the tip of her tongue over it, felt it grow hard. She heard his breath catch, felt his hand comb into her hair and clutch at her curls. And still the energy ebbed and flowed; like waves on a beach, it came in, then out, drawing them closer and closer, pulling them together so that they were bound to each other.

Reaching for his fly, Mairi slipped the button free and pushed the pants down over his hips. He kicked them off, his mouth finding hers, and he kissed her. Slowly, reverently. Like a tender lover, he took her mouth, showing her that this night was not about sex, but love.

Over and over she brushed her fingers along his back, delighting in the shudders that racked his body, loving the way he seemed to cling to her, to hold on to her as if she sapped his strength with her powers.

Emboldened, she kissed his neck, then sucked rhythmically in time to the stroke of her fingers over one of his insertion points. Driving him to the edge with her touch—her love.

Bran could barely think. Mairi's hand, so small and delicate, skated over his shoulder, building his passion, inflaming his body until he thought he might come. But then it passed, and the energy took over, flowing outward and into Mairi. She took him, pulling at him, and he let himself go. Let himself be taken in by her.

"Lanamnas is a sacred act," he said, reaching for her hand. "It's meant to be intimate and beautiful and . . . pure." A white cloth materialized and he reached for her wrist. Palm to palm he fitted their hands, while winding the cloth around their wrists.

"*Anam a Anam*," he said. "Soul to Soul. Not Sidhe to mortal, or male to female. Just two souls."

Mairi threaded their fingers together. His eyes closed, and she couldn't resist touching the crease where his long lashes rested against his cheek. "You were so worth dying for."

His breath brushed her ear, as he nuzzled her lobe. "Will you have me, Mairi, to be your fate?"

"I will."

Trailing his fingers down the smooth column of her throat with his free hand, he watched as his fingers reached her breasts, which were rising above the corset-style bodice, then down lower, to the pendant that was cradled between her breasts. It was his gift. A silver triscale with pale blue stones. It represented Annwyn and the trinity that was theirs—Mairi, Bran, and the raven. To see her wearing it filled him with pride, love, and possession.

Bran watched the rise and fall of her breasts, the droplets of mist that beaded there. In the silver light of the moon, the glistening droplets ran into one another until they were little rivers that trickled enticingly down beneath her corset.

It reminded him of the night in the shower, the night when he knew he'd never be able to live without her.

Lowering his head, he inhaled the heady and lusty scent of her, listened to the erotic cadence of her heart, which beat urgently beneath her breast. The scent of her passion-infused blood was so strong it overtook all his senses. He could no longer hear, could no longer see, because of the lust that was blinding him. He could only smell, and the erotic scent only grew stronger and stronger until his own body was cloaked with it.

He reached for her bodice and pulled it down, revealing her breasts, swollen, heavy. Waiting for his touch. Waving his palm over her, he used magic to unclothe her, and he looked down upon her, naked and beautiful. Just like the goddess he thought she was.

He touched her shoulders, her arms, her hands. He felt her body take him in, felt her energy pulling at him as their joined hands pulsed together at their wrists. And then she began touching him, rubbing her palm along his sensitive skin, loving him with gentle caresses.

Together they touched each other's bodies, quietly listening to the hitching of breaths and the softness of their moans. When he cupped her breast in his palm, he felt the stab of need snake through her body down to the juncture of her thighs, where she was wet and smelling sweet for him.

"You need me," he said as he nuzzled the tender spot beneath her ear. "I can feel it, that need."

Her head tipped back and her hair fell down from its pins, spilling out behind her. Bran had never seen a more erotic or beautiful sight than his wife beneath the moonlight, her eyes closed, her lips parted in ecstasy as he gently fondled her breast.

Needing to taste her, to feel her energy inside him, he took her breast into his mouth and tasted her flesh. Loving her slowly, he watched her uninhibited response. Seeing her arch, hearing her cry of pleasure, made his blood roar in his veins, made the electricity he felt in his body arc wildly.

He could not take his eyes off of her—his wife—she was his fantasy come to life. His erection bobbed, seeking pleasure against her lush belly. He pushed once, feeling his swollen tip cushioned by her soft skin.

"Make me your wife, Bran," she said as she rocked against him. "Make it real."

He followed her down as she slid her legs around his hips, opening herself for him—welcoming him inside her.

She was beautiful there; dark and wet, slick in the moonlight, ready for his penetration. He slid his thumb down her folds, feeling her slickness coating his skin. She writhed, widening her legs, lifting her bottom.

"Invite me in."

Her gaze found his and she smiled, extending her hand to him. "Come to me."

In a moment of sheer weakness, he fell on her, seeking her love. "I love you, *muirnin.* I hope you know just how much."

Her fingers caressed his mouth. It was possession he'd never experienced before. A passion he never could have believed existed.

He slid into her, slow and easy, watching the wonder on her face as he filled her up. His hand came beneath her, cupping her bottom, angling her so that he could penetrate her more deeply with each measured thrust. And she took him in, her thighs clutching his hips, pulling him farther into her.

In the quiet of the grove, they made love. There were no words. Only gentle caresses and the sighs of lovers whispered between them. It was magic, it was sacred, and Bran knew, as he found completion deep inside her, that he had at last found his redemption—in his wife's arms.

"I love you, Mairi. I'll protect you from anything. I'll worship you with my body, and heal you when you're ill. I'll make a life with you and strive to make you happy. You have my heart forever. This I vow to you."

She smiled and pulled him closer. "I can't promise to always obey you, but I'll feed your curse. I'll worship your body, and protect you with mine. I'll love you in sickness and health, richer or poorer, for forever and a day. This I vow to you, Bran, till death parts us."

"It won't," he vowed. "It won't."

EPILOGUE

The incense washed over him, calming him. The sputtering candles soothed him. Clearing his mind, he envisioned what he desired—what he craved. The incantation fell from his lips as he reached out for his brother. The only one who could help him.

"Look upon me."

He raised his head and felt his face cupped in two palms.

"You came," he whispered hoarsely.

"Yes, brother. I'm here."

"Help me," he begged.

"Help to free you?" Aaron asked. "Such a beautiful darkness in you. How you ache. I can smell it. I can feel it. How it must haunt you, brother. No one knows, do they? No one knows the darkness inside you, the darkness you have so cleverly kept hidden. No, do not hang your head in shame, brother."

"Please," he begged. "I need—"

"Salvation. Yes, I know. You are not yet ready, but soon. Soon," he soothed. He kissed each cheek, then his forehead. "When you are ready, I shall come, and I shall rid you of this pain. Together, we will save you. But not yet," he said as he waved his hand over the bowed head before him. "You will not remember this night. You will not remember me—not yet."

He awoke, conscious that he was on his knees in a distant wood. Moonlight shifted over the low-lying fog. Filled with loneliness, he wept. The tears were for his past, the present, and the future. The future of darkness he sensed looming before him. The future that was comprised of hate, loneliness, and rage. A future he felt he no longer controlled, but controlled him. His was a future preordained, a destiny to fulfill, a fate he could not alter.

"Save me," he chanted, as he dug his fingers into the moist, cool earth, needing an anchor to tether him. Over and over he begged to be freed, not knowing to whom he prayed.

"Save me," he whispered, bowing his head until it rested against the earth. "Someone save me."